Greece Actually

BOOKS BY SUE ROBERTS

SUE ROBERTS

Greece Actually

Bookouture

Published by Bookouture in 2021

An imprint of Storyfire Ltd.
Carmelite House
50 Victoria Embankment
London EC4Y 0DZ

www.bookouture.com

ISBN: 978-1-80019-202-7
eBook ISBN: 978-1-80019-201-0

For all my wonderful family and friends, both here and absent.

Prologue

Last night, I barely slept for excitement and this morning I leapt out of bed with a feeling of anticipation and joy. I can hardly believe I'm having a holiday in the glorious Greek sunshine and spending half of it with the friends who have been my rocks recently. I've never been on a girls' holiday before; I imagine sunbathing by the huge pool at the villa, walking over golden sandy beaches to swim in the warm, aquamarine waters, and eating gorgeous food together at tavernas under a balmy, starlit sky. And when they head back to England, I'll spend my days doing a little yoga and reading those books I've been stacking up all year. I feel a little guilty leaving the shop for a while, but everyone needs a break now and then, right? Hopefully after my trip I'll be heading home relaxed and refreshed. Or at least a little less anxious about life. Fingers crossed the Greek island of Skiathos can work its magic…

Chapter One

The smell of lavender and hibiscus fills the air and I inhale the heady aroma deeply. Sometimes when the air is filled with such intoxicating smells, filtering from the annexe in my house where I make my cold-pressed soaps and body creams, I drag my exercise mat out, pile my dark curly hair on top of my head and practise yoga. Or simply sit with a brew and contemplate life. I have dark brown eyes that match my curly brown hair and I once jokingly asked my fair-skinned mum if I was adopted, before she reminded me that I have Dad's curly hair and very distant Italian genes, which I guess would account for my colouring.

My small shop is pretty well stocked at the moment, which although it makes the interior look inviting, also means that sales have been a little slow. When times were busier, I managed to save a little money each month, although my bank balance is not quite so healthy now. The recession and customer preference for shopping in retail parks and online has taken its toll on our little high street. I'm just about holding on to my shop, Love The Skin You're In, which is down a tiny, cobbled alley just off the market square in Ormskirk, a pretty town in Lancashire. I sell all manner of home-made skin products, from rose-scented body butter, wildflower soaps and soothing Himalayan bath salts infused with everything you can think of.

My passion for soap making began as a young child, when I would gather slivers of my mum's colourful soaps from the bathroom and compress them into a tin to make a block of new, rainbow-coloured soap. I also experimented with perfumes made from various flower petals and concoctions of fragrance in bottles of various shapes and sizes, lined up on my bedroom windowsill. Creating new soaps is still my main passion, although I also sell goods made by local suppliers, including hand-made candles and pretty scarves. I opened my shop almost three years ago when I'd managed to save enough money from weekend fairs to secure the rental.

When the council raised the rents, one by one the shutters came down on a lot of the local shops and 'For sale' signs went up. I'm keeping my head above water with stalls at Sunday craft fairs, which means I'm sometimes working seven days a week, but I love what I do. Frustratingly, some days, customers only enter the shop to shelter from the rain, vaguely browsing the merchandise and commenting on the delightful smells but not actually buying anything. Sheila, who ran the wool shop next door, finally closed her doors last month, unable to compete with the huge bargain discount store that opened up a few streets away next to the bus station.

'It won't be the same quality wool,' she lamented. I'd bumped into her in town when I'd closed up for the day, and we were grabbing a coffee. 'That cheap wool isn't good to knit with, but I guess people like a bargain.' She sighed.

'Surely that's good news for you,' I suggested. 'If the customers start itching with the cheap stuff, they'll return to buy from you.

In fact, that could be your selling point. You could make a big sign to have on the market stall. "Buy Sheila's wool, don't risk a rash."'

She spluttered her coffee out and laughed.

Sheila was selling her wool online as well as at the twice-weekly market every Tuesday and Saturday, which by all accounts was being well received. 'I just don't like the cold weather. I'm such a wimp.'

With her pale skin and slight build, she looked as though she might blow over in a heavy gust of wind, so I was impressed with her determination to keep her business going in the outdoor market.

'I might be joining you if things carry on as they are,' I told her. 'I can't keep going for much longer with the high rent and hardly any customers through the door.'

'Times are hard, that's for sure, but there's always a way to survive,' she said, undaunted by the new way she was selling her wool. 'You just have to diversify a little. I've got a Facebook page too; you should get one,' she advised.

'You know, you really are an inspiration,' I told her before we departed. 'And that might not be a bad idea.'

I guess I was missing out not being on Facebook but I didn't want to be too visible on social media, as you never know who might be looking at your profile.

'See you around. Take care of yourself,' she said. 'And remember, there are always stalls on the market for rent, you know, should the worst come to the worst.'

I pop out for a takeaway coffee – one of the few luxuries I allow myself – throwing the hood up on my jacket as a steady drizzle falls onto the glistening pavement. I manoeuvre around a couple huddled beneath a large red and white golf umbrella who are looking at a window display of a famous author's latest crime novel in Waterstones, before heading inside.

The inclement weather means there are hardly any shoppers out today and some of the market stallholders stand under their canvas stalls, including Sheila, stoically sticking it out in the hope of a sale. It's late June and despite yesterday's sunshine, the rain shows no sign of stopping.

I think of Sheila's comments and wonder how long it will be before I am joining the market traders, shivering on a stall beside Sheila throughout the winter months, in the hope of selling some goods. I guess the shop could do with some serious promotion, maybe a full-page ad in the local paper, but then, you never know who might be reading.

A short while later I'm back inside the shop with my caramel latte, pondering my future, when I'm jolted from my thoughts by the tinkle of the doorbell. The door is made of wood and glass, in keeping with the Dickensian-style windows, which wouldn't look out of place in one of those old-fashioned sweet shops.

'Morning,' says the red-haired lady in a smart trench coat who enters the shop. She places her umbrella in a stand near the door. She's probably someone else sheltering from the rain with no intention of buying anything.

'Good morning,' I say brightly, before commenting on the bad weather outside.

'I know, it's awful. I'm glad to be inside. Ooh, these are pretty.' She lifts a gift set of tangerine soaps and hand cream, wrapped in cellophane and tied with a cream bow, from a wooden stand near the door. 'It's my daughter's birthday soon; she loves the smell of tangerines.'

I open a sample pot of the hand cream and offer to smooth some over her hands and she closes her eyes as she inhales the scent. It's a proud moment for me when I introduce people to my merchandise, especially when they give a positive reaction.

'That really is delightful. My hands feel so soft,' she tells me gratefully as she stretches out her hands, showing off her perfectly manicured nails that are painted the same shade as her hair.

I smile to myself thinking of how tangerine goes along with the orange-coloured theme.

'I'll take the set, and these as well.' She selects two magnolia soaps and a vanilla body moisturiser.

As we head to the counter to pay for the purchases, the woman lifts her hand and smells the scent of the body lotion again, praising it once more.

'You have a lovely shop here, I don't recall it being here the last time I was in Ormskirk, although that was quite a few years ago.'

'So you're not local?' I ask as I place her purchases into a brown paper bag made from recycled paper, with the shop logo on the front. I've never seen her around before and in a small market town, you get to recognise a lot of people.

'No, I live in Lytham St Annes,' she replies as she hands over her bank card. 'I'm actually a journalist for *Lancashire Life* magazine. I haven't covered this area for a while, so I thought I would do a piece about independent shops. I'd like to do a feature about you, if you'd consider it. Especially now I've been in and sampled the produce for myself. It could be really good for your business,' she tells me brightly.

Suddenly I freeze. The thought of publicity does indeed sound good for business as, funnily enough, I'd only just been thinking about that, but I can't risk being seen in a magazine.

'I'm not too sure. There's someone who I would rather didn't know of my whereabouts,' I tell her, not wanting to give too much away.

'Oh right, I understand.' She doesn't push, but presses a business card into my hand and I read the name Melanie King. 'In case you change your mind. And if this person lives outside of Lancashire, they'd probably be unlikely to view the magazine. Just a thought.' She smiles warmly before retrieving her umbrella and leaving.

Several more customers make their way into the shop throughout the morning, including a lady with a cute little girl of around six years of age. The lady tells me she wants to buy something to pamper her friend who has been feeling under the weather lately.

'It's my mummy's birthday next week,' says the girl, who has long brown hair and is clutching a little pink handbag.

'Is it really?' I say, and whilst her mum is browsing the merchandise, I slip a little tub of rose hand cream from a basket on the counter into her handbag.

'Ssh. For your mum's birthday.' I wink and her eyes widen in surprise.

'Thank you,' she says, her cute smile revealing two missing front teeth.

She turns and waves when they leave the shop, after her mum has bought a gift for her friend. Thankfully, for the rest of the morning I'm so busy that I don't have time to sit and think about the magazine article. Or dwell on thoughts of Scott.

It's just after twelve thirty when I turn the door sign to closed and head into the small kitchen at the back of the shop to make myself a coffee, mulling over the conversation with Melanie from *Lancashire Life*. Normally I stay open throughout lunch, not wanting to miss a sale, but today I decide to close for fifteen minutes and enjoy an undisturbed coffee. As I flick the kettle on, my other hand instinctively moves to the slightly raised scar across my stomach and I think of how much my life has changed these past few years.

I'm sipping my coffee and pondering things, when there's a banging at the front door of the shop. It's my friend Paige. I became close to Paige very quickly when I ended up living here and she's showed me nothing but kindness, her positivity propping me up when I've wondered where my life was going.

'Open up, Becky. I'm dying for a wee.' She heads straight to the back room, shouting over her shoulder that the toilets in the market are closed for cleaning.

A few minutes later she's emerged.

'Ooh that's better. And I've come to give you this.'

She's holding her bank card and I notice her long nails are painted navy today, to match the trouser suit she is wearing. I admire other people's nails, especially if they're natural as Paige's are, as although my hair is thick and lustrous, my nails never grow to a decent length before they snap. Perhaps it's because I spent so long anxiously biting them, a habit I've only recently managed to stop.

'Just keep hold of it until the end of the month,' she says, handing the card over. 'I'm out of control. I've already gone into my overdraft and I'm out there buying stuff I don't need. I wish shops didn't have so many blinking sales.' She sighs.

'You need therapy,' I tell her, only half-joking. 'And what about internet shopping?' I narrow my eyes as I take her bank card and relive a scenario we have near the end of almost every month. Paige spends a lot of her money on gifts for other people as well as herself, unable to resist a bargain in the sales. She recently bought our friend Abby's twins chunky Aran cardigans that were drastically reduced in a sale, the fact that the twins are only two and the cardigans were for four-year-olds not deterring her, reasoning that a bargain like that was not to be missed, and that they'd 'grow into them'.

'I haven't written the card number down, honest. There's no way I could memorise it. I can barely remember my own date of birth.' She laughs her infectious laugh that often has complete strangers laughing too.

'That's because you're always changing it,' I tease.

'Cheeky. Right, I'm going to have a look around M&S Food Hall now. I'm going to treat Rob to a nice dinner, and a good bottle of Merlot. Maybe a chocolate dessert too.'

She opens her bag and pulls out a small mirror to reapply some pink lipstick.

'It's not Rob's birthday, is it?' I ask.

'No, he just deserves a treat, he's always fussing over me,' she says, pressing her lips together and pouting into the mirror. Looking at Paige with her long poker-straight blonde hair and line-free face, she could pass for twenty-five even though she will be forty next year.

'Won't you be needing your bank card then? And why are you wasting money if it isn't a special occasion?' I ask, like the money police.

'Ah, but I'm getting a dine-in-for-two meal deal. I drew twenty quid out of the ATM before I gave you the card, so I can't spend a penny more,' she tells me triumphantly.

I decide not to mention the fact that there's a huge discount on boxes of Belgian chocolates near the checkout, which I happen to know are her favourites.

Paige and I met at the gym almost three years ago when I first landed here in Ormskirk. She helped me with some weights when I was clueless and we hit it off right away. She gave me the low-down on the local area and said she would help me find rented accommodation if ever I fancied a move, as she worked in an estate agent's. Over the years she's bought me flowers and taken me for cocktails when I've been feeling down, never failing to make me laugh, even when I was at my lowest. She quickly and generously introduced me to her best friend, Abby, and we soon became three. Paige lives with her husband, Rob, who's a builder, in a three-bedroomed semi-detached house close to the park. She struck lucky with Rob, who is utterly devoted to her, although she's something of a catch herself – apart from having a slightly out of control spending habit – but I guess nobody is perfect.

We chat for a while longer before she leaves to head back to work.

'Right, must go if I'm going to M&S. I've dashed out in between appointments. I've got a one thirty showing someone around a five-bedroomed house on St Helens Road.' She glances at her watch.

'Nice,' I say, imagining her heels clipping along the parquet flooring in the hallway of a handsome house.

'It really is. I love showing potential buyers around those big houses. See you later.'

Paige often tells me tales of the houses she shows people around in her role as an estate agent. She's been asked out by blokes selling the family homes in the throes of divorce, been given a precious family heirloom by a confused old lady who thought she was her daughter – said item was returned to the actual daughter – and been surprised by a bloke walking out of a shower in a supposedly empty house. My favourite story, though, involved a dog with a flatulence problem that smelt so bad, the potential buyers almost rescheduled their viewing as it followed them around, farting in every room of the house.

'I don't know what the bloody hell the owners had been feeding that dog, but we all needed a gas mask,' Paige roared as she told me the story. Luckily, the dog was banished to the garden and a sale was eventually agreed.

'Would you believe a doctor lives on that road and his house is *actually* called Bedside Manor,' she once told me, shaking her head. Paige loves her job and is very good at it.

After waving my friend off, I return to my coffee and think about the offer from Melanie again. What would be the chances of Scott seeing *Lancashire Life* magazine? And who doesn't need a boost for their business during difficult economic times? I turn the card over in my hands and vow to give it some thought.

Chapter Two

'Uncle Henry, hi.'

I answer the phone sitting in the cosy lounge of the two-bedroomed house I'm renting near to the train station. The house has a cottagey feel, with its white-painted exterior walls, black front door and a pretty wildflower garden at the rear. I'm lucky enough to have a brilliant landlord too, who agreed a long-term let and is updating the kitchen in a few months. I must admit, though, there's something comforting about the oak units and cream and terracotta wall tiles. I felt at ease here the second I moved in and don't have any plans to move anywhere else.

It amuses Henry that I still call him uncle even though I'm thirty-three years old, but I wouldn't feel right calling him Henry somehow.

'I was just calling to ask if you had any holiday plans for this year?' he asks brightly.

'You're joking. I can just about keep a roof over my head,' I tell him honestly.

'Really? I had no idea, your mum never mentioned anything,' he says, a note of concern in his voice.

There is a reason for that. I never discuss my finances with my parents, as I don't want them worrying about me. I feel guilty enough that they've moved their whole life here to be close to me, despite their reassurances that they have no regrets. Besides, I always manage to get through each day as sales can pick up as quickly as they can go into a slump, just like today.

'I could always send you some money to tide you over, you only have to ask,' Uncle Henry generously offers.

We've had this conversation before, but the truth is I don't need a handout. And my finances have been slightly healthier since I've been selling at the specialist markets. I've come to realise that money isn't everything. I'm slowly beginning to feel at peace here.

'Thanks, Uncle Henry, but I'm alright, really,' I assure him.

'Well, okay, if you're sure. Anyway, back to holidays, I was wondering if you fancied looking after the villa for a while? I'll pay for your flights too, as you'd be doing me a favour. I'm going sailing around the Med in a couple of weeks and I don't like the thought of leaving the place standing empty. I'd ask your mum, but you know how she is with planes,' he says.

Uncle Henry owns a gorgeous villa on the Greek island of Skiathos, and spends most of his time sailing since my aunt Bea passed away suddenly two years ago. I close my eyes and picture the pale-yellow painted villa with the terracotta roof, high up in the hills with a view of the pretty harbour below. I imagine the gorgeous tavernas lining the port and the wonderful food. It does indeed sound very enticing.

'It's tempting, but I don't like leaving the shop for too long,' I explain.

'Oh right. Is the shop busy then? I thought you hinted business isn't so brisk,' says Henry.

'Not very busy, no. In fact, not at all, which is probably why I should stick around and try and put my energy into it,' I tell him. 'I also want to be ready for the next artisan market, although I suppose that isn't until next month.'

Truth be told, I'm not sure what to do. I really ought to be ploughing all my energy into the business, and I wonder if it's fair to ask Mum to look after the shop? I try to remember the last time she and Dad had a holiday, although I tell myself that they have the freedom to go on holiday whenever they like since their retirement.

'Well, I understand how you feel, Becky,' Uncle Henry says. 'But perhaps having a break would do you good, maybe even give you the chance to think up some new ideas for your shop. I'm sure your mum would jump at the chance to help out,' he suggests.

'Maybe you're right.'

'Okay, well think about it, see if a few of your girlfriends want to come along too, there's plenty of room, as you know.'

Four en-suite bedrooms to be precise. And a glorious swimming pool.

'I will, thanks, Uncle Henry. I'll get back to you in a day or two,' I tell him.

'Well, don't hesitate. If you're not interested, I'll stick it on an Airbnb site, but I'd much rather have family here as I can't be doing with strangers sleeping in my bed.' He gives a laugh and I can imagine Henry sitting by the pool with his perma-tan and thick head of still dark hair, sipping a gin and tonic with a slice of lime.

Henry certainly doesn't need the money from the rental but he prefers the villa to be occupied when he's away. He made millions in the gardening industry and ended up owning three huge garden centres around the north-west, which he sold for a small fortune. That's when he and Aunt Bea moved to the Greek island of Skiathos. These days he spends his money dining in fine restaurants and going off on sailing jaunts with his friends from a local sailing club.

When we finish talking, I think about his offer to go and stay at his place. I'm so fortunate to even be offered the opportunity as there's no way I could afford a holiday abroad otherwise and he's even offered to pay my airfare. I don't want to close the shop in my absence but maybe Mum would jump at the chance to help out, especially as her friend – who lives in the same street – runs the hairdresser's next door to my shop. Since his retirement Dad spends most of his days pottering around the huge greenhouse in the garden and Mum once confessed to me that she feels a little lonely sometimes. I do worry at times she misses her old life back in Plymouth.

'I suppose a lot of people who retire have grandchildren to look after,' she once told me, inferring I'd better get a move on. That's the problem with being an only child. There are no siblings for parents to share their expectations with. I must admit, I'd quite like to be a mother one day, but you can't rush these things. Finding a suitable partner would be the first thing, although at this moment in time a boyfriend is the last thing I'm looking for.

It's Sunday morning and the shop is closed today and tomorrow, so I'm wondering what to do with my day, after I've prepared a batch of soaps and hand creams that will be made into gift sets. I flick through the television and onto *Sunday Brunch*, where I wonder how the guests are knocking back speciality gins so early in the morning without slurring their words.

Mum has invited me for Sunday lunch later. It isn't really lunch, as they've taken to eating it around five o'clock, as Mum has decided she and Dad eat too much otherwise. 'I don't know what it is but after Sunday lunch I feel ravenous later in the day and can't seem to stop eating,' she told me, which is probably due to the fact that she bakes enough cakes and desserts to feed the whole street.

It's just after ten o'clock when I finish making the soaps, and a train into Liverpool is due in fifteen minutes, so I decide to head into the city centre. I text my friend Abby to see if she's free, or if I can pop in and say hello for half an hour. Abby lives with her partner, Joe, and has a fifteen-year-old daughter, Heather, and two-year-old twins, Finley and Jack. She was thirty-two when she found out she was pregnant again, and confesses that it was a complete surprise, as she'd always assumed Heather would be an only child.

Five minutes after messaging her, my phone rings.

'Yes, please. Say where, I'll meet you in an hour. Joe's home today, so I can escape for a bit,' Abby says breathlessly.

'Have you been running? Or have I interrupted something…?' I ask with a laugh.

'Pfft. Chance would be a fine thing. No, I've just been running up and down the stairs looking for Finley's dummy. The twins have gone down for a nap; they woke at five this morning.'

'Oh my goodness, you must be shattered. Are you sure you want to meet me? I can pop in if it's easier for you,' I offer.

'No. I need to get out of this house before I go mad.' She's laughing but I'm not sure if it's hysteria.

'Okay. I'll meet you outside Leaf on Bold Street for coffee. I'm having lunch at Mum and Dad's later so I won't be eating.'

'Great, okay, see you in a bit.'

Abby is a freelance writer who works from home. When Paige brought her to the shop, she immediately fell in love with it and treated herself and her daughter to some of the merchandise on offer.

'It smells lush in here,' she said, sniffing the air. 'In fact, it smells *like* Lush, although your prices are cheaper, I can't help noticing.' She lifted a cranberry and lime soap and inhaled the scent, nodding with approval, before telling me about an online blog she wrote about new businesses in the area and asked if I would like to be featured in it. I declined that offer. And it wasn't long before I sitting my new friends down over coffee at a café on a cute cobbled avenue called Church Walks and told them all about Scott and why I had moved here from Plymouth.

'That must have been awful for you,' Abby said sympathetically. 'Especially having to uproot your whole life.'

'Every cloud has a silver lining,' Paige said, with her usual positivity. 'If you hadn't ended up here, we would have missed out on your friendship.' Her words brought tears of gratitude to my eyes. We became good friends quickly and have been pretty much inseparable ever since.

I never dreamt I'd make such great, supportive friends when I left my life behind in Plymouth. Thinking about it, I never had many friends back home, as I spent most of my time with Scott before… well, before things turned sour between us. With hindsight, I suppose there were many opportunities to nurture friendships with women I'd met at work, but Scott never really liked me going out without him. I remember one evening being stressed as I was stuck in traffic and wouldn't be home in time to have dinner with him at six thirty, which was his preferred time to eat. Looking back, I get angry with myself, wondering why I indulged him, but I wasn't even aware I was doing so at the time.

I settle into my train journey and at the third stop along the route, a bloke gets on the train and my heart stops. The man looks so familiar, with dark hair combed to one side and a neatly trimmed beard. His demeanour and height are all similar and I feel my heart rate increase as I bury myself in a newspaper that someone has left behind on the opposite seat. Peeping over the newspaper, I see his full face when he turns around, and, of course, it isn't Scott, but I'm thrown by the similarity. I wonder if this is how it's going to be for the rest of my life? Wondering if he's watching me in a crowd, startled when I notice someone who bears a resemblance. I pull myself together and remind myself that I'm hundreds of miles away and no one, apart from my parents, knows of my whereabouts.

Just over half an hour later, I tell myself to stop being so jumpy, and pull my shoulders back and plaster a smile on my face as Abby waves at me from an outside table at Leaf café. I stride towards her, looking far more confident than I actually feel, as the city centre makes me feel a little overwhelmed at times, but I'm doing my best to overcome my anxiety.

Abby stands and wraps me in a hug when I arrive, her shoulder-length chestnut hair falling over her shoulders. She has large hazel eyes and a smile that lights up her whole face. Today, she's wearing fashionable black jeans, ripped at the knee, and a white T-shirt. Her face is make-up free and she looks stunning.

'Is it too early for a glass of wine?' she asks hopefully, glancing at her watch.

'Mmm, maybe it is for me, but you go ahead if you like,' I say.

I order a coffee from a passing waiter and Abby orders a large glass of her favourite Chenin blanc and a chocolate brownie to share.

'Don't judge me,' she says, taking a glug of her wine when it arrives. 'But it is the weekend and I hardly drink these days since having the twins. Which, don't get me wrong, isn't a bad thing but sometimes' – she takes a long gulp – 'it really hits the spot. So how are you?'

I'm amazed at her cheeriness, given she's had so little sleep. Maybe it's something you get used to.

'I'm okay, thanks. How about you? How's the writing going?' I ask, full of admiration for her, working from home with toddlers under her feet and very little sleep.

'It's a bit of a nightmare, to tell you the truth.' She sighs. 'I mean, working from home used to be a dream but since I've had the twins it's pretty near impossible unless Joe's home, which is often at irregular hours.'

Abby's husband, Joe, works shifts as a manager in a food production factory, although he also does his fair share when he's at home.

'I do most of my work when the twins have a nap, even though I feel like curling up beside them as I'm so bloody exhausted. I was writing a restaurant review yesterday and instead of writing "pepper sauce", I wrote "pepper pig" because bloody *Peppa Pig* was on the TV in the background.' She shakes her head and takes a sip of her wine.

'Oh, Abby, that's hilarious.' I burst out laughing. 'Good job you spotted it before you sent it off.'

'I know! Can you imagine the review? "The melt-in-the-mouth steak was perfectly complemented by the pepper pig."'

We both crease up with laughter.

'Could you put them in a nursery for a few hours a week?' I suggest.

'I've been thinking about it actually. Don't get me wrong, I love being at home with them, but sometimes I do need to work uninterrupted. I was going to wait until they're out of nappies but at the moment they're more interested in wearing their potties as a hat.' She chuckles.

The huge, delicious-looking brownie, dusted with icing sugar with a few raspberries on the side, arrives along with two forks.

'So how's business?' Abby asks.

'A bit quiet but I had a good day yesterday and I'm doing alright for now, thanks. Actually, I had a call from my uncle Henry this morning, who offered to give me a cash injection, but I declined.'

I take a mouthful of the soft gooey brownie and almost wish we'd ordered one each, but I want to save my appetite for Mum's fabulous roast dinner.

'He also asked me over there for a few weeks to look after his villa,' I tell her.

'Is Uncle Henry the one who lives in Greece?' she asks, diving into the brownie and making appreciative noises with every mouthful.

'Yeah. Skiathos. He lives in a villa overlooking the harbour. I'm thinking about it.'

'What exactly are you thinking about?' she asks in astonishment 'I'd be on the first plane over there.'

'Well, you could be,' I tell her as I take a sip of my coffee.

'What do you mean?' she asks, her eyes widening.

'I mean, he's said I can take a couple of friends along with me. So if you fancy it, although I realise you probably couldn't get away, what with the twins being so young and—'

She lets out a high-pitched squeal before standing up and doing a little happy dance, much to the amusement of the other diners.

'Are you kidding me! Of course I'll come, not for the whole time, obviously, but for some of it. Joe's mum is always desperate to spend more time with the kids, so I'm sure she'd jump at the chance to look after them. And it's the school holidays soon, so Heather will help out, of course. If you're serious about going, I'm in.'

She clinks her wine glass against my coffee cup and gives a little whoop.

'Have you asked Paige?' she asks, when she finally calms down. 'I'm sure she'll be on board, if she can prise herself away from Rob for a whole week.' She laughs.

We often tease Paige and Rob for being like a pair of loved-up teenagers, even though they have been married for six years.

'Not yet, no, but I will do. I'm sure she would come over, though, if she can get the time off work at short notice.'

'When are you going?' She flicks her gorgeous long hair over her shoulder, and catches the eye of two blokes walking past.

'It would be in a fortnight, although I've yet to confirm with Henry, or ask my mum if she could watch the shop. I've been thinking it over and the thing is…' I hesitate for a moment. 'I'm not sure I'd be confident enough to travel out there on my own.'

Abby places her hand over mine.

'Well, it's a good job you won't have to,' she says reassuringly.

'Do you think you can organise things before then?' I reply, feeling excited by the possibility of her joining me.

'Of course I can. Ooh, I can't believe it. I've got one or two pieces to write for a magazine, but it will be a damn sight easier writing it from a balcony in Greece than watching the twins playing in the cat's litter tray, I can tell you. This is the best news ever,' she gushes.

'Great! Well, I've just got to make sure Mum can look after the shop. I'll ask her this afternoon over dinner.'

For a second, I feel a bit guilty about asking Mum to help me out, especially when we've not been in the best place recently. I've found her a little, shall we say, claustrophobic in the past with her fussing, which I realise sounds like a terribly ungrateful thing to say. I know she was only worried about me after the incident with Scott, but at times I felt she thought me incapable of tying my own shoelaces. But maybe I just gave in to her nurturing as she had uprooted her life, concerned for my wellbeing, and followed me here, after all. I felt I owed her the opportunity to at least look after me, and although I'm truly grateful for her love and concern, I feel ready to be more independent now.

Henry would have asked Mum and Dad if they'd like to stay at the villa but he knows Mum doesn't fly these days, fearing her next flight will be her last, which is probably fuelled by watching too many of those real-life documentaries about plane disasters. If they do go on holiday, it's to British seaside resorts.

A couple of hours later, after having had a mooch in Shared Earth, a fair trade gift shop on Bold Street, we stroll back to the train station together. Abby tells me she feels invigorated by our meet-up and getting out of the house for a while.

'Imagine how you'd feel after a few days,' I say.

'Imagine sleeping in a bed and having a whole night's uninterrupted sleep. I can hardly wait.'

As we walk, Abby picks up her phone and studies a text that has just pinged through.

'It's Heather, asking where my hairdryer is as hers has just conked out,' she tells me, before giving her a call.

'It's in the top of my wardrobe. I'll be home in half an hour.' She chats to her daughter as we walk along and after finishing the call, heads into Sainsbury's Local at the train station.

'It seems the twins have been happily building a Duplo tower with Heather since they woke up, whilst Joe has Sunday lunch on the go. He's asked me to pick up a dessert.' She selects a strawberry cheesecake from a fridge and says she wishes she hadn't eaten the brownie now.

When Abby reaches her stop on the train, she says she will let me know about the holiday after she talks to Joe, so I just need to get in touch with Paige now, and, of course, ask Mum how she feels about looking after the shop. But all things considered, I think we might just be on, and the very thought of it gives me a tingle of excitement!

Chapter Three

Mum's dining table is groaning with the usual Sunday roast fare, including a mountain of golden roast potatoes and fluffy Yorkshire puddings.

'Who else have you invited?' I ask with a smile, before tucking in.

'I know, I always make too much.' She laughs.

'I bought her one of those pasta-measuring devices once from the Lakeland shop when we went to the Lake District for a weekend,' says Dad, 'but she never uses it.'

'Well, the amount those things suggest wouldn't feed a child,' Mum says dismissively.

'So, it's in a kitchen drawer along with a load of other stuff we don't use, ordered from a Sunday supplement magazine.' Dad rolls his eyes and smiles and Mum chuckles.

'It's true. I had to put those magazines straight in the recycling bin so I wouldn't be tempted. I think I used a plastic "Good morning" imprint for toast once. There's one with sunshine on it too.'

'And a whole load of other stuff. I'm frightened to go into that drawer.' Dad laughs.

'I suppose so, although remember a couple of months ago, when you couldn't find your tape measure? That one from a Christmas cracker came to the rescue,' says Mum triumphantly.

'Actually, Mum, that toast stencil sounds fun – I'll have that if you don't mind,' I say, thinking it will be a cheerful way to start the morning with a slice of sunshine toast.

'Of course. Have a root through the drawer later, see if there's anything else you fancy,' Mum says.

'Take the whole drawer if you like,' says Dad, with a grin on his face.. It's testament to their love that they are still together as Dad is a minimalist, practical guy who would declutter the house every week if he had his way, whereas Mum likes lots of things around her, thinking it homely. Over the years they've kind of met somewhere in the middle, although I've spotted Dad furtively chucking things into bin liners from time to time when Mum's out at her hospital volunteering.

Over lunch I tell Mum about my conversation with Uncle Henry and how he's invited me over to look after the villa.

'Well, that sounds wonderful. And, of course, you don't need to worry about the shop, I'll be happy to help out,' she says with a smile on her face. 'In fact, any time you feel like a break, you only have to ask. It's such a lovely shop to work in and it gets me out of the house. Evelyn's hairdressing shop is next door too, so we can have a natter at lunchtime,' she says, really warming to the idea. 'Oh and I really like that charity shop near the market square, there's lots of bargains to be found in there.'

I'm sure Dad pales a little at the thought of Mum bagging more bargains to fill the house with.

'Thanks, Mum, that's great, I was hoping you might like to help. The shop's pretty well stocked, but I'll make plenty more products over the next week or so, just in case there's a sudden rush.'

Well, I can only dare to hope.

'And if you need a break, I'm sure Dad might pop in and help. Fancy that, Dad?'

'I might just do that. I can't spend all day in my greenhouse, can I?' He chews a slice of roast beef thoughtfully.

'It doesn't normally stop you,' Mum mutters under her breath. 'Actually, Henry was talking about coming over here for a visit in the autumn, which will be nice as even though we speak on the phone I haven't seen him for almost three years. I feel so guilty about not flying out there to see him.' Mum sighs.

'I'm sure he understands,' I reassure her. 'Although maybe you should stop watching those programmes about planes crashing into mountains,' I add.

'Maybe you're right,' Mum says quietly. 'I don't suppose any of us are getting any younger. I'd have to renew my passport, though.'

I find it encouraging that she's at least thinking that way. Mum and Uncle Henry were close growing up, before she married and moved to Plymouth. She met my dad when she went there on holiday one year with friends, fell in love and eventually moved to his home town. Henry is two years older than Mum and as kids he was quite the protective big brother by all accounts. She has many fond memories of them growing up together and spending days on the beach at Blackpool, where they were raised, and has an album full of photographs of them at family picnics and splashing about in the sea.

I worry Mum misses her life back home in Plymouth, but she assures me she loves it here and always imagined living in a small market town. She was also happy to learn that there are beaches, which she loves, within a half-hour drive of here. When I decided to move to Ormskirk, Mum couldn't bear the thought of me moving so far away, so they sold their house and followed me here, buying a pretty bungalow with a huge garden and have never really looked back. She told no one of her address, but gave her friend and old neighbour Doreen her phone number so they could catch up with an occasional chat.

Mum and Dad are in their late sixties now; in fact, Dad will be seventy next year, Mum in two years' time, although they could both pass for much younger. There's no sign of a grey hair on Mum's head – due to her attending her friend's salon and regularly having it tinted a warm brown shade. Dad still has a good head of dark, slightly curly hair, peppered with grey that gives him a look of Monty Don, which is fitting, given his passion for spending hours in the garden or greenhouse.

Two hours later, and resisting a second slice of lemon drizzle cake and chocolates from a box of Thornton's Continental selection, I stand up to leave. 'Right, I'm off. I want to call in on Paige before I head home and ask her about the holiday.'

I kiss my parents goodbye and set off on the ten-minute walk to my friend's house. I messaged Paige earlier and asked if she'd be around if I called in and she said yes as her and Rob would be home all day, enjoying a lazy Sunday.

Their modern, sandstone-coloured semi is at the end of a small, pretty cul-de-sac, with a neat front lawn and a sage-green wooden front door, flanked by two bay trees in silver pots. Paige answers the door wearing a pink velour tracksuit that matches her nails, with a glass of white wine in her hand.

'Hi! Come on in,' she greets me warmly.

'Alright, Becky.' Rob is wearing grey lounge joggers and a black vest that shows off his toned, muscled arms. 'I'll leave you both to it.' He smiles as he heads off upstairs.

I notice the rugby is playing on the huge flat-screen wall-mounted television.

'Gosh, I hope he hasn't left on my behalf, I didn't realise he was watching the rugby,' I say guiltily as we head into the kitchen.

'No, don't worry about it. He'll be watching it upstairs, which he'll be secretly pleased about as the telly is bigger there.' She giggles. 'Fancy a glass of wine?'

'Go on then. Just a small one, thanks. I won't be staying too long, I just came to ask you something.'

'I know, you mentioned that in your text. This all sounds intriguing,' she says as I follow her into the kitchen, which has glossy cream units and a central island with bar stools.

Paige sloshes a generous measure of wine into a glass and tips some peanuts into a bowl and we return to the lounge, which is dominated by a huge cream corner unit and colourful cushions.

'I came to see if you fancy a free holiday to Greece,' I tell her as I take a sip of my wine. 'Well, you'd have to pay the airfare and a bit of spends, but that's it. I've spoken to Abby and, hopefully, she's on board if she can sort the childcare. To be honest, I think she's desperate for the break,' I tell her.

'Greece? Wow. Sounds amazing. How come it's free?' she asks.

I tell her all about Uncle Henry and how he's going off sailing so the villa will be sitting empty.

'The only thing is, I'd be going in two weeks' time so it is pretty short notice. I'm staying for around two and a half weeks. I think Abby is only planning on staying for the first half, maybe even less,' I tell her.

'Ooh, I'm sure I could do a few days, maybe even a week. I've actually got lots of my annual holiday left as me and Rob never went away this year as we had the extension done. And I don't think anyone at the office has any leave planned until mid-August. I'll let you know tomorrow when I've checked in with work and had a chat with Rob, if that's okay?' She claps her hands together in excitement. 'A holiday in Greece with the girls, how exciting! We've never been away together before.'

It's almost eight thirty, and it's a fine summer evening with a pink-streaked sky, so I decide to walk home via the park. It's quiet now, apart from a group of teenagers sitting on the grass and chatting, making the most of their time together before the daylight fades. For a second, I envy their youth and the possibilities they may choose for themselves in the future, although life rarely turns out exactly as we planned. A couple of boys on the skateboard area of the park put on a display of daredevil stunts as a couple of teenage girls walk past.

During daylight hours, the park is filled with families, some with small children who enjoy feeding the ducks on the pond. In the summer months, pensioners linger on the benches, chatting and watching the children play with smiles on their faces as they lick ice creams purchased from the pink and white van that is a permanent fixture in the warmer weather. It's not the largest park around, but big enough for everyone in the community to find something that appeals to them.

Passing a general store on my way home, I call in to pick up some milk and my eyes fall on the magazine section of the shop and there on the middle shelf is *Lancashire Life* magazine, with a picture of a church in Slaidburn in the Ribble Valley in all its glory on its front cover. I purchase a copy to take home.

Chapter Four

The following lunchtime, I've had messages from Paige and Abby to say they are both coming on holiday so I call Uncle Henry to confirm and, during my break, I book the flights. They're both able to come and spend the first ten days with me, so we are going to travel over together, which I'm thrilled about. Suddenly I can't wait to be away from the unpredictable weather here in England, where the sun is struggling to break through a grey sky most days and I can't wait to be covering myself with sun oil and sunbathing beneath a brilliant blue sky.

As I sit in the shop waiting for customers I turn the card the journalist gave me over in my hand and, before I have time to change my mind, take a deep breath and bravely dial the number.

'Hi, Melanie King speaking.' Her cheerful voice rings down the phone.

'Hi, Melanie, this is Becky from Love The Skin You're In,' I tell her.

'Becky, hi, how nice to hear from you. What can I do for you?' she asks brightly.

I can imagine her smiling face, framed by her glorious mane of long, red hair as she speaks and wonder if she's still wearing matching orange nail varnish.

'I've been thinking about your offer to run a feature on my shop. I think I might have changed my mind about it. Do you fancy coming over sometime? It would have to be in the next week or so, though.'

I tell her about my plans to go on holiday.

'Marvellous, I could come over on Tuesday, if that suits?' she says enthusiastically. 'I've got a meeting with the Women's Institute in Parbold, which is over that way.'

'Tuesday's fine. It's market day too, if you like a bargain,' I tell her, before wondering why I said that as the last time I saw her she looked expensively dressed.

'Perfect. See you Tuesday then, around eleven o'clock, if that's alright?'

'That's fine, see you then.'

I hang up and hope to goodness I've done the right thing as my stomach does a little flip. I flicked through the *Lancashire Life* magazine last night and even though it is available in other areas of the country, it's highly unlikely to be the type of magazine Scott would even glance at, and even more unlikely to be available where he is right now. Besides, it's not as if I'd be plastered over the front page. I think of all the positives, thinking how the exposure might drive more sales to the door and cross my fingers that I've done the right thing.

Scott is currently three years into a five-year sentence, which means he'll be out before I know it and the thought fills me with dread, even though he has no idea where I live and I'm almost three hundred miles away. Yet even so, I dread the day he's released. I thought, after all this time, I was finally beginning to put the past behind me, but seeing the bloke on the train the other day brought a lot of buried emotions to the surface.

I remember that evening as if it was yesterday. I arrived home an hour later than I'd said I would from a friend's house and a row erupted. Scott paced the room asking me where I'd been over and over, refusing to believe I'd been with a work colleague at their flat. I'd vaguely mentioned a pub we'd be going to for a drink after work, but at the last minute we went to my friend's new flat instead, armed with wine and snacks, so she could show off her new décor. Scott had been to the pub and when I wasn't there, he'd bombarded me with texts, which I hadn't noticed as my battery had died. I'd been increasingly worn down by Scott's controlling suspicious nature anyway, and was about to call time on our two-year relationship.

He was like a pressure cooker ready to explode by the time I returned home and, during our argument, he grabbed a knife from a block in the kitchen and waved it at me menacingly. I tried to remain calm and when I eventually asked him to leave, he seemed calmer too. I never saw that he'd concealed the knife and as we approached the front door I felt a sharp pain in my stomach, then the warmth of blood oozing through my fingers as he ran off.

The doctors said I'd been lucky the blade hadn't pierced a major organ in my body and I survived the attack, although the emotional scars took longer to heal. Scott was picked up by police a few days later, several miles away at a friend's house after a tip-off, and locked up.

After appearing in court, he was sentenced to five years in jail for the assault and I naively thought that would be the last I ever saw of him. Yet he wrote to me constantly from prison, saying he couldn't wait for us to be together again and how much he missed me, as if nothing had happened. It was then that I realised I would never be free of him. One afternoon, I stuck a pin in a map and it landed on the market town of Ormskirk in Lancashire, which turned out to be a lucky strike, as I quickly made friends and was able to find a small empty shop unit to sell my bath products. The busy market scene, along with the increasing frequency of the artisan markets throughout the year, have been ideal for me and I quickly settled in. I remember those early days, constantly looking over my shoulder and jumping like a frightened rabbit if I spotted an unfamiliar car parked close to my house, even though I knew Scott was in prison. I even have a pay-as-you-go phone and I paid my rent in cash to my landlord when I first arrived here. I'm as careful as I can be not to leave any clues to my whereabouts, but there's no denying the shop could do with some publicity to improve sales.

Next morning I finish my breakfast, and take the short drive to the shop in my battered old black Corsa that I use to transport stock to the shop; the rest of the time I walk or take the train. I unload several boxes of soaps and gift sets and, half an hour after arriving, take delivery of some hand-made candles and picture frames from a local supplier, which fills an empty shelf perfectly. When everything is set out, I look around the shop with a feeling of pride. It's well stocked with the addition of the hand-made gifts from local suppliers and once I've made up a few more gift sets there should be plenty of stock to cover sales in my absence. In the unlikely event that there's a rush, I'll leave details with Mum about the local stockists.

It's a steady day sales wise, and, before I know it, I'm turning the shop sign to closed as I settle up for the day. Mum's blonde friend

Evelyn appears from the hairdresser's just as I'm leaving, locking the front door of the shop.

'Hi, love, how's things?' she asks.

'Good thanks,' I reply. 'How's things with you?'

'Oh alright, thanks, love, busy enough thankfully. Especially as another hairdresser's has opened on the other side of the market. I've got my regular customers, though, so I should be alright.'

I hope so too, as I've heard the new hairdresser's is offering cuts at very competitive prices.

My thoughts turn to Sheila and I hope her customers remain loyal too and visit her at the market stall to buy her wool.

'I believe you're off to Greece next week. Lucky you,' says Evelyn. 'At least you'll be guaranteed some sunshine there.' She looks up at the grey sky above and tuts.

'I know, that's the bit I'm really looking forward to.'

'Well, I'm looking forward to having a cuppa with your mum when she looks after the shop. It will give me a reason to take a proper lunch break. I'm so jealous. I'm not going away until October.' She sighs.

'At least you'll have something to look forward to when the rest of us are here shivering in the cooler weather,' I say and she nods.

'That's true. I love getting away in the autumn. That Tenerife sunshine really gives me a boost before winter sets in. Anyway, have a great holiday, Becky love, have a safe journey.'

I head home to pack my suitcase with a growing sense of anticipation, as talk of sunshine holidays has whetted my appetite. I can hardly believe that this time next week I'll be sunning myself beside the pool at Uncle Henry's villa in Greece!

Chapter Five

Melanie arrives just before eleven o'clock on Tuesday wearing a stylish khaki shirt dress that complements her red hair perfectly. I notice her nails are still orange.

'I just love walking through that door,' she gushes as she inhales the smell. 'It's so gorgeous, I might have to buy something else.'

'Feel free,' I say with a smile.

'I arrived a little early and had a good look around the market. I've bought my mum some lovely slippers that were a real bargain,' she tells me, which goes to prove there is something for everyone in a market.

She takes a couple of photos of the shop interior and I pose outside the shop front for a final picture. Inside, I tell her all about my business and she takes notes.

'Great,' she says when she's all done. 'You'll feature in the next edition of the magazine and I'm going to write a piece about the market too. What a great place. There's a real feeling of community here.' We chat for a while longer, and she purchases some rose-scented body moisturiser before glancing at her watch.

'Right, I must be off then. I'm going to hear all about a local bake off the WI are organising for charity. I'll be in touch. Have a great holiday.' She breezes out of the door, leaving the scent of her floral perfume lingering in the air.

As she leaves the shop, I'm overcome with doubts and feel a sudden sense of panic. I'm about to chew on my nails, but consciously stop myself as they're finally beginning to grow. I pace the floor of the shop, wondering if I've done the right thing in allowing myself to be photographed for a magazine. For a second, I consider haring after her, before breathing deeply and telling myself to calm down. I can't live like this, and besides, the shop could do with the advertising.

The day drags today, as many customers seem to bypass the shop for a wander around the market as it's such a bright, sunny day. Some are sitting outside cafés sipping cold drinks and making the most of the pleasant weather. I've had a few customers who purchased a few small items but as it's generally quiet, I decide to close a little earlier than usual.

Business seems to be booming on the market stalls outside, in such contrast to a few days ago when it was pouring with rain and the traders stood forlornly beneath their canvases. I pass Sheila's stall on the way to Costa to pick up a coffee and she's chatting to a group of women, who are lifting the wool and inspecting it, and I wonder if they are returning customers who used to buy from her shop, or new ones. She lifts her arm and waves when she sees me and I wave back, feeling pleased that she appears to be having a busy day.

The window of Dorothy Perkins is plastered with red posters advertising a summer sale so I head inside and buy myself a new bikini for my holiday, along with some wedge summer sandals that are half price and look really stylish. I resist the urge to buy a couple of dresses as I have a suitcase at home filled with summer clothes, which, luckily, I can still fit into, even though I haven't been abroad in the last three years, but succumb to a pair of pretty sandals that have a thirty per cent discount.

As I walk home, passing through the market again, the buzzing atmosphere lifts my spirits. I love watching the stallholders change their produce as the seasons change, from the flower seller displaying sunflowers in the summer, right through to December where they are replaced with sprigs of holly, ivy and bright red poinsettia plants. The summer dresses displayed on the clothes stall today will be swapped for chunky jumpers and coats once winter sets in. Even the cheese seller sells different cheeses in the winter, infused with chilli and winter spices. I purchase a mixed bunch of colourful summer blooms from the flower stall for Mum to give to her when I see her tomorrow to run through a few things about the shop. I'm so excited at the thought of my holiday and I can't thank Uncle Henry enough.

The day has finally arrived and I leapt out of bed this morning with excited butterflies dancing around in my stomach. At the airport, two blokes are queueing behind us at check-in, and Paige strikes up a conversation with them. They tell us they are heading to Skopelos to meet their parents, who are already there viewing a house they are hoping to buy and all use as a holiday home.

'I'd love a holiday home in the sun.' Paige sighs. 'Imagine just being able to jump on a plane and head for the beach during our rotten summers,' she says.

Once we've headed through security, Paige seems determined to buy something from every shop in the terminal, including a new bikini, even though she told me she has already packed four.

'I can't resist these airport shops and wish they didn't have so many sales.' She lifts an iPod docking station and I remind her she won't need it, as there is surround sound in every room at Uncle Henry's place. 'Do you want me to take your credit card so that you're not tempted to buy any more stuff?' I offer.

'Thanks, but don't worry, Rob gave me a little extra money for spends, and told me to enjoy myself,' she explains. 'Although maybe that's enough for now.'

On the plane we settle down to enjoy the flight with a gin and tonic, Paige continuing the conversation with one of the brothers we met at check-in, who happens to be seated behind. Paige gives him some tips on what to look out for when viewing the holiday home, so no wonder he's happy to share his nuts.

I have a window seat and as we prepare for landing, I look out to see the shortest of runways beside a strip of water and silently say a prayer that we land safely. As we descend, a group of plane spotters loom into view, reaching their arms in the air as if trying to touch the bottom of the plane.

'Have that lot been on the ouzo?' asks Paige as she leans across and stares out of the window when I tell her about the people on the ground, whereas Abby covers her ears and asks me to stop the running commentary, especially the bit about being so close to the sea. Apparently, there are only two airports in the world where it's possible to get up so close to the planes on the runway. One is Skiathos, the other Saint Martin in the Caribbean.

After getting through arrivals, we head outside into the searing heat, Paige finishing her chat with the bloke from the plane, to find Uncle Henry leaning on his black Range Rover and puffing on a cigar, looking every inch the successful businessman.

He's wearing designer sunglasses, white shorts and navy polo shirt combo. He looks slimmer and ten years younger than the last time I saw him, so living out here is obviously doing him the world of good.

'Ladies, welcome to Greece.'

He greets us all with a kiss before loading our suitcases into the boot of the car.

We chat easily and he asks after Mum and Dad and I ask him about his forthcoming sailing trip.

'I'm really looking forward to it.' He beams. 'There's nothing like being on the open water and watching the sun go down with a nice gin and tonic.'

It sounds like Uncle Henry really is living the dream.

Paige is taking in the sights and comments on how different it must be selling property over here than it is in the north-west of England. 'At least we wouldn't have to stare at the garden from the front lounge when it's pouring down outside.' She laughs.

The winding road takes us past sparkling water and houses dotted about, and the occasional glimpse of an infinity pool with views over the edge of the mountains.

'I mean, who owns places like this.' Paige sighs.

'I do,' pipes up Uncle Henry, laughing.

'Of course you do. I can hardly wait to see your place,' says Paige excitedly.

Abby appears to be in a daydream as she glances out of the window at the lush landscape.

'Penny for your thoughts?' I ask her.

'I'm just taking it all in. Imagine getting married in a place like this,' she comments.

'People get married at the Bourtzi,' says Uncle Henry. 'It's built into the rocks overlooking the old port. They have concerts there throughout the summer months,' he tells us. 'It's a beautiful place.'

I wonder if she's dreaming of getting married herself as she's been with Joe for fifteen years with no mention of marriage on the cards despite having a family together, although I always got the impression that they were happily unmarried.

We climb the mountain road, and before long the pale yellow walls of the villa with its terracotta roof tiles looms into view. It's more beautiful than I remember and we step out of the car onto a driveway that is surrounded by a landscaped garden with palm trees.

'Oh, my word, this is the stuff of dreams,' gushes Abby as we all help to unload the car and make our way towards a huge sun terrace, set with a long table and a shaded seating area. For a few moments we just stand and stare at the view below. There's the port with its many restaurants, and boats bobbing in the harbour, with pine forests rising in the background. The sparkling sea stretches out with a distant view of mountains.

'Right,' says Uncle Henry when we've finally stopped admiring the view. 'I thought gin and tonics on the terrace first, and then I'll show you to your rooms.'

We take seats under the shade of a huge parasol, seated on comfortable cream sofas, and are soon tucking into delicious snacks of cured meats and cheeses, olive bread and oils and balsamic vinegar for dipping. I slide my sandals off and stretch my toes as I sip a gin and tonic with ice and a slice of lime and think to myself that this is a life I could get used to.

Uncle Henry tells us he is setting off tomorrow, so this evening he will treat us to dinner at his favourite restaurant.

The girls marvel at the interior of the cool villa, which has floor-length windows with far-reaching views. The main lounge is painted white, filled with antique vases and modern pieces that blend together seamlessly, showing Henry's good taste for design. A vast kitchen with glossy grey cupboards leads to another veranda and each light and airy bedroom has a balcony. The whole place manages to combine traditional Greek style with ultra-modern and it works perfectly.

'I can't take all the credit for it,' Henry tells Paige when she compliments him on his good taste. 'I commissioned an interior designer for a lot of it.'

I notice quite a bit of it has changed since my aunt's death, and wonder whether it was painful for him having too many reminders of their life together in the house.

As soon as we are settled in our rooms, Joe phones Abby and Heather and the twins are waving at the camera saying 'Mamma'.

'Say hello to my friends,' she says, and the twins wave and smile. After the call, Abby is plagued with guilt.

'Oh God, I think that's going to kill me every time I see them,' she says, closing the lid of her laptop. 'I suddenly feel so selfish being here.' She sighs anxiously.

'You'll be back with them before you know it,' I tell her. 'Everyone is allowed a break, you know. The boys are with their dad and Heather, not to mention their grandmother. They'll be just fine,' I try to reassure her.

'I suppose so. I just haven't been away from them before. I hope it doesn't confuse them, seeing me on the camera like that.' She ponders. 'I think I just might have to call Joe without seeing their little faces in future.'

I give Mum a call before handing the phone to Uncle Henry and they have a quick chat, Mum telling him how one day soon she'll surprise him and brave a flight out to Skiathos to visit him.

Half an hour later and we've all changed into our swimwear and are lounging around the most beautiful pool.

Lying on the sunlounger in my bikini, I run my hand over the scar on my stomach. I decided a long time ago that I wasn't going to cover up in swimsuits, as I've always preferred wearing a bikini. This is how I look and I can't change things. Besides, the visible scar is a reminder to me of how things can turn sour and has made me so cautious about relationships that I haven't really been involved with anyone since Scott. But I think I'm doing just fine on my own and try not to think about it too much. I breathe deeply and surrender to the wonderful, soothing effects of the sun and before long I'm snoozing contentedly in the glorious sunshine.

We all doze, feeling tired after our early flight and an hour later we are showered and ready to have a little walk around the surrounding area. We pass Villa Marina, a large, gated house, similar to Henry's but with white painted walls and bright pink bougainvillea snaking over the wall near the blue gate. Paige immediately notices the 'For Sale' sign.

'What I wouldn't do to live here and sell houses like this.' She says dreamily.

'Don't you sell enough swanky houses back home?' I remind her, thinking of all the glamorous homes she sells in the UK.

'That's true, but the surroundings don't compare to this.' She glances around her and sighs. 'I've always loved the sun. I'd love to buy a plot of land and have Rob build us a house here, but I know he'd never leave Britain,' she reveals.

Maybe they've never really discussed it, as I'm pretty sure Rob would build Paige a house on the moon if she asked him to.

As we head down towards the harbour, winding through narrow roads of houses with wooden doors, interspersed with the odd café, we stop at a viewing point close to the old port. To the left, high on a peninsula with pine trees below, is the Bourtzi, which Uncle Henry told us about. At the summit, white restaurant chairs and tables can be glimpsed, with cream-coloured canopies stretched out above them.

There's a pathway leading down from the restaurant, towards the harbour, that is dotted with benches where people are seated, some sitting alone reading or taking in the gorgeous surroundings. I imagine spending lazy mornings there reading books and watching the sailboats arrive in the harbour before heading off to a taverna for lunch.

After ten minutes, we take a short stroll through some backstreets to the new port, where a huge red and white ferry is just arriving.

We buy a refreshing iced tea from a kiosk and watch the mixture of day trippers and holidaymakers alight from the ferry.

We walk along the harbour, which is lined with restaurants, and heaving with tourists, some dragging their cases and searching for taxis. Various boats line the harbour offering trips. A middle-aged man wearing a light blue shirt and a pair of dark trousers is stood outside a car rental shop, handing the keys to a smiling young couple, before he mops his brow in the heat.

'Fancy getting a car for a few days?' asks Abby. 'Unless the use of Henry's Range Rover comes with the villa,' she asks hopefully.

For a second, I wonder whether Henry will trust me with it as, let's just say, I've had a few bumps in my car over the years that he is well aware of.

'Or maybe he's aware of your terrible driving,' Paige pipes up as if reading my mind. 'In which case, I'll take the driver's seat. I haven't had a single accident in ten years of driving.'

Paige told me once that she passed her driving test on her first attempt and immediately went on a road trip to Leeds, whereas I passed on my third attempt and limited my driving to the local area for months before I had the confidence to venture further afield.

'I hope you haven't gone and jinxed it.' Abby laughs.

Heading along the port, we pass luxurious yachts with cream leather seats, some offering private hire for groups of people, complete with their own chef on board. A tanned, good-looking man around fifty years of age offers us a card with a telephone number, and we gulp at the cost of the trip as we chat to him, trying not to look shocked.

'Gosh, that's over a week's salary for a day out,' says Paige as we walk along. 'I think we'll have to stick to the tourist boats with the masses.' She laughs as she tosses the card into a dustbin.

Presently, we pass exactly the type of tourist boat Paige meant, a blue and white wooden sailing boat, with a glossy poster displayed on a nearby board proclaiming it to be the 'best and original *Mamma Mia!* tour'. A young bloke wearing a white sports cap and smiling broadly approaches us and begins his sales spiel.

'Hello, ladies. Take a look. Today I can offer you a special price.' He fixes us all with a dazzling smile and points to a map of some blue caves and beaches, the church used in the film, and, of course, the island of Skopelos.

'Well, it's definitely something we'll do while we're here,' I tell the man, who introduces himself as Renos.

It's Saturday today and Renos tells us the trips take place every two days, and he's taking bookings for the next one tomorrow. I tell him we will have a think about it, but more than likely take the Tuesday trip, and he scratches his chin.

'Hmm. I think the weather is set to change on Tuesday. Maybe there will be a storm. In fact,' he continues, 'I am almost sure of it. Maybe it's better to take the trip tomorrow.'

'We'll take our chances, thanks,' I tell him, thinking he's probably keen to sell the last of the spaces on the boat before tomorrow's trip. 'Can I take a card with your number?'

He hands over a business card with a smile and a shrug.

'Remember, this special price is for one week only,' he calls after us as we head off.

Cutting through side streets on the way back to the villa, we stop to admire some pretty sale dresses hanging on a rail outside a boutique and I am instinctively drawn towards them. I imagine what is must feel like to have enough money to lavish on private yacht hire and shopping sprees in designer stores, rather than rummaging through sales for a bargain. I'm content with my life back home, but think it would be nice to go wild every now and then and not have to consider the cost.

We pass a gorgeous gift store; its wooden shopfront painted in the familiar bright blue that can be seen throughout Greece. Apparently, the blue and white theme of the houses is not the colours of the Greek flag as many people think, but rather derives from the loulaki blue cleaning substance people had readily in their homes, which was mixed with lime and used to paint over volcanic stones, which were too hot and dark to be used in house building.

A display of the most beautiful silver jewellery in a glass case entices us inside the shop and the interior has an almost magical feel. A low ceiling has wind chimes suspended from it and the old, dark wooden floor creaks as we walk on it. The space is filled with jewellery, pretty household ornaments – some made of beaten copper – and colourful, vibrant cushions and throws, draped over stylish chairs showing them off to their best advantage.

Abby buys a pretty silver-and-jade necklace for her mother, whose birthday is coming up in a couple of months, and the assistant wraps it in tissue paper before placing it in a pretty shimmery drawstring bag, adorned with moons and stars. It's a shop you could very easily spend a long time browsing in and parting with your cash, so after Abby makes her purchase, we head off.

I can feel the pull on my calves as we make our way back uphill to the villa, briefly wondering whether we ought to have got a taxi, although maybe the exercise will do me good. I got out of the habit of going to the gym and my yoga classes with my friends in Plymouth, as Scott would interrogate me when I returned home if I was longer than a couple of hours. I really must make an effort to at least dig out my old yoga mat and do a few stretches to keep in shape.

'It's a bit different to the downhill stroll, isn't it?' says Abby after fifteen minutes, echoing my thoughts.

'Yeah, but in a taxi you wouldn't get the chance to stop and admire all of this.' Paige waves her hand at the stunning scenery below, where the sun is gently shimmering on the water as a boat glides into the port.

'That's true. We're definitely taking a taxi home after dinner this evening, though,' I say and the others agree.

It's a little after six when we arrive back at the villa and as I shower I find myself thinking of the upcoming magazine article back home and for a second I feel a little uneasy again, wondering if I have done the right thing in giving the interview. There's no doubt it will be good publicity for the shop but I suddenly feel exposed, and even a little anxious. I consider phoning Melanie and asking her not to run the story, before deciding again that I can't have Scott ruling my life like that. I won't let the past dominate my future, as those inspirational quotes that pop up on social media often remind me. I decide to put my fears aside as I rifle through my wardrobe and decide what to wear for dinner this evening, thankful to be here, with the people I love.

Chapter Six

'It doesn't sound very Greek,' I comment as we take a seat in a taverna called Jimmy's, on Uncle Henry's recommendation.

'Ah, but the food is completely Greek. Wonderful. The best around here,' Uncle Henry assures me.

'So, who's Jimmy?' I ask.

'I'm not sure there is a Jimmy. Maybe there was once. Although, sometimes an English name entices English customers in.' He winks.

Jimmy's is on the beach road close to Troulos beach and next to a supermarket. The interior of the restaurant has rough textured white walls and stripped wooden tables with blue painted chairs. Grapes are threaded through the pergola above and the tables are set with candles inside little vases, giving it all a cosy and welcoming feel.

'You're so lucky living in your beautiful villa,' says Paige as she munches her way through a delicious aubergine and halloumi starter drizzled with a balsamic glaze. 'I could never get tired of living in a place like this.'

'Well, nobody's life is perfect, but I must admit it's easier to shrug away a bad day in a beautiful place, when the sun is shining,' he agrees.

I suppose it's true that no one has a perfect life and I think of how sad Henry must have been following Aunt Bea's death, so feel happy he has such good friends here with whom he is able to indulge his passion for sailing.

'Henry, good evening. How are you?'

A Greek man in his sixties shakes us each warmly by the hand as Henry makes introductions.

'Well, I am delighted to meet you all. I hope you enjoy your time here in Skiathos,' he tells us.

We dine on delicious dishes of moussaka, and a baked feta dish served in a clay pot. It's so delicious that I ask the chef how it is made.

'Slowly,' he tells me. 'Always slowly. Olive oil, oregano, garlic and feta. Just a little black pepper. Baked in the pot.' He holds four fingers up. 'Four hours.'

I recall the last time I was over here, how the chefs are so generous sharing their recipes, proud that you enjoy their food so much that you want to replicate it yourself, unlike back home where it can be like a closely guarded secret in some restaurants.

After finishing up with baklava and ouzo, it's easy to see how this is Uncle Henry's favourite restaurant as the food was absolutely delicious and the service wonderful. The owner excuses himself from a group of people he's chatting with at a nearby table to say good night to us, shaking our hands warmly once again.

'We can head back in a taxi if you like, but if you want to party, I'll drop you at the port on the way. I want to be up early tomorrow,' says Henry, who's off on his sailing trip after breakfast.

'Great idea! Are you all up for it?' asks Paige excitedly. 'I'm not ready for the evening to end just yet.'

'You know, I've had a wonderful evening but I'm absolutely ready for my bed. I've averaged around four hours a night unbroken sleep since the twins have been born and I'm fantasising about climbing into that bed in the villa and sleeping until the sun rises,' says Abby. 'Maybe even until lunchtime,' she adds.

'Well, I completely get that. Right, Becky, is it just us two then? Don't let me down,' Paige pleads.

'Oh, go on then,' I say and Paige gives a little squeal of delight.

Henry and Abby drop us at the harbour front as they continue on to the villa and we're soon sitting outside a bar, lured by the pulsating music and bright lights. A young, good-looking waiter wearing his hair in a man bun takes our order for two mojitos and we settle back and enjoy the music.

'Ah, this is nice,' I say, sipping the refreshing drink. 'I can't remember the last time I went to a nightclub. I've been to a few music bars, but not like this. I must be getting old before my time at the ripe old age of thirty-three.'

'No, you're not. Maybe you just got out of the habit of letting your hair down with your friends when you were with Scott,' Paige says honestly as she sips her mojito. 'Anyway, I prefer bars. Nightclubs these days are filled with teenagers who are barely out of school.'

Just then, I notice a couple of guys staring over at us and smiling, in between scrolling through their phones.

'Which one do you fancy then?' asks Paige mischievously.

'They are equally attractive,' I reply, glancing at the handsome blokes, who look in their mid-twenties. 'Although you shouldn't even be noticing other men. You've hit the jackpot with Rob.'

'Oh, don't worry, I know I have. I never thought I'd want to settle down, to be honest, but everything just felt right with Rob,' she says, a big smile crossing her face at the mention of his name.

Paige married Rob after being with him for just over a year, and she once told me that she worried they were marrying during the lust phase. She wondered whether it was better to get to know someone long-term, because then you would know whether you actually liked them, which made me laugh. Thinking about it, though, it was a sensible thing to say as once you're in a long-term relationship there is often no urgency to get married. You only have to chat to Abby to get that perspective. And, of course, Scott was the perfect boyfriend when we first met and look how that turned out. I'm pretty sure it's put me off marriage for life.

We enjoy another cocktail and the handsome young blokes stroll over and ask if they can join us. They are from Essex and turn out to be good company.

It's their first day on the island and I recommend a few places to visit. Skiathos is dotted with beaches along a coast road and I recommend Koukounaries beach, which is considered the best beach on the island, if you like a party vibe. It's filled with cool, good-looking young people and a great beach bar that pumps out club tunes. I also recommend Jimmy's where we just dined. The blokes thank us, and head off, their eyes wandering towards a pair of attractive women, more their own age, who have just sat down at a nearby table.

'What a great evening.' I take a seat in the taxi and stifle a yawn.

'I know. I was thinking I hadn't lost my touch with the young blokes, but it turns out they were only bothering with us until someone younger came along. Maybe I reminded them of their mother.' Paige roars her infectious laugh that even has the taxi driver turning around and smiling.

It's one thirty when we arrive back at the villa, its twinkling lights beckoning us forward as we head up the mountain road towards it, the bends on the road feeling a little scary in the dark.

Once home, I kick my shoes off and take a glass of water to bed. It's been such a lovely first day, I can't wait for tomorrow to come and see what adventure the day brings!

Chapter Seven

Abby and Uncle Henry are downstairs when I tread down the modern open staircase, feeling the beginnings of a slight headache.

They're in the huge kitchen with floor-to-ceiling windows that overlook the swimming pool and Abby has just brewed a pot of fresh coffee. Two minutes later, Paige appears, fully made up and looking as fresh as a daisy in a pretty white cotton dress.

'Morning! How are we all?' she asks brightly as she pours herself a glass of orange juice.

'I feel fabulous,' says Abby. 'I slept for seven hours straight, which is totally unheard of. I can't believe it,' she says as she tucks into some croissants. 'I feel like a new person.'

Henry tells us to help ourselves from the fridge and the freezer, which is fully stocked.

'Oh and, of course, you can have use of the Range Rover to get up and down from the port.'

Paige gives a little squeal.

'Just be careful approaching the bends.' He looks directly at me.

'Oh, I will, don't worry. Although truthfully, I think Paige can hardly wait to get behind the wheel.'

I glance at Paige, who is nodding her head furiously. She's used to handling a large car as she owned a large SUV for several years back home, before doing a complete one eighty and buying a sports car.

At midday, we give Henry a lift down to the port where he is meeting his friends, before they head off on their sailing adventure. He introduces us to his three friends – one who has film star looks – who will take it in turns to skipper the boat.

'Have a wonderful time,' I tell him as I hug him goodbye.

'No wild parties,' he tells me jokingly, wagging his finger.

'I promise,' I reassure him, but feeling excited that this is the start of my holiday with the girls.

Back at the villa, we discuss heading down to Koukounaries beach for a few hours. Abby has called home and is reassured to learn that the twins are fine and her mother and father-in-law are taking them for a day out to an animal play farm today. She has stuck to her decision to call rather than video call in case the twins get upset, although I think it's to protect her own feelings too.

'I should really be getting on with some writing,' Abby admits reluctantly. 'That was my plan whilst here, but I must admit I'm dying to get to the beach,' she says, her resolve weakening as we toss sun cream into our bags. 'I wouldn't mind going home with a bit of a tan.'

'Well, we'll be back around five,' I tell her, glancing at my watch, which shows the time as just after twelve. 'Maybe you could do a couple of hours' writing then, if we have a late dinner tonight,' I suggest.

'Oh go on then,' she says excitedly, easily persuaded. 'I'll just grab a beach towel,' she says.

'Then if you have a full writing day tomorrow, we can do the *Mamma Mia!* boat trip on Tuesday,' I remind her.

'That sounds like a plan. Perhaps we'd better book the trip today, though; they might be sold out otherwise, with it being high season.'

Twenty minutes later, we're heading along the coast road to the beach, passing wooden signs for several other beaches en route and catching the occasional glimpse of the shimmering sea, which is obscured by trees. On the opposite side of the road holiday apartments, in varying pastel shades with pools outside, are interspersed by the occasional bar and restaurant. I feel such a sense of freedom here that I briefly imagine living with Uncle Henry in his villa and making a new life for myself. But maybe that's just running away from reality.

Fifteen minutes later, we park the Range Rover in a car park and head along a wooden boardwalk to the soft sandy beach.

'Wow, this looks gorgeous,' says Abby as we scan the sunbeds for the best spot. There's a stand nearby offering activities including surfing, water skiing and banana boat rides.

The beach is full of holidaymakers, some seated on white wooden chairs with turquoise canvas seats enjoying lunch in the shade of the beach restaurant. The place is heaving, but we're lucky enough to get some beds close to the sea as a family of four gather their things, and head off.

We settle down and before long, an older guy with weathered brown skin approaches us for payment of the sunbeds, closely followed by a young man who hands us a menu and tells us we can order from our sunbeds and have waiter service.

'Ah, this is the life,' says Abby as she settles down onto her bed after ordering us each a cocktail and some bottled water. 'I can't remember the last time I did anything like this. I just need to get over my slight feelings of guilt,' she confesses.

'Why? I bet Joe didn't feel guilty on that lads' trip to Vegas a few months ago, did he?' Paige reminds her.

'No, you're right, he didn't, did he? Five nights of the kids up all night teething and he was there in Vegas having the time of his life,' she says firmly.

'Well, you're only here for a short while so try and relax. The twins are being looked after by family. It's not as if you've gone and left them with a babysitter or something. People who have nannies do it all the time,' I remind her.

'You're right,' she says as a Greek Adonis appears with our drinks.

'Ladies, would you like something to eat?'

Abby takes a second too long looking him up and down before tossing her hair over her shoulder and ordering a Caesar salad. Realising I didn't really eat breakfast, I opt for a burger and fries, as does Paige.

'No problem.' As he strolls to the bar, he looks over his shoulder and smiles warmly at Abby.

'I think you're in there,' jokes Paige. 'He couldn't take his eyes off you.'

'Don't be ridiculous.' She dismisses the idea, but I can tell from the smile on her face that she's flattered by the attention from the young man, who looks around his mid-twenties.

'Anyway, as if I'm interested in other men; I'm practically a married woman,' she says.

'Practically,' adds Paige, taking a long sip of her mojito.

'What do you mean?' asks Abby, a little seriously.

'Well, you're not married, are you? I'm just saying.'

Paige laughs off her comment but I can see Abby is a little stung by it.

'Well, I know we don't have a piece of paper, but we've been together for sixteen years, and we have three kids. What more of a commitment do you need than that?' She sniffs.

'Is that what Joe says?' Paige laughs, never quite knowing when to stop.

'It's what we both say,' Abby replies a little stiffly.

A few seconds later a beach ball lands on Abby's knees and she shrieks in surprise and laughs. Two young boys appear and retrieve the ball, before apologising and running off giggling, and the conversation about marriage appears to be over. For now, at least. Shortly afterwards, our delicious food arrives and we tuck in hungrily, listening to club tunes pump out from the bar and watching the sparkling, inviting sea. As I feel the searing heat on my body, I massage some more sun oil into my skin. I know I'll return home with a lovely tan, as my skin is smooth and tans easily.

An hour later, I decide to head into the water for a swim, and rub my eyes in amazement and wonder as if I'm seeing things. I didn't think I'd been in the sun long enough to be hallucinating, but there, before my very eyes, is a huge white swan gliding along in the water. People are snapping away with their cameras, nudging their sunbathing partners to sit up and take a look.

'It is not such an unusual sight,' says the barman, who has returned to deliver us a second round of drinks. 'But seeing it for the first time always amuses tourists.' He smiles.

I ask where it came from and he explains that the swans live in a nature reserve, just behind the beach, and often head out into the open sea.

'Oh and they are also very friendly. They won't bother you if you swim,' he informs me.

I decide to wait until the swan has completely drifted past before I head into the water and enjoy the most wonderful swim. As I roll onto my back, glancing above at the searing sun, I toy with the idea of spending a whole summer here with Uncle Henry next year. Maybe I could open a little market stall near the harbour selling my soaps and bath products. Or maybe there's more chance of flying pigs, although I have just witnessed a swan swimming in the open sea.

We spend the rest of the afternoon swimming, chatting and listening to the music coming from the beach bar. It's almost five thirty when we gather up our things and head towards the car park. As we pass the bar, our handsome waiter is leaning on it.

'Bye, ladies. Have a nice evening. If you are dining out tonight I can recommend Mistrali's.' He hands a card to Abby with a small map of the restaurant.

'Thanks. See you again,' says Abby.

'I hope so,' he replies, with a slow, sexy smile.

'I bet that's his family's restaurant. Either that or he's on commission,' says Paige as we stroll along.

'Do you have to be so cynical about everything?' asks Abby, rolling her eyes.

'I'm not a cynic, just a realist.' She shrugs; it's true, I suppose.

As I only had one cocktail at lunchtime, followed by water through-out the day, I take the wheel as we head home. The sun is still warm when we leave, and people continue to arrive at the beach, some with older family members who may prefer not to be out in the midday sun. The long days that seem to stretch out forever mean the beach is full for most of the daylight hours throughout the summer months.

The car journey only takes fifteen minutes and soon enough we are heading into the sweeping driveway of the villa once more. Whilst Abby and Paige head inside for a shower, I linger over the perimeter fence near the pool and take in the breath-taking view below. I close my eyes for a minute and breathe, enjoying the brief solitude. I've always been the type of person who needs time alone to re-energise, whether it's an hour on the yoga mat in my lounge or going for a long walk; I always feel invigorated afterwards.

Later, we're sitting on the terrace, showered and dressed for the evening as lights come on around the pool area. I can feel the pleasant tingling sensation on my skin as I clutch a cold Mythos beer in my hand and all is well with the world. Abby is turning the card over in her hand of the restaurant recommended by the waiter at the beach.

'So are we going to give this a try then?' she asks.

'I don't mind,' says Paige. 'We could do. Shall we take a taxi, though?'

'Definitely. Maybe we'd better book a table too, rather than just turning up,' I suggest.

Abby successfully manages to book us a table, although it's for nine o'clock, which Paige grumbles is a little late to eat.

'It's the Greek way,' says Abby, pushing a bowl of olives in front of her.

'I'm not Greek,' says Paige. 'I'll go and grab some snacks to tide me over.'

Paige heads into the kitchen and returns carrying a huge bag of crisps and some assorted nuts, which she tips into a bowl. She happily grazes on the snacks for the next hour and I honestly don't know how she manages to maintain such a svelte figure.

Whilst we're sitting chatting, Abby nips inside to give Joe a call.

'That was quick,' I comment, when she emerges a few minutes later.

'Joe wasn't home. I spoke to Heather and she said he'd just nipped out. I might try him again later,' she says, looking slightly disappointed.

Mistrali's is along the coast road away from the main town, and tucked down a little side street. There are two other restaurants down the same street, and I spotted the neon lights of a cocktail bar from the taxi, just a short walk away. Other than that, it's a little off the beaten track.

'Hardly the throbbing centre of Skiathos, is it?' Paige comments.

'Maybe, but we can stay around the harbour tomorrow night. It's good to discover other places,' I tell her and she nods.

'Suppose so. And I don't mind really, as long as the food's good. I'm starving.'

Abby and I look at her in disbelief.

It's quiet as we head down the narrow street, which has some residential properties close by. We can hear the chirrup of cicadas as we walk, the sky above us darkening and the beginnings of a silvery moon are visible.

'I love that sound,' I say as we stroll along, linking arms and navigating a bumpy stone road as we're wearing heels. After a few minutes we arrive at the wooden front of Mistrali's, where we are greeted by a moustachioed Greek man who looks in his fifties.

'Welcome, ladies. We have an outside table for you, is this okay?' He smiles warmly, his brown eyes crinkling at the corners.

There is a large inside dining area, with ceiling fans, but on an evening like this, dining outside is perfect.

'*Efcharisto*,' we reply as he puts his arm out and guides us to the table on a terrace, set with a candle inside a storm vase.

The majority of diners on the terrace are couples; one couple at an adjacent table are holding hands and gazing into each other's eyes. We strike up conversation and the couple tell us they are on their honeymoon.

'What a lovely place to spend a honeymoon,' I say.

The couple tell us they got married on a yacht in the port and are having a rare night out alone, away from the rest of the family who had attended the wedding and are staying at a nearby hotel.

'They're off clubbing in Skiathos, but we wanted somewhere quiet this evening,' says the woman, threading her hand through her new husband's.

'Everyone needs a little time alone,' says Abby, no doubt relishing her freedom away from her family, despite doting on them.

We dine on the most delicious food, including a mixed meze of hot and cold dips, including creamy hummus and warm aubergines, and soft pitta bread, followed by a tasty meatball dish.

'You'd better not have too many ouzos, Abby, we don't want you falling down those stairs.'

I gesture to the flight of steps at the entrance and Paige laughs.

'Don't remind me.' Abby pulls a face. 'In my defence, it was the first night out after the twins were born so I hadn't touched any alcohol in almost a year.'

She lost her footing at the top of a flight of stairs at a club in town – thankfully a short flight – and landed in a heap at the bottom. The doorman who had rushed to her aid made sure she was alright, before asking her for her name and contact details.

Paige picks up the story. 'And you slurred indignantly, "Excuse me, but I have a boyfriend. He's on his way here now to take me home."'

I finish the story. 'And the hunky doorman looked at you and said, "Erm. I meant for the accident book. We have to record everything. Health and safety."'

We roar with laughter, even though Abby covers her face with her hands, still mortified at the memory.

We're so full that we decline dessert, but are presented nonetheless with a shot of ouzo that we quickly down.

'How far do you think that cocktail bar that we passed in the taxi is?' asks Paige as we settle the bill, leaving a good tip for a fabulous meal.

'I'd say ten minutes. Shall we try it?' We head off, vowing not to eat for a week.

The road ahead is dimly lit and the bars that seemed close by in the taxi are actually a lot more spaced out on foot. After ten minutes walking along the dark road, there's no sign of the cocktail bar.

'Are you sure we're even walking in the right direction?' I ask as we stop and try to get our bearings. All of a sudden, a moped startles us as it roars out of a side road and Paige waves it down.

'Are we walking in the right direction of a cocktail bar?' she asks the rider.

'Yes, two minutes. Do you want to hop on?' he offers, with a wink.

'I'm not sure we'd all fit.' She gestures to me and Abby, who emerge from the shadows near the roadside.

'No problem. You are very close anyway.' He speeds off into the distance and literally two minutes later, we hear the gentle pulsating sound of music and the pink neon sign of the cocktail bar appears before our eyes.

Chapter Eight

'What time is it in England?' Abby checks as we take a seat on bar stools near the bar and order espresso Martini cocktails.

'Two hours behind. Why?' I tell her.

'I think I'll just nip and phone Joe,' she says. I can't help noticing that he didn't return her earlier call. She heads outside and returns a few minutes later looking slightly worried.

'Is everything okay?' I ask. I don't think I've ever seen Abby look so distracted and it concerns me.

'I think so. Heather said Joe had just nipped next door. That's where he was earlier, though.'

'Is that unusual?' asks Paige.

'I think so. At least I've never known him do that when I'm at home,' she tells us.

'Who lives there?' I ask, intrigued.

'Priya. Our beautiful, Indian single-parent neighbour.' She takes a sip of her cocktail. 'Oh, that's good. Much nicer than an after-dinner coffee,' she says appreciatively.

Paige and I exchange a glance.

I wait for Abby to say something more but as usual Paige dives right in.

'You don't think he fancies her, do you?' she asks, with a slight frown.

Abby takes a while to answer. 'No. Actually… no, of course not,' she says, dismissing the idea. 'She's a really lovely neighbour.' She's smiling now. 'She's lived next door for five years, so I'm pretty sure I'd know if anything was going on. Occasionally, she'll knock and ask to borrow Joe for a minute to help her lift something heavy.'

'So it's his muscles she's after,' says Paige and I shoot her a look and she shrugs before taking a sip of her drink.

Abby laughs but I hope she doesn't have doubts about Joe. As far as I can tell, he's totally devoted to Abby and the kids, but maybe his reluctance to marry is a sticking point between them. I realise that despite my close friendship with Abby, Paige has known her a lot longer than I have, and her earlier comments appear to have struck a nerve with Abby.

We're enjoying a second, final cocktail, when in walks the guy from the beach at Koukounaries. He recognises us and comes over to say hello.

'Evening, ladies, have you been to Mistrali's for dinner?' he asks.

'Yes, and you're right. It was absolutely perfect,' I tell him.

'It's easily the best restaurant in this area. I'm glad you liked it. Maybe I'll see you at the beach again.' He seems to direct this at Abby with a dazzling smile, before he heads off to join some blokes who are sitting at a table in the corner laughing and drinking beer.

If the villa wasn't halfway up a hill we might have walked home as it's such a beautiful evening, with a glorious pink-streaked sky and a white full moon, but as it is, we call a taxi and enjoy the ride home, chatting to the taxi driver, who recommends various places to visit, some of which I've visited before. Fifteen minutes later we pull up outside the villa, having enjoyed a lovely evening out.

Tomorrow is Monday, so we've all agreed to have a day lazing around the pool and plan to set off on Tuesday morning on the *Mamma Mia!* boat trip. Abby needs to get some writing done, as she failed to do any today after we returned home from the beach.

We're just out of the car, when Abby takes a phone call from Joe on the terrace. They chat for a few minutes and she seems lighter when the call ends.

'Everything okay?' I ask.

'Yeah, it's fine. Joe had nipped next door to help Priya's son fix something on his laptop. He's been home for hours, but Heather has only just told him that I'd called,' she explains.

'Typical teenager,' I say, happy he called before she retires for the evening, although I can't help wondering if something has changed between them to make her troubled by Joe being at the next-door neighbour's house.

'Right, I'm off to bed,' she says brightly, grabbing a bottle of water from the fridge.

Paige and I follow suit and head upstairs.

Chapter Nine

The dawn chorus of birds can be heard as I breathe deeply and stretch my body into warrior pose. Practising yoga here on the terrace this morning before the others wake up has been a complete joy and reawakened my love for it. I take a long sip of my water and view the mist as it continues to ascend from the mountains, while an already warm sun pokes through a cloud. I'm just finishing up, sitting cross-legged on a yoga mat and feeling completely relaxed, when I hear the chatter of voices coming from the kitchen.

'You're up early this morning,' says Paige as she emerges from the kitchen eating a strawberry.

'I fancied doing a little yoga. It's done me the world of good.' I beam, feeling energised and happy.

As the mist clears and the sun beats down on the terrace, we decide to eat our breakfast outside.

'Gosh, I feel bad helping myself to food and a free holiday,' says Abby as she tucks into some fruit and Greek yoghurt.

'I was thinking the same. Maybe we ought to go and shop for food tomorrow?' says Paige. 'Fill the fridge up again before Henry returns from his trip.'

'There's nowhere to put any more food. Besides, I'm here for another week when you two leave, remember. I'll do a big shop when Henry gets back,' I tell them and they offer to leave some money towards it.

'There's enough food to feed an army here. Maybe we should invite the neighbours over for a party,' suggests Paige.

'What neighbours?' I ask. There is a villa opposite, but apart from that there's only one or two houses in the distance. 'Besides, I'm under strict instructions to look after the place and have no wild parties.'

'I'm just joking.' Paige laughs. 'Well, we should at least buy Henry a nice present,' she says. 'Maybe something with a nautical theme. It's the least we can do for inviting us to stay here.'

Later, when we're all settled sunbathing around the gorgeous pool, I nip into the air-conditioned lounge and give Mum a call.

'Hi, Mum, how are things going?' I ask brightly.

'Oh hi, love, I'll call you back in a minute, there's a customer here.'

It feels strange knowing Mum is looking after the shop and I hope she is enjoying herself. Ten minutes later she calls me back.

'Ooh there was a bit of a rush on just then. Well, when I say rush, there were five customers in the shop all at once. I had to keep my eye on a couple of teenagers who seemed to be loitering around the basil and lime candles. They're a real bargain, those, and they smell as good as the Jo Malone ones. They eventually left without buying anything once they realised I was watching them,' she says with satisfaction.

'Really? That is good news, I don't mean about having potential shoplifters, I mean the shop being busy. Gosh, I hope you don't run out of stock.'

'No, there's plenty,' she reassures me. 'Besides, two of the purchases were from other suppliers, a scarf and some organic bath bombs. One lady bought some discount soaps from the till, though, three bars, along with a pretty gift set.'

'You've discounted the soaps?' I ask in surprise.

'Only those loose ones in the baskets that weren't selling. I've reduced them to one pound and sold a dozen already today.'

The soaps contain expensive organic ingredients and usually retail for three pounds each, but I don't say anything to Mum as she's looking after the shop after all, and perhaps she's right, they were just sitting there unsold.

'Thanks, Mum. Just don't go discounting the gift sets,' I tell her. 'They're already a good price.'

'Of course I won't.'

'So, is everything okay? Any other news?' I ask.

'No, what kind of news?' Mum says a little abruptly.

'I don't know, just general gossip.'

'Have you heard something?' she asks.

'About what?' Mum has got me puzzled now, as well as a little worried.

'Oh nothing, I just wondered what you meant by other news,' she says dismissively.

'I just meant as in you and Dad, the market, you know, just general news.'

Mum is quiet for a minute, confirming to me that there is something she isn't telling me.

'Mum, what's the matter?' I ask, now feeling increasingly concerned.

'Oh, it's nothing, but I was chatting to Doreen from Plymouth on the phone last night. She told me her daughter Claire is getting married next year.'

'Surely that's happy news, not something to worry about?' I know at once that isn't the thing she is thinking about.

'Oh yes, and she did happen to mention something else.' She hesitates for a moment. 'Scott has been released from prison,' she says in a low voice.

Despite the heat of the day, a sudden chill runs through my body.

'He's been released?' I reply, hardly able to believe what I'm hearing. By my calculation he's only served three years of a five-year sentence.

'Yes. Doreen said he knocked on her door and asked about your whereabouts. He's out on good behaviour, apparently.'

'He did what? Oh my goodness, what did she tell him?'

My heart is thumping, yet I tell myself I'm being irrational. Scott has no idea where I live after all and Mum reminds me of this.

'Nothing, of course. How could she? She doesn't know where you are; she only phones me for an occasional chat.'

'Yes, I know, Mum, but I can't believe it. What if he finds out where I am?' I ask, my heart galloping wildly.

'He won't. You're not listed anywhere,' she tells me reassuringly.

I feel as though I've just been delivered a bombshell. Even though I knew that Scott would be released from prison sometime, I didn't expect it to be just yet. Released early on good behaviour. I shake my head at the thought, although thinking about it Scott could be charming when he wanted something. It was the thing that attracted me to him – apart from his good looks admittedly. He was attentive and charming and would organise surprise days out and once set up a table in the garden with little candles and fairy lights strung through the trees for my birthday, where he served dinner. Everyone loved him and told me how lucky I was to have a boyfriend like that, and I think I was rather proud of the fact that people envied me.

I head outside and join the girls around the pool, my thoughts spinning, and tell them all about the conversation with Mum.

'Try not to worry,' says Paige. 'You're literally thousands of miles away. Even when you get home, he has no idea where you are,' she tries to reassure me.

'I know, but I'll be going home in less than two weeks,' I remind her, trying to quell the knot of worry forming in my stomach.

Abby and Paige try to comfort me, telling me I have nothing to worry about and as the morning wears on, I allow myself to relax a little. A little after two o'clock, we decide to head down to the Bourtzi for a late lunch.

We are lucky enough to find a table near the railings overlooking the harbour below, with the rugged pine forests rising in the distance. Colourful boats are bobbing in the harbour, alongside tourist boats, one of which is making its way back to the harbour, packed with people.

We dine on fresh fish and Greek salad, which is completely delicious. I've decided to put all thoughts of my chat with Mum out of my mind and so I concentrate on enjoying the spectacular views. I can see the villa from here, sunshine bouncing from the glass walls like a beacon in the mountains. It's all so beautiful.

Paige, looking stylish in a straw hat and designer sunglasses, takes a selfie and sends it to Rob. A few minutes later, he returns a photo of himself at work on a building site in a hi-vis jacket and hard hat beneath a grey sky, a heart emoji covering the photo.

'Ah, I miss him already and it's only day three.' She sighs. 'Although, I must admit, I absolutely adore it here.' She removes her sunglasses and turns her face to the sun, sighing contentedly. 'Your uncle Henry is so lucky to live in a place like this.'

'I suppose there was a certain amount of luck involved, not to mention a lot of hard graft,' I remind her.

I recall Mum telling me how many hours Henry put in when he was building his gardening business and Aunt Bea complaining that she sometimes felt like a widow, although, added Mum, she didn't seem to mind when he'd amassed a load of money and bought up several huge garden centres, allowing her to spend her days shopping and going to lunch with friends whilst Henry toiled away.

'You should bring Rob out with you for a holiday,' I suggest. 'Henry loves having visitors at his place; he's always telling Mum he rattles around the place since Aunt Bea died. You know how sociable he is.'

'So sociable that he's buggered off sailing when we come to stay.' Paige laughs and once again people nearby can't help smiling at the sound of her unique laughter.

'Seriously, though, that's not a bad idea. Maybe he'd fall in love with the place, and build us our dream home here.' She sighs, glancing out to sea.

We order coffee and then saunter down to the port to book the *Mamma Mia!* boat trip. Threading through old cobbled side streets, we stop to admire clothes in shop windows and a restaurant that has herbs in grey boxes attached to the exterior walls as the smell of rosemary drifts through the air. There's a cute gift shop, its wares spilling out onto the pavement, including baskets of tea towels and wooden gifts and I resolve to take a better look inside another time, as Mum loves traditional holiday souvenirs and still cherishes a paperweight that I brought back from a school trip to France.

When we arrive at the boat, the same bloke who was here the other day, Renos, is sitting chatting to a thin woman with cropped blonde hair wearing a black vest and tiny white shorts.

'Ladies, welcome back.' He smiles and stands to greet us.

So many tourists pass along the harbour front, I'm surprised he recognises us, but maybe it's a skill he's developed to remember everyone who has shown an interest in the trip.

'Do you have any seats for the trip tomorrow?' I ask.

He leafs through a folder and taps his pen on the small counter in front of the boat as we wait patiently.

'Yes, okay, we have three spaces only. You are very lucky.' He smiles at us.

'Will the weather be alright?' Paige asks the woman. 'It's just that we were told there might be a storm tomorrow.' She glances at Renos with a mischievous grin on her face.

The woman looks at her blankly. 'Who on earth told you that? It will be perfect weather for sailing,' she says, handing her a ticket for the money we have just paid.

Paige glances at Renos and he gives a cheeky smile.

As we walk along, despite me resolving not to think about Scott, my thoughts suddenly turn back to the news I received from Mum. Scott is out of prison. I wonder what went through his mind when he turned up at my old family home and found my parents were no longer living there. Doreen has no idea where we are, which I'm relieved about, as although she's a lovely woman, Scott might have been able to wear her down with his charm if she knew my whereabouts.

I received a letter almost every month from prison in the beginning. The last one I received from him was just before I moved away, saying he was counting the days down until we could be together. Me telling him there was never going to be a future for us only seemed to fuel his determination to have me forgive him. It was never going to stop. My heart still pounds just thinking about it.

'So what do you think then?'

'About what?' I ask as Paige snaps me out of my daydream.

'About which beach we should head to.'

'They all sound nice,' says Abby. 'Or I don't mind if we head back to Koukounaries, it was lovely there.'

'You wouldn't want to run into a certain barman, would you?' teases Paige.

'What do you mean? Of course not,' she replies indignantly. 'Although he is pretty fit. And anyway, as you pointed out, I'm not married, am I? Only practically.'

Paige and I exchange a look.

We pass a bar and Abby gestures to an outside table and we order a drink.

'So come on, what's this all about?' I ask as we sip an ice-cold beer in the blazing sunshine.

'It's just what you said the other day about me not being married, it struck a nerve, that's all,' says Abby.

'I didn't mean to upset you,' says Paige apologetically.

'I know you didn't.' Abby covers Paige's hand with her own. 'I know that whatever you are thinking comes straight out of your mouth, but you were right. We're not married and, the truth is, I would like to be. Especially since we've had the twins,' she confides.

'And Joe?'

'He clearly doesn't want to. He comes out with all kinds of excuses, saying isn't it nicer that we want to be together of our own free will, who needs a contract blah blah blah, but at the back of my mind I think he just thinks things will be less messy if we ever break up.'

'Oh, Abby, have you told him how you really feel?' I ask, feeling bad for my friend.

'Once or twice, yes, but I'm never going to mention it again. What's the point in forcing him into something he clearly doesn't see the need for?' She shrugs. 'And I do love him, so I guess I have to respect how he feels.'

'And what about your feelings?' adds Paige, trying for a sensitive voice. 'Is it causing problems between you both?'

'I'm not sure.' Abby sighs. 'I guess I'm so busy with the twins I never really confront my feelings. I tell myself it doesn't matter, but truthfully it does a little. We have three gorgeous kids together but he doesn't want me to be his wife.' She gulps down a long drink of her beer.

'Well, you need to be honest with yourself as well as Joe. There's two people in this relationship; it's not all about him,' says Paige.

'You're so right,' Abby says. 'I'm glad I've spoken about it; I think I needed to. Thanks, Paige, for making me face the situation.'

It would appear Paige's honesty isn't such a bad thing sometimes.

Finishing our drinks, we head off out of the port slightly and walk to the nearest bus stop where buses head along the coast road passing several beaches. We've decided to head to a closer one, which I googled and looks beautiful and less crowded than Koukounaries. The bus is almost full and we're lucky to get a seat. The door stays firmly closed as we pass several more stops, the passengers on the bus, many standing, are packed together like sardines in a tin. The people who are left behind at the bus stops, raise their arms in disappointment as we sail past.

'They're every fifteen minutes,' says a woman, whose ample bosom is squashing into my arm as she tries to navigate a blown-up alligator for the beach. 'It's for my grandson.' She waves at a boy a few seats behind. 'One of the waiters at the hotel helped me pump it up,' she explains. 'I nearly had a heart attack last time I tried it at the beach.' She chuckles.

The beach is smaller but every bit as beautiful as Koukounaries. There's a beach bar and restaurant and at the far end of the beach another bar. We settle down and fish our books from our bags. Paige is applying sun cream when her phone rings. It's Rob.

'Hey, gorgeous, what you up to then?' She pans the phone around and we all say hi before she chats away to Rob. He takes in the glorious blue sky and sandy beach and pushes his bottom lip out and pans his phone around to show the cloudy sky outside the window. It looks like an autumn day back home and I feel so lucky to be here enjoying the warm sun. Paige makes lots of kissing noises and says, 'I love you,' before she finishes the call.

'Are you missing each other by any chance?' I tease.

'Like crazy. Rob's off to the gym for a workout, probably to burn off some testosterone; I think he's missing the sex.' She sighs. 'So am I, to be honest.'

A gorgeous bloke strolls past at that very moment in navy shorts, his muscular body gleaming with sun oil. He glances at us and smiles as he sweeps back his dark hair.

'Pop your eyes back in,' I tell Paige.

'I think I'm definitely missing Rob's body.' She sighs. 'No harm in just looking.' She winks.

Paige and Abby's stories couldn't be more different. Rob and Paige walked down the aisle just over a year after they met and still seem to be in their honeymoon period, six years later, and Abby and Joe have been together for sixteen years and still haven't tied the knot.

'Bloody hell, you've only been away from each other for three days. I'm not sure Joe would miss that side of things unless weeks went by,' Abby reveals.

'It's a bit different when you've got toddlers hanging around, though, I would imagine,' says Paige.

'You're not kidding. Even when we do manage to get intimate, there's usually the patter of tiny feet bounding into the bedroom to share our bed.' She laughs.

'According to my mum, I never slept as a child,' says Paige. 'She said I'd have an hour or two and then I'd be wide awake rattling the spindles of my cot, demanding to be released. I can laugh about it now, but my poor mum said she thought she was going mad due to sleep deprivation. She told me she survived on black coffee and reading *Woman's Own* magazine in the middle of the night when I was wide awake playing with my toys.'

'Your poor mum. You two do realise you are putting me off ever having children?' I tell my friends, although I can't ever imagine settling down with someone and having children, at least not for a long time.

'Sorry about that. Anyway, don't worry, all kids are different and, would you know it, as a teenager I could never get out of bed and was nearly always late for school. I think I was catching up on all those years of lost sleep,' Paige says.

As we're chatting, Abby's phone rings and Joe's face appears on the screen, smiling broadly, and we all wave and say hi just as we did with Rob. For a second it stabs at my heart when I realise there is no one at home calling me. Apart from Mum, of course. I wonder when I'll be able to trust another man after everything that went on with Scott. I'm thinking all this when I hear Abby's voice.

'Joe, what the hell are the twins doing?'

I glance at her phone and there, in the background, are the twins, naked and about to dip their hands into a pot of moisturiser from a dressing table.

'Bloody hell, I've only just got them dressed. They've been doing that these last few days,' he tells her, before grabbing the cream and placing it on a high shelf. 'As soon as I've got them dressed, they decide it's funny to strip off again. I'd better go. I'll call you tonight,' says Joe.

'Oh before you go, how come you're not in work?' asks Abby.

'I came home early to collect the twins from Priya. She was watching them for a few hours,' he tells her.

'Priya?' asks Abby, her tone changing slightly.

'Yeah, Mum caught a bit of a stomach bug, so Priya stepped in and helped out. Heather's gone out for the day with her friends to

Southport. I can't expect her to help out every day – it's the summer holidays and she's a teenager.'

He's right of course, Heather has been a great help but she has her own life too.

'No, no of course you can't, it wouldn't be fair. Well, that's kind of Priya to help out,' she says, smiling into the camera but the colour seems to have drained from her face.

She wraps up the call, but seems quiet as she settles down on the bed and immerses herself in her book. Thankfully Paige doesn't offer her any pearls of wisdom and we enjoy the afternoon reading and swimming on the beach, before we set off a little after six. Passing a supermarket, we head inside and buy chicken and steaks to fire up the BBQ at the villa. There's a ton of salad in the fridge that needs using up too and I also spied some cartons of pineapple juice so I purchase a bottle of vodka and some Chambord.

'To make us a French Martini with dinner,' I tell the girls.

'Ooh, can't wait,' says Paige.

Back at the villa Mum phones checking I'm okay after the news about Scott and, feeling calmer, I reassure her that I'm fine. She tells me she's been busy today and has sold eight gift sets, along with lots of bars of soap, and that she might have to contact the local suppliers to replenish an empty shelf.

'Gosh, Mum, I should leave you in charge more often,' I tell her.

'Oh anytime, I can't tell you how much I'm enjoying myself. Your dad has made a lovely grey wooden blackboard for outside the shop, and he's written on it in chalk, announcing special offers inside.'

'What special offers?' I ask, a little shocked.

'Oh, don't worry, only more of the soaps and some cinnamon body butter that wasn't shifting. Cinnamon isn't everyone's cup of tea, you know,' Mum says firmly. 'Your dad hates the stuff.' She chuckles.

'Well, he's hardly likely to be using body butter, so he isn't my target audience, but I take your point. Maybe I should appoint you my product manager,' I tell her jokingly, wondering if she's right. Maybe cinnamon is a love or hate thing.

I'm happy Mum's enjoying working in the shop. I knew she was growing a little bored at home so it might be just the thing for her.

That evening, I marinade the meats in oregano and garlic and later we enjoy a simple tasty BBQ on the huge terrace, enjoying harbour views, and the French Martinis are going down a treat. We decide to limit ourselves to no more than two, as we have to be down at the harbour early tomorrow morning for our boat trip, which we are all looking forward to.

Abby has been a little quiet this evening and it's clear something isn't sitting right with her. Apparently, Joe never nipped out anywhere when she was at home, she reveals, when I ask her if she's okay.

'You do trust him, don't you?' asks Paige as she sips the last of her Martini through a straw.

'Yes, I do. Sixteen years together and I've never had any reason to doubt him in all that time,' she answers.

'I wonder what's making you feel a little insecure now then?' asks Paige, always one to get to the heart of the matter.

'I honestly don't know. Maybe it's because we don't go out together anymore, which I don't expect it to be as frequently with the babies obviously, but I worry we've stopped looking after own relationship,' she tells us honestly.

'Well, if you can manage to get away for over a week, I'm sure you can arrange a babysitter now and then. Surely Heather's old enough to watch them for a few hours in the evening if they're in bed? When you get home, book dinner at a fancy restaurant and buy some sexy lingerie, put the romance back in the relationship,' Paige advises. 'Would your in-laws have the kids overnight? Or I'll have them if you're really stuck.' Abby's own parents live in London.

I can't imagine toddlers in Paige's pristine house, but it was typically kind of her to offer.

'Me too,' I say, although I know nothing about looking after two-year-olds.

'Thanks, girls. And maybe you're right about getting a spark back. Maybe Joe is sick of seeing me slobbing around in leggings and T-shirts, but I don't see the point in dressing up when I'm working from home.'

'Oh dear, sounds like you're in a right old rut. All the more reason to dress up and go out to dinner together. You definitely need to have a chat when you get home,' says Paige.

'I know, you're right, we will.' Abby nods her head and I pray they manage to sort things out between them.

We're about to head off to bed, when Uncle Henry gives us a Skype call from the deck of a yacht. It's strung with lights and there's a table littered with glasses and leftover food on plates. Henry is puffing on a large cigar.

'Just checking you're not having any wild parties,' he jokes.

'Looks like you've done a bit of that yourself,' I reply, laughing, taking in the scene.

'And don't worry, it's just us three,' I tell him as Abby and Paige wave at the camera.

His friends, who are wearing loud patterned shirts, wave at us in return and raise a glass. The tanned, fair-haired bloke that looks like a movie star smiles a dazzling smile and Paige flicks her hair over her shoulder and pouts at the camera.

'Do you think we could get an invite on that yacht? It looks amazing,' she says with a deep sigh when we finish the call.

'I'm afraid you'll be gone by the time they return,' I remind her. 'So you've missed the boat there.'

'Very funny.' She rolls her eyes.

There's no denying the guy on the boat is attractive especially for someone in his sixties, but even if a gorgeous bloke was sitting here right now, flirting with me, I'm not sure I would raise a flicker of interest. I like being on my own. I like my independence and my female friendships, plus I'm not sure I could ever commit to a relationship again after being involved with Scott.

We clear up and head off to bed, feeling relaxed after a lovely day on the beach and then just hanging out back here this evening. I'm so glad Henry seems to be enjoying himself too. He's such a kind, generous man; he deserves all the happiness in the world.

Chapter Ten

We wake the next morning to another sunny day and it's already warm at only nine thirty, the sun having risen early over the mountains. I'm standing on the terrace watching cars weaving their way along the mountain road towards the harbour, surrounded by patches of green from the pine forests in the background.

I'm sure it would be easy to just sit here all day and while away the hours if I had nothing planned for the day. No wonder Henry chose this place to retire; it's absolutely perfect.

Half an hour later we're all ready to head down to the harbour to pick up the boat for the trip, filled with anticipation for the day ahead.

'Ooh I'm excited about this,' says Paige. 'I'm keen to have a look around Skopelos too, even though it's only for a couple of hours.'

'Me too,' says Abby. 'And I hope there's a toilet on the boat. My bladder's been a nightmare since I've had the twins,' she complains.

'You know, I've heard taking pumpkin extract is good for that. It strengthens the bladder apparently,' I inform her. 'I learned that particular nugget of information from the woman on the health food stall at the market back home.'

'Really? Well, who knew?' says Abby.

'Someone who ate a lot of pumpkin and never had a wee for three days,' Paige chimes in and has us all laughing.

'It does make you wonder how things were first discovered,' I say. 'I mean, who first discovered aspirin is derived from willow bark? Were they sitting there sucking a tree or something when their aches and pains disappeared?'

'And don't even ask how someone thought peeing on a jellyfish sting would help. That must have been one crazy beach party,' roars Paige. 'And it's a myth apparently. I learned that on a nature programme,' she adds.

'Well, I'm glad you told us that,' says Abby. 'We won't have any embarrassing scenes on the beach now, should someone get stung.'

At the harbour we join a small queue before boarding the boat and after fifteen minutes head upstairs to the top deck.

Luckily there are three seats at the front of the boat and we settle in, after saying hi to the other passengers who are already seated. There's a couple who look in their late forties. The man is wearing designer shades, and determinedly hanging on to his thinning hair, with a few strands gelled upright. The woman, wearing a pink sundress, has bottle-blonde hair piled on top of her head, and skin as bronzed as David Dickinson. There's a family with two bored-looking teenagers, who look up and half smile, and a jolly, smiling, dark-haired mum. The bearded dad, wearing a cap, continues his conversation about cars with the bloke with the thinning hair, after saying hello to us and his teenage children immerse themselves in their phones.

We sit in the harbour for another ten minutes, awaiting a couple of late arrivals who eventually turn up before we finally set off, skimming the water and leaving foamy trails in our wake. Ten minutes into our journey, the soundtrack of ABBA fires up and can be heard in the background.

The jolly, dark-haired mum engages us in conversation before commenting that the ABBA soundtrack in the background isn't very loud, and the teenage boy mutters, 'Thank God,' under his breath. She tells us she finds it a bit disappointing, as she was rather hoping to have a bit of a singalong with likeminded ABBA fans.

We sail across the striking turquoise water, passing green forest behind golden beaches and soon enough any feelings of tension melt away as the boat continues its journey. A speedboat skims along in the distance and a water skier can be seen bouncing along the waves, enjoying the freedom on the water. It's exhilarating and a world away from real life, for a few hours at least.

Paige is studying a little map of the trip. 'I think that's where there's a scene with Sophie in *Mamma Mia!*' she says, pointing to a stretch of beach. The other passengers listen as she tells us a little more. 'I think it's called Glysteri beach.'

'Well, it's a good job you're here,' says the bronzed blonde, who stands to take a photograph of the beach. 'There's no commentary from the captain,' she says, a hint of disappointment in her voice.

We glide along the waves, soaking up the sun and chatting, everyone in a happy holiday mood when Renos skips upstairs and asks if we would like a drink from the bar. Settled down with ice-cold beers, we continue to chat to the other passengers, who are a friendly bunch. Well, apart from the teenage son, who has obviously been dragged along, although the daughter is happily humming along to the ABBA soundtrack. After a while, the captain announces that we will be pulling into a little beach for half an hour to take a swim.

The sand and shingle beach has white cliffs rising in the background behind, with clear, shallow waters that are perfect for swimming. The boat drops a ladder into the water, for those who would like to swim the short distance to the shore and the teenage boy, encouraged by his sister, climbs down the ladder and into the water, where a few minutes later he is splashing water over his sister and laughing, his face completely transformed by his smile. The boat gently glides to the water's edge for the rest of the passengers to disembark, before the staff sit on deck, chatting around a table.

'What a great job they have,' says Paige as we head into the warm sea.

'I know, imagine having this as your office.' I glance around at the beach, and vast, open sea. 'It's a bit different to looking out over rooftops back home, although maybe any job gets a bit monotonous after a while. They have to listen to ABBA songs on a loop all day in the boat, which must be torture if they're not actually fans,' I say, as we splash about in the water.

'Gosh that's true,' says Paige. 'Maybe they're only in it for the "money, money, money".' She howls with laughter at her own joke, and some of the people nearby in the water laugh along too.

I gaze at the bright blue sky above, feeling the burn of the sun, and wishing I could stay in this moment forever. For a second, my mind flits to Scott and I wonder what he will do for work now that he's out of prison, before feeling annoyed with myself wondering why I even care. I let the warm waves wash over me and will myself not to let thoughts of him ruin my holiday.

'Talking of work,' says Abby as we dry ourselves off. 'I've still got that magazine article to write. I should have done it yesterday really. Tomorrow, without fail, I'd better get stuck in. Would you believe the article is all about the reasons why we procrastinate.' She laughs.

'And why do we do that?' I ask.

'I'll tell you later,' she says, and laughs at her own joke.

'You'd better make the most of today then if you're spending tomorrow writing,' says Paige, stretching her arms out in the sun.

We settle back to enjoy the scenery and after a while we sail into a patch of striking blue-green water with white caves in the background, which is the blue cave. Everyone on the boat is standing up snapping photos, although the inside of the cave is inaccessible, which is slightly disappointing as I recall sailing through blue grotto caves on holidays elsewhere.

A short while later, Abby returns from the toilet and from the look on her face, I can tell at once that something is wrong.

'Abby, is everything okay?' I ask. Paige is snoozing gently, her book on the floor beside her, lulled asleep by sunshine, beer and the gentle rhythm of the boat chugging along on the water.

'I'm not sure,' she says. 'I just video called Joe to show him the gorgeous surroundings, and Heather answered saying he'd nipped next door again and his phone was on charge. I couldn't contain my annoyance so I asked her to go and get him, which didn't go down well at all. Instead of being pleased to see me, he muttered something about him being halfway up a ladder. I don't know, something just doesn't feel right.' She sighs.

'Abby, just think about this,' I say, trying to be rational. 'Do you really think he would be sneaking off next door for a quick leg over, leaving Heather with the babies? Surely he's not that type of man?'

I try to reassure her, although normally I'd say pay close attention to your gut feelings as they are usually right. But I don't think right now is the time to share that point of view. Besides, Joe has always seemed to be great guy who, if I'm honest, I could never imagine cheating on Abby, despite his apparent reluctance to tie the knot.

'No, I'm sure you're right. Gosh, what's got into me?' She places her hands on her cheeks and exhales. 'I've never been the jealous type. It's just that I've never known him to pop next door quite so frequently. And it doesn't help that she's so bloody pretty.' She manages a half smile, and I hug her.

'Er, hello? Have you looked in the mirror lately?' I say, as Abby is the definition of good looking, with large brown eyes and a tumbling head of auburn hair. A natural beauty.

'Well thanks, Becky, I just don't feel very confident lately, that's all, I'm not even sure why.'

'Just because he isn't keen on the idea of marriage, it doesn't mean he's jumping into bed with the next-door neighbour. Maybe he's just perfectly happy the way things are and doesn't want things to change between you.'

'Maybe you're right.' She sighs.

'Who's jumping into bed with the next-door neighbour?' Paige yawns and stretches her arms over her head, before sitting up.

'No one. Go back to sleep.' I laugh.

'I wasn't asleep,' Paige protests. 'Was I?'

'Ask the teenagers; they were laughing at your snoring.' I point to the teenagers sitting opposite. Paige puts her hand over her mouth looking mortified, before I tell her I'm only joking. She narrows her eyes and vows to get me back.

The boat glides into another beach, as the captain makes the announcement that we are nearing the church of Agios Ionnis Kastri used in the filming of the *Mamma Mia!* movie. Passengers are on deck, pointing up at the church that sits at the top of a promontory and taking photographs. It looks tiny from here, its roof and white walls like a beacon on the headland. I find myself trying to imagine a bridal group making their way to the top in the summer months and still looking fresh for the wedding photos.

As we disembark the boat, Paige asks Renos if it's possible to walk to the church from here, as she had rather hoped to.

Renos points to a staircase cut into the rock at the rear of the small beach, which looks narrow and a little precarious, if I'm honest. This leads to a pathway, ending at the foot of the winding steps that lead to the church at the top. Renos tells us that this is not the best route to get to the church, which is more easily accessed from the other side of the island by car.

'Most people just take a photo.' He shrugs.

'Are you really so keen to get up there?' I ask Paige, glancing high up beyond the rugged grey rocks to the little white church, its chapel seemingly suspended in the clouds.

'Of course I am. Did you think I was coming on this trip without a photo of me standing outside that little chapel? Are you two coming with me? I like someone to chat to as I walk along.'

'Mm, sorry, Paige, I think I'll stick to taking a photo from here?' I say and Abby agrees. 'I don't think I have the right walking shoes,' I add, pointing to my pretty sandals.

'Me neither,' says Abby, who is wearing similar footwear. Paige is dressed in shorts and a vest and a pair of white Nike trainers on her feet, so is suitably dressed to scale the steps.

'You can walk up with me if you like, I'm going up,' a voice behind us says.

We turn to find a bronzed six-footer, with tousled brown hair, smiling at us.

'What? Really? Well yes, if you're sure you don't mind.' Paige lowers her sunglasses, then tosses her hair over her shoulder.

'Rather her than me,' says Abby as they head off and start scaling the narrow steps from the beach. 'But I'm sure Superman can carry her back down here if she can't make it.'

The small shingle beach is almost identical to the last beach we stopped at, so this time we stay on board, finding a table on deck, beneath the shade of an umbrella and sip an ice-cold cola.

I send Mum a quick text, asking if all is well and she replies with a thumbs up, saying she will call me this evening for a proper chat.

Five minutes later we glance to the top of the staircase, where Paige is waving at us. We watch her make her way along a path, the handsome six-footer in front of her, until she is at the bottom of what looks like a never-ending staircase up to the tiny church, where a queue of people are steadily snaking their way to the top.

'Do they actually still perform wedding ceremonies?' Abby wonders as she sips her drink.

'Why, are you thinking of popping the question to Joe?' I jok-ingly ask.

'No. He knows I'd like to be married so I'll wait for him to decide on that one. I was just thinking, imagine asking all the guests to climb up there?' She laughs. 'Do you think Meryl Streep really ran up them? How the bloody hell did she manage to sing as well?'

'I have no idea. Maybe they used a younger double in those parts, although she does seem really fit for her age.'

Renos appears and asks if we are okay for drinks, and we chat for a few minutes, me asking him if he ever tires of doing these trips throughout the summer months.

'Never. I love the sea,' he tells us. 'Maybe, sometimes, if I tell the truth, I could do without listening to ABBA all day long.' He laughs. 'But the season is so short I am grateful for the work. There is not a lot to do in the winter, so we welcome the tourist trade. I also get to meet a lot of interesting people that I keep in touch with. I like to practise my English.'

'It's very good,' I tell him.

'To speak, yes, it's okay. When I write email to my friends, it's maybe not so good. I visited a friend in Scotland once and mes-saged him when home. I told him I found Scotland revolting, but of course I meant to say refreshing. I'm surprised he ever spoke to me again.' He laughs.

'So you've been to the UK?' I ask, chuckling at his story.

'Only Scotland. I became friends with a tourist and he invited me over to his place in Inverness in the winter. It was freezing. How do people live in that cold?' He gives a little shiver.

'It can get cold in the North of England too. You get used to it, I suppose,' I tell him.

A short while later, we glance up to the small chapel and Paige is waving furiously, so I zoom in with my camera and take a photo, wishing I'd worn my trainers and joined her as I'm sure my mum would have loved a photo, being a fan of the movie.

Half an hour later, Paige returns to the boat, looking as cool as a cucumber with her new friend, who heads off to join his friends on the lower deck.

'See you around,' he says with a wink, before he departs.

'That was brilliant,' gushes Paige, ordering a drink from Renos. 'The chapel is so tiny. It's beautiful, though, with pretty stained-glass windows.' She gratefully gulps down a cold orange juice, then we head to the top deck to resume our sunbathing. 'I heard someone say the inside wasn't used in the actual movie, that was somewhere else apparently. But the outside was.'

The teenage boy has his earphones plugged in again and every now and then he raises his head and takes a look at the water, before resuming his obsession with his phone.

On the way to Skopelos harbour we coast past hills, lush and green, with chapels and houses dotted in the background. Everything is just so serene here and a world away from home. I think of Henry and hope he is enjoying himself with his friends at sea and admire once again how he got on with his life after he lost Aunt Bea. I never knew Bea that well as a child, because Henry tended to visit our house alone, which is a little unusual, now I come to think of it. He'd always bring me a small toy or a bag of sweets and

I remember his warm, outgoing personality filling the house with sunshine, even on the dullest of days. And how I'd run down the path and he would sweep me up into his arms saying, 'How's my favourite niece?' Even though I am his only niece.

I think of his marriage to Bea and wonder how it must feel losing someone after being with them for over thirty years, but I guess we have an instinct to adapt and survive, and there's no doubting that Skiathos is certainly a beautiful place to heal.

Chapter Eleven

As the boat sails into Skopelos harbour, the sight of waterfront cafés and restaurants, in white and pastel shades, beckon us forward and we approach a space in the line of fishing and sailing boats docked in the pretty bay.

Walking down the wooden gangplank to disembark, Renos tells us we have two hours for lunch before the boat leaves. The island looks so inviting as we glance around; two hours doesn't seem nearly long enough to explore it properly.

'And may I recommend this restaurant.' He gestures to a restaurant a few yards to the right. 'It is the best on Skopelos. I live in Skopelos, so I know this for sure,' he says with certainty.

'He's probably on commission too,' Paige whispers in my ear, before turning to Renos with a smile and thanking him warmly.

Heading away from the harbour, we find ourselves in a jumble of pretty side streets, with terracotta pots overflowing with colourful flowers, outside brightly painted wooden doors. Women dressed in black sit outside on wooden chairs chatting as stray cats roam past. Moving on, we find ourselves in backstreets with baskets of goods displayed outside shops that sell olive oils and herbs, and the smell of dried thyme hanging from a doorway hits our nostrils as we pass by. Our circular walk takes us past more shops selling souvenirs of every description, and as we approach the harbour once again, the smell of tantalising food drifts out from the busy restaurants. On the harbour front we find a table at a fish restaurant overlooking the water.

'This is just so gorgeous. It's a shame we have to move on in an hour; I could happily sit here all afternoon.' Abby sighs, looking out across the water.

'Me too. This is definitely somewhere I'd like to return to and explore properly,' I reply.

Sea bass cooked in garlic and lemon is the speciality of the house and we all enjoy a delicious meal, served with sautéed potatoes and a crisp, green salad, all washed down with a glass of cold white wine.

'I still can't believe we're all here together on holiday in Greece,' says Abby as she forks the tender, delicious fish into her mouth. 'I feel so invigorated by the sun and a couple of full nights' sleep. I'm sure I'll go back a different person on Sunday,' she says.

I wonder whether sleep deprivation has been responsible for making Abby a little oversensitive to things back home, as she does seem a little more relaxed today.

'I'm really glad you're enjoying yourself. You deserve a break,' I tell her.

'You do,' agrees Paige. 'To be honest, I think we all do. It's nice to step off the treadmill for a while, although I feel bad that Rob is out working outdoors in all weathers. He's talked about having a break in the winter sun to the Canary Islands, though, so at least he will have that to look forward to. In the meantime, I'm going to save and surprise him with a lovely mini-break in October to the Lake District. It's so pretty there in the autumn when all the leaves change colour,' she says dreamily.

'You're going to… save?' I ask in disbelief.

'Yes, I can do it if I put my mind to it,' says Paige. 'I'll even hand my bank card over to you again. I'm not going to buy any more clothes, I have enough at home, so I'll save money there and I have enough make-up to open my own beauty salon, too,' she says, a determination in her voice. 'I think it's time I turned over a new leaf. Being here makes me think I ought to appreciate the simple things in life a little more.'

She pulls a mirror from her handbag and examines her forehead. 'Although I won't rule out Botox in the future.'

'In the future?' teases Abby.

'Well, yes, okay, I've had it once before a wedding that I knew a load of my old classmates would be attending and I wanted to look my very best,' she admits. 'It's not something I'd necessarily do again.'

'Until the next big event,' I reply.

She gives a shrug. 'Maybe I'll try anti-wrinkle cream instead; it's cheaper.'

'That's because it doesn't work,' says Abby. 'If it did, there'd be a load of wrinkle-free pensioners walking around and I haven't seen too many of those.'

'Maybe you should write about that in your blog,' I suggest.

'What? That the beauty industry has been ripping women off for years? I don't think I'd ever work again.' She laughs.

'Maybe not then.'

'That reminds me.' I turn to Paige. 'Are you going to be able to resist those special offers on the beauty websites that are always sending you emails?' I ask.

'I'll unsubscribe. I'll do the same for the craft gin club too,' she says firmly.

'You'll have enough money for that weekend in no time, if you give up the gin,' Abby says.

'Cheeky.' Paige scrunches up a paper napkin and flings it at her playfully.

'Well, good luck with the saving,' I tell her genuinely. 'Think of that luxury hotel break whenever you feel a spending splurge coming on.'

'I will. Just you watch. Rob and I will be lounging in a luxury suite overlooking Lake Windermere in a couple of months,' she says with conviction.

A short while later we pay the bill and head off for a walk. There's twenty minutes left until the boat leaves, so we hope to walk off some of our huge lunch. Passing a boutique, Paige's eyes fall on a beautiful blue and silver kaftan in the window.

'Ooh look at that, I'm just going to nip inside.'

'Well, that lasted all of ten minutes,' I remind her and she protests that it's not really clothes, as it's a beach cover-up and she'd intended to buy one here anyway.

We all head inside and the shop is filled with so many pretty clothes that I'm impressed with Paige's resolve as she buys the kaftan and nothing else.

I purchase a pretty silver bangle for Mum, set with a single topaz, which is her birthstone, and a hand-fashioned trowel with a brightly painted wooden handle that I think will look good in Dad's potting shed. When we've finished browsing the shops, with just ten minutes left until the boat sails, we head to an ice-cream kiosk and walk back to the boat licking our delicious ice creams.

'What a gorgeous place,' says the bronzed blonde, who is laden down with shopping bags, when we take our seats back on the boat. 'I'd definitely like to book a week's holiday here.'

Her husband nods. 'Beautiful place,' he agrees.

We discuss our couple of hours and where we went for lunch, all recommending different restaurants in case any of us return in the future.

When we dock back at Skiathos around five o'clock, we say goodbye to the other friendly passengers and wish them all a happy holiday and even the male teenager is smiling, probably invigorated by his time spent snorkelling and swimming in the sea.

'Well, that was well worth doing,' says Paige as we stroll along. 'Although it's a shame we weren't able to sail inside those blue caves. And I would have liked a bit more commentary about the surroundings, but never mind.'

Arriving back at the villa, we shower and chill for the evening on the terrace. The sunset is a vivid orange this evening and a gentle breeze wafts across the terrace, which feels just wonderful. I feel tired yet invigorated by our day out today, but the news of Scott's release is annoyingly still there at the back of my mind.

Abby has vowed to write her magazine piece tomorrow, whilst Paige has opted for a day lounging around the pool and topping up her tan, so I decide to explore the island alone. I have a vague knowledge of the area, although Henry has always escorted me to places in the car, so maybe I'll do some walking and take the local buses. I head off to bed, thinking that today has been a really good day.

Chapter Twelve

The next morning after practising some yoga and then breakfast, I walk down to the harbour with my book and find an empty bench near the Bourtzi, where I take a seat and watch the world go by, in between reading.

The harbour is busy with tourists today, some sitting outside restaurants and cafés, others boarding boats for trips around the harbour, or simply strolling along admiring the scenery. Sitting here, reading a book about a husband who is keeping a secret from his family, makes me think of how little we really know about someone beneath the surface. To the outside world, Scott was a jovial, easy-going bloke, yet he controlled almost every aspect of my life. I never realised it at the time, of course, and I thought it sweet when he said he was 'worried something had happened to me' if I didn't answer my phone when he called, or arrived home from work ten minutes later than normal, if I'd been stuck in traffic. He fell embarrassingly silent when I introduced him to a male colleague we'd bumped into one Saturday afternoon whilst out shopping, and quizzed me about him when we arrived home later.

Even if I had realised his behaviour was unhealthy – which I unbelievably didn't, for a while at least – and spoken out to someone,

I'm not sure anyone would have believed me as his alter ego was so at odds with how he treated me at home. He was so charming. Well, apart from the day he met the male co-worker and, thinking about it, he was probably more engaging with women. I sigh, wishing I hadn't been such a pushover although maybe my confidence had taken such a knock, I was happy to just let the relationship continue. Maybe I thought his behaviour was normal, as I didn't have too many past relationships to compare it with. I decide I don't want thoughts of Scott to ruin this lovely day, so I return to my book, when a good-looking Greek man approaches and asks if I mind him taking a seat at the other end of the bench. I look around and notice that all the other benches are full. Before I even have a chance to answer, he pushes my bag towards me, a little impatiently I feel.

'You're welcome,' I say sarcastically, which he doesn't appear to pick up on as he sits down.

He's wearing his black hair up in a man bun, which if I'm honest I'm not a fan of, but he pulls it off, managing to look really sexy.

'This is where I like to take my break,' he informs me as he sits down. 'Although as you can see, it's a very popular spot.' He gestures to the full benches all around.

I place my book down on the bench beside me.

'Really?' I try to feign disinterest as I stand and gather my things to leave.

He exhales deeply and raises his hands.

'Sorry if you thought me a little rude. Things are a little crazy in work at the moment as we are short-staffed. Please don't leave on my account.'

I sit back down and he introduces himself as Kyros.

'I'm Becky. Do you work locally?' I ask.

'A restaurant on the front,' he tells me, before taking a long swig from a water bottle. 'The one with the orange front. The Two Brothers' .' He points to the restaurant on the harbour. 'I've been up since first light running errands, then working in the kitchen as our new chef has been taken ill.'

'The Two Brothers' ? My uncle actually recommended I have dinner there,' I tell him, remembering Henry mentioning several restaurants he particularly liked. 'We must try it some evening. Are you one of the brothers?'

'Yes, my brother Linus and I co-own the restaurant. Although, recently, it's just been me and the staff as Linus and his wife have had a new baby.'

Despite his initial bad mood, he's so easy to talk to and I find myself telling him all about holidaying here in Uncle Henry's villa and his face breaks into a smile.

'Ah yes, Henry, I know him. He visits the restaurant regularly. What a lovely man,' he says kindly.

'He really is. I was a little worried about him after my aunt Bea died, but he's lucky to have some good friends. And a place like this to live in.'

'Yes, I was sorry to hear about your aunt. I didn't know her as well as your uncle, as he often came into our restaurant alone,' he tells me, which I find a little strange as I had the impression Henry and Bea had done everything together.

'So, where are your friends today?' Kyros asks, removing his sunglasses and placing them on the top of his head. He has large, deep brown eyes that hold your gaze when he speaks. His mouth is full and almost cupid-bow shaped, which might have given him a feminine look if it weren't for his strong aquiline nose, the combination giving him striking good looks.

I tell him all about Abby trying to write her magazine article and Paige choosing to spend the day lounging around the pool.

'Well, be sure to pop down to the restaurant one evening. I am sure you won't be disappointed with the food,' he says confidently.

'I might just do that.' I smile.

There's something quite captivating about his presence, and I'm surprised at myself for wishing he could hang around for a bit longer.

'It was nice to meet you, Becky,' he says in his strong Greek accent. 'I hope to see you around.' He drains the last of his water and throws the bottle into a recycling bin, a few yards away.

I watch him walking away, noting his tall, well-built frame, and how his white T-shirt hugs his body tightly and when he turns and waves, I realise I'm staring after him and quickly push my nose into my book.

After another half hour reading, I just sit watching the activity in the harbour. Some people are returning from trips, and I note that one of them was a *Mamma Mia!* trip and find myself wondering if it was any different to the one we went on yesterday, and whether the people enjoyed it.

I decide to walk up to the Bourtzi and enjoy a frappé under the shade of a parasol, once again enjoying the stunning view of the sparkling water below. Later, I potter around some of the shops and purchase some fresh baklava from a bakery to enjoy with the girls later. Much as I enjoy the company of my friends, I find I'm enjoying spending time alone, which is something I've always loved doing.

I've spent many an hour alone at galleries and museums back home, sometimes striking up a conversation with a stranger, sharing our thoughts on a piece of art. Maybe I just enjoy the freedom of doing my own thing, having spent two years in a suffocating relationship.

Around an hour later, I glance up at the villa, and debate buying some water and walking up, before I decide to head to the taxi rank, where I join a short queue. I'm looking around, people watching, when I hear a voice.

'We meet again.' It's Kyros from the restaurant, carrying a bag of groceries.

'Hi. Are you taking another break already?' I tease.

'No, I've actually nipped out to the market. Would you believe we ran out of aubergines at the restaurant,' he tells me, lifting the bag. 'Maybe it's because my aubergine dip is so popular. Where are you heading?' he asks as I shuffle forward in the taxi queue.

'Back to Henry's villa; I had intended to walk but the sun is rather hot now, and it's all uphill.'

'Please, walk with me to the restaurant while I drop these off, then I will give you a lift,' he says.

'No, really there's no need,' I protest, but he insists and gently takes my arm and leads me down the road to his restaurant. When we enter, the smell of something delicious reaches my nostrils.

'Maybe I'll try some of that aubergine dip you mentioned before I head off,' I tell him.

'It would be my pleasure.' He shows me to an empty table under an awning and speaks in Greek to a waitress, who quickly despatches a jug of iced water with lemon to my table. He then takes the bag of aubergines into the kitchen, before returning and taking a seat opposite me.

We chat for a few minutes, then the waitress places a plate of warm aubergine dip and soft, warm pitta bread in front of me, along with a small Greek salad. I dip my bread into the tasty, creamy dip and make an appreciative noise.

'Oh that really is good,' I tell him. 'I think that's the best aubergine dip I've ever tasted.'

'Thank you. That doesn't surprise me,' he replies proudly.

'Modesty isn't one of your strong points then?' I laugh.

'No,' he says, taking a sip of water. 'If I tell someone my food is the best, then it has to be the best. I see no point in false modesty.'

I admire his honesty, thinking of how often I've walked into places that boast unbeatable service only to be presented with mediocre service and a feeling of disappointment. It occurs to me that Kyros and I are similar in our quest to make the best possible product, as I take my soap making seriously, sourcing the best organic ingredients, and spending hours experimenting with fragrances before trying them out on my friends.

'So what do you do for a living?' asks Kyros as he picks at some bread, diving into my thoughts.

I tell him all about my little shop back home and he listens with interest, his dark eyes holding my gaze as I speak. My breath feels a little short under his intense look.

'That sounds like a nice job. Maybe not as stressful as running a restaurant,' he suggests, although I have to admit he doesn't look too stressed, sitting here with me, chatting. I mention this.

'Maybe sitting opposite a beautiful woman is good for my blood pressure.' He raises an eyebrow as he takes a sip of his drink.

Is he really flirting with me?

'It's been pretty full-on since my brother has been away for a while,' he explains. 'But he's back now and he's been training a promising new chef, so hopefully we can both take equal breaks in the near future.'

I imagine it's more difficult to take paternity leave for too long when running your own business, so it makes perfect sense to train someone up who you can trust.

'So you're an uncle?'

'I am indeed. A proud uncle to ten-month-old Antonio. I'm looking forward to taking him walking and fishing when he's a little older.'

'Are you sure you've time to drive me to the villa?' I ask as we finish up and a group of people stop to peruse the menu on a board outside the restaurant.

'Yes, of course. I'll be there and back in ten minutes. Are you ready to go?'

'I am, if you're sure.'

'Of course.' He stands up and speaks quickly in Greek to a young man who is setting a table, who then heads towards the entrance of the restaurant.

Back at the villa, I plan to have a swim and maybe a siesta before we head out for dinner this evening, as I'm sure the girls will be ready for a change of scenery having spent the day at the villa. I think we'll definitely head to the Two Brothers' restaurant one evening, but maybe not tonight. For some reason I don't want

Kyros to think I'm so keen to see him again, before wondering why on earth I am thinking like that.

As the car climbs the mountain road, I can't help glancing at Kyros, and thinking how good he looks, even in profile. I wonder if his behaviour is unusual in escorting me home, although maybe it's simply part of a friendly service that the restaurant provides to advertise their business. It is only a few minutes' drive away after all. When he deposits me outside the gates of the villa I thank him warmly.

'No problem. I hope to see you at the restaurant some time. If you let me know when you are coming, I will reserve the best table for you and your friends,' he says.

'I'm certain we will dine there one evening. I'll be sure to let you know.' I smile, before thanking him again and heading inside.

Chapter Thirteen

Paige is snoozing on a sunbed; her straw hat is covering her face and her book is on the floor beside her. She's wearing a zebra-print bikini and her body is already sporting a light golden tan.

I head straight into the kitchen and enjoy the welcoming blast of the air conditioning as it sweeps over my body. There's no sign of Abby, who must still be on the balcony of her bedroom, writing. I head upstairs for my bikini and I glimpse Abby working away on her laptop from my bedroom on the wraparound balcony.

'Fancy a drink?' I pop my head around the corner and ask.

'Hi, Becky. Yes, actually. I'll come down and get one, I'm just about finishing up here,' she says as her fingers tap away on her laptop.

Ten minutes later, Abby appears in the kitchen, having sent her piece off to her editor.

'Thank goodness that's out of the way, I can relax now.' She smiles broadly. 'So how was your day?' she asks as she reaches into the fridge for a carton of orange juice.

I tell her all about exploring the harbour and chatting to Kyros.

'Wow sounds like you had a good time. Is that what happens when you go out alone, hey?' she teases.

'I know. He gave me a lift home actually,' I tell her casually.

'Ooh tell me more,' she gushes.

I tell her all about Kyros inviting me into the restaurant to try the aubergine dip and her eyes widen.

'What are you like? You go out without us for the first time and end up getting chatted up by a local.'

'I wasn't chatted up, just chatted to. And anyway, he was probably just trying to advertise his restaurant. There's nothing wrong with drumming up business,' I say, although secretly hoping he did find me attractive.

'Yeah right, because all restaurant owners give people free food and a lift home.' She raises an eyebrow.

'Who's been getting free food?' Paige walks into the kitchen, stretching her arms over her head and yawning.

'Trust you to surface when you hear the word "food".' I laugh.

Abby tells Paige all about my afternoon.

'Ooh great, are we going to try the restaurant then? I love aubergines.'

'Yes, maybe not tonight, though. I don't want to appear too keen.'

'So you do fancy him,' says Abby. 'I knew it!'

If I'm honest with myself, I did find Kyros attractive. He was so easy to talk to and there's no denying his good looks, but I'm not interested. I've never been into holiday romances.

'You are entitled to be happy, you know,' says Abby gently.

'Yes, not all men are psychos like Scott,' adds Paige as diplomatically as ever.

'Well, thanks for that, Paige, but even if I did like him, I live in a little market town in Lancashire, and Kyros runs a restaurant in

Skiathos. Besides, he might not have even fancied me.' I shrug, yet find myself wondering if he did.

It's almost five o'clock now, so we decide to get ready and head out to a little restaurant that I spotted when Kyros drove me home. It's down a side street and has a lovely view of the harbour. I gauge it's no more than a ten-minute walk but hope we don't end up walking in the dark, like we did when we'd been to Mistrali's and were looking for the cocktail bar.

We shower and change, and a couple of hours later we meet on the terrace. Paige has just been Skyping Rob and she looks a little flat.

'Are you okay?' I ask.

'Yeah fine, it's beautiful here and I'm having the best time with you two, but I guess I'm missing Rob a bit. I can't remember the last time we slept apart.'

'You mean you're missing the sex?' says Abby candidly.

'No. I just miss him. Well, okay yes, maybe a little. We're still in the honeymoon phase.' She laughs.

I get the impression they will be for the rest of their lives.

'Well, it will be all the sweeter when you get home then. They do say absence makes the heart grow fonder,' I remind her.

'You're right,' she says. 'That's if he still fancies me when I get home.' She glances at a family-sized empty packet of crisps she's munched her way through before dinner. 'All this fresh air seems to be to be giving me an appetite,' she says, and I wonder if she's substituting food for sex. 'Right, let's go eat. Lead the way.'

We link arms and head off, and I hope to goodness I can actually remember where the restaurant is.

It's a beautiful evening and as we stroll along I glance back at the villa and feel immensely proud of Uncle Henry and all that he's achieved in his lifetime, especially as he came from quite humble beginnings. Mum told me how he'd always had a knack for selling things and combined with his love of nurturing plants he set up a stall on a local market, selling plants and garden ornaments. Pretty soon, he moved to a shop and the business went from strength to strength, securing a loyal band of customers due to his product knowledge and sparkling personality. Twenty years after setting up the stall, he'd made his first million.

We walk for around ten minutes before a string of fairy lights and a waft of garlic leads us to the wooden door of the restaurant, which is open wide to reveal the homely interior. Dark brown furniture offsets the white tablecloths and a single red rose is in a vase at the centre of each table. Along with carefully placed lanterns, the place has a romantic feel and I hope it won't make Paige miss Rob even more.

We are shown to an outside table by a young man who looks as though he might be around eighteen years of age.

'Ladies, welcome. You are lucky as we still have some of our lamb casserole left. It is the speciality of the house tonight, prepared by my grandmother and cooked slowly for hours.'

'Sounds amazing.'

I love how the grandparents are often involved in the restaurants in Greece, giving the food a traditional, authentic feel.

The table gives a view of the sea, which is inky black now, with a silvery moon casting ripples on the surface. Our local restaurants back home, although many of them very good, could never offer a view like this and once again I envy Henry living here.

'So, girls, what shall we do tomorrow?' I ask. 'Does anyone fancy going to the monastery up in the hills? Evangelistria, I think it's called.'

'I think I've read about that in a brochure. It has its own café and gift shop. Yes, that might be a nice day out,' agrees Abby.

'Oh yes, I was reading about that too,' says Paige. 'They make their own wine and olive oil and sell it in the gift shop. And before you say anything about my spending habits, souvenirs on holiday don't count.' She laughs.

'I'm sure Rob would like nothing more than a bottle of fortified wine made by monks,' says Abby and we all laugh.

'And perhaps we could head to the Two Brothers' restaurant in the evening?' I suggest.

Abby and Paige agree as they exchange a knowing look, but they refrain from teasing me.

'I'd love to drive us up those twisty mountain roads to the monastery tomorrow, if no one minds me taking the wheel,' says Paige, and Abby and I agree.

The food is so delicious that we ask our waiter to send compliments to the chef and he thanks us before disappearing into the kitchen. A few minutes later, an elderly lady appears from the kitchen and heads towards our table. She's wearing a pinny over a black dress and her hair is twisted up into a bun. Her smile reveals several missing teeth, and the warmth of it radiates from her soft brown eyes.

'I am happy you enjoy the food. *Efcharisto.*'

Her grandson tells us she doesn't speak much English, so he translates our compliments to her. I ask her what gave the casserole a slightly lemony flavour.

'Sumac,' she tells us, before making her way back to the kitchen.

'You are privileged,' says our young waiter. 'My grandmother usually never reveals recipes, saying they are a family secret.' He smiles. 'She must be in a good mood this evening.'

He tells us the restaurant is family run, and points to his mother, who is front of house on the other side of the restaurant, chatting to a group of diners.

'It seems like you have the perfect set-up,' I tell him.

Abby has taken some photos of the restaurant and our food from her phone and says she might do an article on her blog about traditional family-run restaurants and how they compare to the huge chains.

I wonder if my little business back home could become a family concern. Maybe one day I could rent more premises and hire someone to help make the skin products? My parents might even like to help out in the new shop from time to time. I smile to myself, realising anything seems possible on holiday and maybe I'm just getting carried away.

We opt for a Metaxa brandy for dessert and our waiter presents us with some fresh watermelon, which rounds things off nicely.

It's just before midnight as we head home, feeling relaxed and happy as we link arms and walk along companionably. The sound of cicadas humming once again fills the air and the lights from the town below have disappeared, apart from the lively bars at the other end of the harbour where the nightlife will continue into the small hours.

Later, as I drift off to sleep, the moonlight bathing my bedroom in a soft light, I realise I haven't really thought about Scott all evening. I'm determined not to let thoughts of his prison release consume me. I have a life that I happen to be enjoying very much at the moment. And I thank my lucky stars for that.

Chapter Fourteen

Paige and I are in the kitchen the next morning a little after nine when Abby finally surfaces. She looks a little strained.

'Morning, Abby. How are you?' I ask.

'What? Oh yeah, fine. I just had a bit of a restless night's sleep, that's all. I probably just need a coffee.' She plasters a smile on her face and pours herself a coffee from the pot I've just made.

Paige puts a pile of pancakes on a plate, before wiping her hands on a pinny she'd found on the back of the kitchen door, then sits down opposite Abby.

'Right, spill. What's up?' She refills Abby's cup with coffee.

'I don't want you two to think I'm whining, but I just spoke to Joe on the phone and he seemed so distracted. It's as if he couldn't wait to get me off the phone.' She lets out a sigh.

'It's two hours behind in the UK, remember, perhaps he was just getting ready to go to work,' Paige suggests diplomatically.

'That's what he said actually. Oh I don't know, maybe I'm getting paranoid. It's probably because I haven't been away from the family before,' she considers.

'Well, maybe you ought to do it a little more often. Joe has his overnight fishing trips, doesn't he? When do you ever get a break?' Paige probes, although gently.

'When the twins nap, although I'm usually furiously writing then. Or when Heather's home I might go for a coffee or get my nails done. I really enjoyed our meet-up in town that Sunday,' she says to me.

'And did the house fall down when you were out?' asks Paige.

'No, of course not. Actually, Joe got Sunday lunch on the go and Heather entertained the twins. Maybe you're right.'

'There you go. You need to allow yourself a little "me" time and stop feeling so guilty.' She pats Abby's hand gently, before munching her way through a pancake. 'I know you have a young family, but you mustn't neglect yourself,' she advises, whilst I nod in agreement.

'I know, you're right. Of course you are,' says Abby.

'Listen. You'll be home in a couple of days; you should try to stop worrying and relax,' I suggest softly.

'I am relaxed, really, honestly, I'm loving being here, who wouldn't? Maybe I'm just overthinking things.' She smiles brightly, but the smile doesn't quite reach her eyes and I wonder what's actually been going on to make her feel so insecure.

After the breakfast things have been cleared away, I study a map that I'd found in a drawer and tuck it into my bag. I know the car has sat nav, but I also like to get my bearings from a paper map, just in case there's ever a problem with the electrics in the car and the sat nav crashes, which has happened to me before in the middle of nowhere.

We climb into the car, Paige only too happy to be at the wheel, and head down the hill, before turning right onto a fairly busy road. A car appears from a side road without indicating, and we all gasp at the near miss and Paige hoots the horn long and loud and shouts, 'Bloody idiot,' as she waves her fist out of the window.

The roads are fairly busy today, so it's a relief when we head off the beaten track slightly and onto a narrow country road, passing fields, forests and streams and follow the winding road as it climbs higher into the hills.

'Why are monasteries always near the top of hills or mountains?' asks Paige, and I'm half expecting a punchline to a joke.

'Ah, I happen to know the answer to that,' says Abby. 'They have to be built in natural surroundings so that the mind is free from thinking about material possessions. It needs to be in an environment that encourages meditation and prayer,' she explains. 'Some people think they're built high in the mountains to feel closer to God in heaven, although I'm not too sure about that one.'

'How come you know so much about it?' asks Paige, bemused. 'Have you finally seen the light?'

'Heather did a topic on places of worship for her RE studies once at school, and told me some facts about monasteries. I must admit, I found it all very interesting, although I can't ever imagine being so cut off from the rest of the world.'

We climb higher until eventually we see a sign pointing to the entrance of the monastery. Through a forest below, we glimpse the sparkling blue sea and spy a red and white boat making its way across the water. When we climb out of the car, the first sound we are greeted with is the sound of a motorbike haring along the mountain road, followed by two others in convoy, briefly shattering the silence of the peaceful surroundings.

We scale a stone slope and are soon standing in front of the attractive building that has a pretty stone archway that leads to a courtyard with beautiful flowers in pots bursting with colour. I feel enveloped in a feeling of peace as soon as I enter the space, and surprisingly the road noise can't be heard from here. Strolling on, we pass huge bottles and demijohns filled with preserved lemons, apricots and blackberries that are grown throughout the grounds lined up along a low wall.

The monastery itself is an imposing light stone building, with arch-shaped wooden doors and we snap away with our cameras, before heading into a small museum that displays old farming tools and gives a brief history of the monks, with black and white photographs displayed on the wall. It also proudly houses the loom that made the very first Greek flag.

The chapel of the monastery is only small, yet ornately decorated with faded frescoes on the ceiling and tall, gold candle holders and beautiful stained-glass windows. The black and white floor fans out into a pretty pattern and it's hard not to admire the workmanship that must have gone into building such a lovely place and it gives me an almost spiritual feel when I step inside. I wonder what makes people choose a life of exile from the outside world, although knowing Scott has been released from prison, I do see some of the appeal. He'd never find me in a place like this.

'This really is gorgeous, isn't it?' says Abby as we stand on a stone terrace and glance at the lush greenness of the valley below, and we all agree.

'I thought about becoming a nun once,' says Paige, and Abby and I stare at her in disbelief.

'But maybe it was because I was going through a rough time and just wanted to run away from my problems,' she reveals.

'Things must have been pretty bad to think about joining a convent,' says Abby, still shocked by the revelation.

'I suppose they were,' says Paige matter-of-factly. 'I struggled a bit when my mum died as I was only nineteen and Dad, well, I was never very close to him but after Mum's death he assumed I would look after him and my two lazy, ungrateful brothers.' She strokes the leaves of a nearby fig tree as she speaks. 'Joining a nunnery seemed like a better prospect at the time. In the end, I moved in with the first bloke that came along, which turned out to be a disaster, but I was desperate to get away from home,' she reflects.

We walk around the grounds a little more, stopping to admire various plants and flowers, and explore the nooks and crannies of the building tucked away in the gardens.

'Shall we head to the shop now?' suggests Paige, when she has had enough of sitting on a bench soaking up the solitude. It makes me smile to think that she even considered living somewhere like a convent.

The shop has an old, heavy wooden door, which creaks slightly as we open it and we step into the interior, which has a stone-flagged floor. All manner of religious memorabilia is on sale, from small statues to keyrings. An alcove at the far end of the shop is lined with shelves holding bottles of wine, olive oils and ouzo, all made by the monks.

'Would you like to try a sample?' A young, dark-haired man puts down the mobile phone that he'd been glancing at, the device somehow feeling at odds with this calm, natural environment.

He holds up a small bottle of pink coloured liquid. 'Strawberry flavoured ouzo. And this one is melon,' he says, holding up a pale green coloured liquid.

We accept, and he pours us each a sample into a plastic shot glass. They are both delicious, particularly the strawberry one, which we all buy a bottle of, along with some wine and olive oil. My eyes fall on some handmade soaps fragranced with frankincense and myrrh. I buy a couple, wondering if the scents might work in my soaps back home.

Armed with our purchases, we're thanked by the young man before he returns to his mobile phone. We head to the outdoor café and find a table beneath a parasol, as the sun reaches higher in the sky, grateful to be sitting in the shade. A pretty, dark-haired waitress takes our order, and a few minutes later we are sipping frappés and eating huge, sticky iced almond buns. Paige is slightly disappointed that they only serve snacks, despite only having had breakfast around two hours ago.

'Although maybe it's best if I save my appetite for your friend's restaurant tonight,' she says, with a wink.

'Kyros is hardly my friend. I've only met him once,' I tell her, realising I'm really looking forward to visiting the restaurant this evening and seeing him again. 'Actually, I think I ought to book a table. It's probably popular with its location on the harbour front, and it is high season after all,' I say as I take my phone from my bag.

I nip inside the café for a minute, where the phone reception is better, and manage to make a reservation for eight. I mentally run through my outfits, pleased I've brought some pretty dresses with me, as for some reason I don't want to admit to, I want to look good tonight.

'All sorted,' I tell my friends as I return to the table. 'I've managed to get us a table for eight o'clock. I think we were lucky they weren't booked up.'

'I'm sure Kyros would have fitted you in somewhere,' says Abby, with a glint in her eye.

Sipping our drinks here in the sunshine overlooking the valley is just so peaceful and relaxing that I'm sure I'll miss doing these things with my friends when they return home in a few days' time, although I hope to enjoy some walks along the beach and explore the backstreets more when the girls leave.

When we leave the monastery, it's three o'clock in the afternoon and we decide to spend a couple of hours on the beach before heading back to the villa. We pull into another small beach en route. It's quiet, although still with the gorgeous soft sand and a snack bar for refreshments. We buy some water and settle down on our sunbeds and soon enough Paige and Abby are taking a siesta and snoozing beneath the shade of the straw beach umbrellas.

Despite the relaxing and soothing effects of the sun, I'm unable to drift off, so I head into the crystal-clear water for a swim. I lie on my back and stare at the sky, suddenly feeling very small in the universe. I imagined I'd be worrying about the shop, yet as the days go by I find my mind embracing my surroundings and, at times, home feels like a million miles away. I check in regularly with Mum, of course, but she seems to have everything in hand, so I've allowed myself to switch off a little.

It's almost six when we arrive back at the villa, feeling refreshed. Me after my relaxing swim and a read of my book. Abby and Paige after having enjoyed a long siesta. We head to shower and get ready and an hour later we meet on the terrace.

The sun is beginning to drop in the sky behind the mountains and after some indecision, we decide to take a taxi down to the harbour, as none of us fancy the downward walk in high-heeled wedge sandals.

Arriving at the Two Brothers' restaurant we are greeted by a smiling middle-aged woman, who shows us to a table. I glance around and I'm surprised to feel a pang of disappointment that Kyros is nowhere to be seen, when a few minutes later he emerges from the back of the restaurant, dressed smartly in a blue shirt and a pair of black trousers. His slightly curly hair is down and almost reaches his shoulders and I catch my breath at how handsome he looks, when suddenly a pretty dark-haired woman around the same age appears at his side.

'Becky, hi,' he says casually as he stops at our table. 'It's good to see you again. I hope you and your friends enjoy your meal. I can personally recommend the red mullet, pulled fresh from the sea today,' he says, smiling at my friends but suddenly I've lost my appetite. He doesn't introduce the woman standing beside him, who discreetly tugs at his sleeve and tells him they must leave. 'Maybe I will see you later,' he says, but not directly to me and we all nod politely. In that moment, I realise that Kyros is obviously just someone who talks to all potential customers. I was no one special to him and I was a fool to think that I was.

'Right then. Shall I order some drinks?' asks Paige, smiling brightly as a waitress appears at our table. She seems oblivious to my disappointment or maybe she's just trying to lighten the mood a little. Or she's being unusually diplomatic.

We order drinks and I bury my head in the menu whilst the waitress goes off to retrieve the drinks.

'Well, he's certainly as handsome as you described.' Abby is the first one to mention Kyros.

'He is,' says Paige. 'No wonder you were smitten.'

'Hardly,' I say a little sharply. 'You two came to that conclusion yourselves. He gave me a sample of the food here and a lift home in the heat. Hardly a declaration of undying love, was it?' Despite my protestation, I feel a little stung that he was here with another woman, proving I was indeed reading too much into things.

When the waitress returns, we place our food orders and talk of Kyros is over.

Abby and Paige opt for the red mullet recommended by Kyros, whilst I try a traditional moussaka, which, although it's creamy and delicious, I find myself picking at half-heartedly.

I wonder whether Kyros's brother is in the kitchen tonight. Kyros appeared to be in rather a hurry when he left earlier and I find myself wondering where he went, and who the girl with him was, before wondering why I even care. I remind myself that he behaved perfectly courteously towards me the other day and never gave me the slightest hint that he was attracted to me.

Maybe that's my problem. When a guy is being friendly or just kind, giving me a lift home for example, perhaps I read something more into it. As I recall, Scott came to my rescue when I was walking near the shops and a flimsy plastic bag I was carrying gave way and my shopping tumbled to the ground, several oranges rolling down the street. Scott popped into a nearby shop and purchased another bag for me, after he'd retrieved the rolling oranges. If I had been less charmed, and less quick to give him my phone number when he'd asked for it, I wonder what my life would be like now?

We finish up with coffees and, after settling the bill, head along the harbour front. It's almost ten o'clock and the twinkling lights from the restaurants illuminate the water softly. There are sounds

of chatter and laughter ringing out from restaurants and the gentle
sound of music from a bar further along.

'Right, where to now? The night is young,' says Paige.

'I think I saw a board advertising karaoke this evening at a bar
near the harbour,' says Abby. 'Does anyone fancy it?'

'Lead the way,' says Paige. 'It's ages since I've done my Dolly
Parton impression and sung "9 to 5", which pretty much sums up
my job.' She laughs.

'You love your job, though, don't you?' I ask her.

'I do, I'm lucky. Some days I dream of lying in bed and not having
to open the office up, especially in the freezing winter months, but
I'm not sure I'd have the discipline to work freelance from home,
like you, Abby. I need set hours.'

'I'm not sure I have that discipline either,' confesses Abby.
'Although that's only since the twins were born, I suppose. I squeeze
some writing in when Joe or Heather are home. Maybe I'll see if
our local newspaper has any jobs going when I get home, get a bit
of structure in my life too,' she muses.

I think of how lucky I am having my own little business, even
though my income can be a bit unpredictable. I love what I do and
wouldn't change it for the world.

I'm not really in the mood for karaoke but I follow the others
towards the bar Abby spotted earlier. We're about to turn a corner
into a cobbled street, when I hear someone shout my name. I turn
around and to my astonishment I see Kyros jogging towards us.
He seems slightly out of breath when he speaks.

'Hi, ladies. I'm glad I spotted you. I saw you in the distance
and had to run to catch up before you disappeared,' he says. 'I was

wondering if I could buy you a drink. All of you, of course.' He smiles at my friends.

'We're just off to a karaoke bar actually,' says Paige. 'Although, it's not really your thing, is it, Becky?' She looks at me and smiles.

'Truthfully, no not really.' I shrug.

'Then, in that case, may I steal you away for a drink?' He looks directly at me; once again, his piercing eyes make me catch my breath.

'Where's your friend?' I ask, wondering exactly what he is up to.

'I'll explain. Come.' He guides me away, arranging to catch up with my friends a little later.

Kyros leads me down a narrow, cobbled side street to a bar that has a yellow painted front and a few wrought-iron tables and chairs outside. It's fairly busy, but as we arrive a couple vacate a table and we sit down. The table has a small candle in a vase at the centre that illuminates Kyros's large brown eyes. He really is gorgeous.

'I'm sorry I had to leave earlier,' he tells me, after he's ordered us a drink from a waiter. 'I didn't want to be late for a memorial service at church. For my late mother,' he informs me.

'Oh, Kyros, I'm sorry,' I tell him as my heart goes out to him.

'The lady I was with was my cousin Zoe. She was giving me a lift to the church across town. I wanted to ask you out for a drink, but it didn't seem appropriate earlier, as I was heading to my mother's memorial service.' He takes a sip of his bottled beer that has just been placed in front of him.

'No, of course, I understand that.'

I ask about his mother and he tells me it is the second anniversary of her death and that his father lives alone in a house not far from the restaurant.

'Occasionally he calls in to help, or should I say chat to the customers.' He smiles. 'He has tried to take things easy on his doctor's advice, yet I know he finds it difficult. He is a man that needs to be busy.'

'I suppose that's only natural after the death of your mother. He must feel a little lonely at times, so it must be nice to have people to chat to,' I suggest.

'You're right. Everyone in town knows my father. He could sit on a bench and spend all day chatting to people who walk by and greet him.'

'Actually, I think I may have seen him near the Bourtzi when I've been there myself. He has the look of you, if it's the right man.'

'It probably was. Everyone comments on our likeness. Linus is more like our mother.'

I think it must be lovely to grow up in a place where everyone knows you and there is always someone to pass the time of day with. No wonder Uncle Henry likes living here.

Kyros tells me that his father opened the restaurant in the nineteen eighties, just as holidays to Greece gained popularity. He ran it with his brother Dimitri, who has since sadly passed away.

'I think he would still be working there now, dashing about, had it not been for a mild heart attack he suffered last year, which forced him to slow down,' Kyros tells me as he sips his beer. 'Although he still likes to get up with the customers and do a little Greek dancing from time to time. It makes us a little nervous when the tempo gets really fast, though.' He pulls a face.

'Well, he's lucky to have you and your brother to keep an eye on him.'

'I suppose so. Not that he always listens to us.' He raises an eyebrow.

'What was Skiathos like before the tourists came?' I ask.

'Little more than a working fishing port originally, I believe, before bars and restaurants opened up to meet demand as foreign holidays became popular. The Brits in particular liked to party, according to my father. He has lots of photographs from back then. I'd like to show them to you sometime if you are interested.'

'Yes,' I tell him. 'I'd like that. I'm surprised you don't have some displayed on the walls in the restaurant, as customers love nostalgia.'

'That's a good idea,' Kyros replies.

We smile at each other, before I look away, and take a sip of my drink. We chat easily for an hour, Kyros telling me stories his father told him about how Skiathos has changed over the years, and how the restaurant business flourishes during the summer months. He asks if he can take me to dinner tomorrow evening and I eagerly accept his offer, before we head to the karaoke bar so I can re-join my friends.

Nearing the bar, the sound of Paige's half-decent voice can be heard ringing out and unbelievably the crowd are on their feet, waving their hands in the air and joining in the chorus of 'Sweet Caroline'.

'I told you Brits like to party.' Kyros nods towards Paige and I laugh. Abby is sitting at a table in the crowded bar and raises her arm and waves when she spots me.

'Fancy a duet before you go?' I ask Kyros jokingly. 'I'm thinking Jason and Kylie?'

'I'm afraid I would empty the bar with my singing voice. I know the owner and he would never forgive me.' He smiles and I notice his straight white teeth. 'I am pleased I found you again, Becky.' Kyros steps towards me and as his lips brush my cheek, a thrill shoots through my body and I find myself wishing my evening with him could continue.

'Enjoy the rest of the evening with your friends. I will collect you from the villa at eight tomorrow evening,' he tells me before he departs.

Paige steps off the stage to rousing applause and joins us at the table with a huge grin on her face.

'I'd forgotten how much fun that was,' she says. 'Is anyone else up for it?'

'Not for me,' says Abby. 'And by the look on her face, I'd say Becky's had enough excitement for one night,' she teases.

Not nearly enough, I think to myself, already counting down the hours until tomorrow night.

Chapter Fifteen

We have breakfast on the terrace the following morning and as Paige glances around at the stunning views, she asks, 'Who's up for a day trip to Skopelos? We barely had any time to look around when we went on the boat trip, did we?'

'I'm definitely up for that! I think we might have to take the ferry, though, as the other boats are part of a trip,' I say.

'The ferry it is then. I've googled it, and it takes around an hour to get to Skopelos from the new harbour.'

We head upstairs to gather our things and, half an hour later, we purchase a ticket from the ticket office and sit waiting for the next ferry, which is due in around twenty minutes. I take in the surrounding pine forest beyond the expanse of calm, blue water. Below, I spot a shoal of tiny silver fish swimming towards the pier, before scattering into the distance.

'Hey, isn't this where Harry and Sam miss the ferry to Skopelos in *Mamma Mia!*?' I ask, recalling the scene where Harry races along the pier in vain as he tries to board the ferry.

'Yes, that was the ticket office in the film.' Abby points to a small white building on the pier that has a ladder outside and looks like it might be used as a storeroom. Paige moons over how lucky Meryl Streep was to snog Pierce Brosnan in the movie.

'Colin Firth for me. Well, in his younger days anyway,' Abby says with a sigh. 'When he was in *Pride and Prejudice* would do it.'

'Nah. I just can't that image out of my head of him wearing those hideous Christmas jumpers in the Bridget Jones movies.' Paige laughs.

We all snap away with our camera phones as we stroll along the fairly short pier and take in the turquoise water. In the movie, Harry's yacht was an attractive sailing boat, rather than the hulking red and white metal vessel that can be seen in the distance, making its way steadily towards the pier.

Our return ticket will have us arrive back at six, which will give me time to change for dinner this evening with Kyros and I feel a little rush of excitement at the thought.

The ferry is fairly crowded, but we manage to find seats on the top deck and settle down for the journey that will have us arrive in Skopelos before noon.

Abby immerses herself in a book and Paige plugs her headphones in to listen to some music, whilst I simply gaze out to sea, watching the rush of the waves and the white foam from the huge ferry as it sails on, the gentle drone of the engine interrupting the calmness. I turn my face to the hot sun, feeling the burn, and must have dozed off, as a short while later I hear the deep sound of the ship's horn as we head into Skopelos harbour once again.

When we disembark, Abby flicks open a little map of the island.

'I thought as we only have today to explore Skopelos we should really make the most of it,' she says. 'Shall we head uphill first?

There's the ruins of a thirteenth-century Venetian church, with a little café next door, where we can grab a drink,' she says. 'The views are meant be really something from up there.'

We take Abby's lead and head off to find the church.

We stroll along happily enough, but as the path climbs higher, the sun really gets up. Old ladies are sitting outside pastel-coloured front doors, chatting, and they smile as we walk past. I notice that the houses are immaculately kept, with scrubbed wooden windowsills and pots of flowers spilling from balconies above, the residents taking an obvious pride in their homes. Mopeds lean against the walls of some houses and the sound of children's laughter can be heard ringing from back alleys and side streets. I envy the freedom of not having to lock their doors here, or worry about the children who seem to run free.

The climb uphill seems to go on forever, and in the heat we question the decision to visit the church, which still seems quite a long walk up.

'Don't give up. Let's grab an ice cream and sit in the square here for a bit,' suggests Abby, pointing to a shop displaying around a dozen different flavour ice creams in a freezer outside. We purchase our ice creams and find an empty bench and sit beneath the shade of a lemon tree.

The square is pretty, flanked by a small white church, a café and stone houses with blue shutters.

'I might just stay here, whilst you two shoot up and see the church.' Paige winks, enjoying her ice cream. 'You can take a photo for me.'

'Not a chance. We're nearly there now,' says Abby decisively. 'Anyway, you climbed those steps to the church on the boat trip;

this should be a breeze to you. Or maybe the charming company motivated you to keep going.'

'Fair enough.' Paige giggles.

Five minutes later, we arrive at the pretty church and take a photo, but the reward is more the view of the harbour and the pine forests beyond. Whilst we are there, on the hour, the church bell rings out as locals begin to arrive for a church service, mainly women dressed in black, although one or two families with young children make their way inside slowly.

'I hope all the church bells don't go off at once,' says Abby, burying her nose in the information leaflet. 'Or we might need to buy some earplugs. It says there's three hundred and sixty churches in Skopelos.' She laughs.

I find it funny that as a tourist I enjoy exploring churches and monasteries, yet wouldn't think of driving around exploring churches back home, although perhaps it's not the same without the view from the hilltops. And the sunshine.

Making our way back down towards the harbour, we turn in to narrow side streets and discover tiny bakeries and gift shops with painted wooden doorways, selling jewellery and gifts. An artist is sitting midway up a flight of steps painting, some of his work spread out and exhibited on the floor beside him. My eye falls upon a painting of a beach scene, with an unusual moody-looking grey sky, streaked with purple, and a solitary sailing boat in the water. I pay the man twenty euros for the painting and he thanks me gratefully.

We eventually end up back down at the harbour front and find a table at a fish restaurant overlooking the water, where we order a sharing seafood platter including squid, which I've never tried before and to my surprise, I find it delicious.

'I've heard people say it's rubbery, but it isn't,' I say. It's cooked in a light batter and I drizzle it with lemon juice.

'I think it's easy to overcook it,' says Paige. 'Oh and did you hear about the down-and-out octopus?'

'No?' I say, glancing at Abby, who is already rolling her eyes waiting for the punchline.

'It ended up on squid row.'

We devour our delicious food served with a side order of salad as we watch day trippers alight from one of the tourist boats in the harbour.

'Looks like we got here at just the right time,' Abby comments as the throng spills out onto the harbour in search of somewhere for lunch.

'This is just heavenly,' says Abby as she sips a glass of crisp, cold wine from a bottle we ordered along with some water.

Abby's skin has taken on a light golden glow and I'm happy to see that she seems to be finally relaxing and enjoying herself. Joe works hard, but has his fishing trips to switch off with, so I hope being here reminds Abby that she's entitled to some time for herself too, without feeling guilty.

A while later, we stroll along the harbour linking arms, sated and happy. 'That restaurant deserves all of those five stars,' says Paige. 'Good choice, Becky.'

'It's only a couple of miles to Loutraki beach, if anyone fancies it?' says Abby, consulting her guidebook once again. 'We don't have to be back on the ferry for another three hours.'

'We haven't brought our swimming gear but I don't mind chilling out under an umbrella after that lunch,' I say, so we head to a nearby taxi rank and ten minutes later our friendly driver drops us off.

The beach is dominated by a trendy-looking bar set back from the beach with an arched stone entrance, from which gentle music is pumping out. It's a shingle beach with a pretty pine forest backdrop and the most stunning, emerald green shallow waters. We settle down on our beds with the straw umbrellas, ready to relax for a couple of hours.

As I watch a waiter deliver some food to a nearby couple, I find myself thinking about Kyros, and wondering if the restaurant is busy this afternoon and how he'll manage to find the time to sneak out on a date with me later, although he did say he's been running the restaurant almost single-handedly these past few months, so maybe he feels entitled to a little time off now and then.

The gentle swish of the waves caressing the pebbles at the water's edge almost lulls me to sleep, and I hope we have at least some sunny weather when we return to England so I can spend some time on the long sandy beach at Crosby. I've been known to spend a whole day there, breaking for lunch at one of the many restaurants in nearby South Road, my particular favourite being a Lebanese restaurant. The beach is a beautiful place to take an evening walk, and when an orange sunset casts its glow over the iron men in the sea at Antony Gormley's 'Another Place', there's nowhere else I would rather be.

I'm almost asleep when I hear a male voice and I sit up to find a smiling Abby talking to Jonas, the barman from Koukounaries beach.

'Fancy meeting you here,' he says to us all and introduces his friend, Luca.

'Hi, Jonas, how are you?' I ask.

'I'm okay, thanks. It's my day off so I came to Skopelos to visit Luca. I see you have discovered the best beach.'

He's wearing red swimming shorts, revealing a muscular, toned body, and Abby seems a little flustered as Jonas's eyes flicks over her body and she instinctively wraps a beach cover-up around herself.

'Are you heading back later?' Jonas asks us. 'It's just that a friend of mine is having a BBQ this evening for his birthday on Koukounaries beach. Luca is coming too.'

'Yes, and you are welcome to join us,' adds his good-looking friend.

'That sounds nice, but I'm not sure what our plans are for this evening,' says Abby.

'Okay, well if you are undecided, it would be lovely to see you there.' He locks eyes with Abby.

'He's really got a thing for you,' says Paige as she picks up her book. 'Isn't it funny how all the hot guys appear when you're already in a relationship,' she ponders. 'I mean, before I got with Rob, I never saw anyone I fancied and was approached by middle-aged men with paunches who obviously thought they were still in their prime. I've had more offers from handsome men since I've been married. Good job I'm happy,' she adds.

'Is infidelity okay if you're unhappy then?' asks Abby.

'That's a difficult question to answer,' I say. 'Personally, I'd say it makes things even messier if you're not happy and you go with someone else. End the relationship if you're not happy, but don't cheat.'

'I must agree,' says Paige. 'It's not fair on anyone otherwise. Why do you ask, are you lusting after Jonas?' she teases.

'No, no, of course not, I was just thinking out loud,' Abby says dismissively. 'I agree it probably complicates things even more.' She immerses herself in her book, telling us the conversation is over.

All too soon, our time on the beach has come to an end and we gather our things and take a taxi back to the harbour, having enjoyed a wonderful day out. And of course, the day isn't over yet, as I still have the evening with Kyros to look forward to. I feel a tingle of excitement at the thought of spending the evening with him.

Chapter Sixteen

I'm just out of the shower, when I receive a video call from Uncle Henry. He is sitting outside a bar with palm trees in the background, nursing a cocktail.

'Henry, hi! Where are you? It looks amazing there,' I say as I scrunch hair mousse through my curly brown locks.

'Alonissos. We're spending two days here. I've been reliably informed there's a rather marvellous restaurant here that has the best belly dancers. I can hardly wait.' He beams into the camera. He tells me his friends have gone off to spend the day at the beach, but he's staying local to catch up with some reading and make a few phone calls.

I tell him about my date with Kyros from the restaurant this evening.

'Kyros? Yes, I know him, he's a wonderful young man. I know his father too. He often sits on the benches near the Bourtzi watching the world go by,' he tells me. 'I think his whole life was the restaurant before he retired.'

'Well, it's a great place to retire, that's for sure. I can't imagine sitting on a bench back home for hours on end.'

'It sure is, although I don't think Alex has fully retired, as he often makes an appearance at the restaurant just to make sure his sons are keeping up his standards, I think.' Henry laughs.

'Yes, I've heard that. And that he enjoys doing a spot of Greek dancing.'

I suppose it must be difficult to lose your role in life and feel surplus to requirements as you get older. I guess we all have a desire to feel needed.

We chat for a while longer and Henry asks me what's new, and for a second I think he's alluding to the news about Scott, and I wonder if Mum would have discussed that with him?

I avoid the subject with Henry, as I don't feel the need to discuss it. At least not yet. Not when I'm having such a good time here in Skiathos and I don't want my thoughts dominated by Scott once again.

'Right, my dear, I must let you go. We're heading out for dinner in an hour and I have to go and get ready.' He beams at the camera. 'I'm glad you're having a good time at the villa. I look forward to seeing you next week.'

He signs off and I think about what to wear for my own evening out. I wonder where Kyros will take me this evening? It occurs to me that this is the first date I've been on since Scott and I'm surprised by how nervous I feel.

I head upstairs as Paige emerges from the bathroom, wearing a white towelling robe.

'That bathroom is something else. It's definitely my favourite one in the house as the views are amazing. And it's so huge! I love the fact that you can wander around naked, with it having one-sided glass, it's so liberating.' She sighs.

The bathroom in question is a huge marble affair with views of the hills. It's also the only room in the house that directly overlooks an outside balcony of the villa opposite.

'You're right about that view, although I bet the people on the balcony of the villa opposite have an even better view when you shower in there.' I can barely stifle my giggles.

'What are you talking about?' asks Paige, her eyes widening.

'The windows in that bathroom.'

'What about them?' Paige seems to have gone a little pale.

'They don't have one-way glass.'

Chapter Seventeen

Paige and Abby are sipping a cold drink on the terrace when I join them. Tears are streaming down Abby's face, as she has just heard about Paige's unintentional naked dance show for the neighbours.

'I wouldn't mind, but I was dancing around like that woman at the beginning of *Tales of the Unexpected*, swirling my arms above my head, Oh the shame.' She sinks down into the chair, covering her eyes, and Abby laughs even louder.

They both turn as I approach the terrace and Paige lets out a little wolf whistle.

'Wow, look at you, you look amazing,' she says and Abby agrees. 'Black really suits you.'

I'm wearing a simple black, linen dress that really shows off my tan and have accessorised it with some silver jewellery.

'Your hair looks lovely too. I'm so envious that you just scrunch dry your hair and you're ready to go. It takes me hours to do my hair,' moans Paige, who blow dries her hair, then meticulously straightens it to achieve her trademark long, poker-straight look.

'It's just as well, as I don't think I'd have time for all that in the morning before I open the shop,' I tell her. Paige once told me that she sets her alarm half an hour earlier than needed every morning so she can straighten her hair.

I head inside and grab myself a bottle of mineral water, as I want to take it easy with alcohol, especially on a first date. I can't believe I'm actually going out on a date with Kyros, and suppress a sudden feeling of apprehension wondering where he is going to take me. Should it be somewhere very public? I don't know anything about this guy after all, or maybe I'm just being paranoid given my past history.

'Have you two decided where you are dining this evening?' I ask my friends as I take a sip of my water and try to shake off the rising panic.

'Actually, we might head down to the beach bar at Koukounaries for that BBQ Jonas was talking about,' says Abby. 'Neither of us can really be bothered dressing up, so a beach party sounds nice and casual. The buses run past there until after midnight from the harbour.'

For a second, I wonder whether Abby is playing with fire, accepting an invitation from a bloke who so obviously fancies her. Especially as she's feeling unsettled about Joe's recent jaunts to her next-door neighbour, but then I guess she'll be with Paige. And she's a grown woman after all.

'Right, well, have fun. Kyros should be here any minute to collect me.' I glance at my watch, which shows just after eight and, right on cue, I see car headlights snaking around a bend towards the driveway of the villa.

My heart skips a beat as Kyros gets out of the car and, like a gentleman, opens the passenger door for me to step inside. He looks even more handsome this evening, dressed in a black short-sleeved shirt and smart stone-coloured shorts.

'You look amazing,' he whispers as I stand next to him before I step into the passenger seat. I can smell his musky, masculine aftershave and something stirs inside of me.

'So do you,' I tell him honestly and he smiles warmly.

I ask him where we are going, as when we reach the bottom of the hill we appear to be heading a little out of town, away from the harbour.

'A little place I think you will like,' Kyros tells me, without revealing any more as we drive along.

Kyros expertly weaves his way along the coast road, which has lots of bends, until we eventually park up alongside what looks like a forest. The moon is shining brightly on a stretch of water and as we get out of the car, I recognise it as the nature reserve at the rear of Koukounaries beach.

'Come.' Kyros guides me along a forest footpath. I have a moment's hesitation as I look ahead and spy the forest, shrouded by tall trees, the only light guiding us being from the moon above. I stumble on a tree root and he takes my hand, which reassures me and even gives me a fuzzy feeling inside, somehow calming my doubts. I tell myself that he's a well- known figure in the town and my friends know he has taken me out for the evening, so I allow myself to relax a little.

Presently, we see some lights up ahead and we approach what looks like someone's house, but is in fact a small restaurant.

'They serve the best lamb kleftico here,' Kyros assures me. 'I was lucky to get a reservation.'

We are greeted at the entrance of the unremarkable-looking building, where a couple of people are enjoying a drink on the terrace, before we are led to a gate at the side of the building. When the young woman with long dark hair opens the gate, the sight that greets me almost takes my breath away.

It's almost as though we have stumbled across a magic garden, as half a dozen or so tables take up the space on the neat lawn. Trees are threaded with lights and an ancient oak tree takes centre stage. In one corner, a man is seated on an intricately carved wooden chair that reminds me of a storyteller's chair, playing a gentle tune on a guitar. The tables are also hand-fashioned from solid wood that looks as though it may have come from the surrounding forest.

'Kyros, this is beautiful,' I gasp, taking in my surroundings, noting stone statues of various shapes and sizes, including fairies and nymphs, dotted about the garden. We are shown to a table with a grey stone phoenix for company, nestled in the shrubbery beside us.

We place a drinks order with the dark-haired woman and she goes off to retrieve them.

'I don't remember seeing this place when I googled local restaurants,' I tell Kyros, completely captivated by my surroundings.

'That's because it isn't on the internet. It's something of a closely guarded secret in these parts. The owner wanted to keep it as somewhere special, not to be overrun with tourists, although of course if someone is on holiday celebrating an important anniversary, then they may have a chance of booking a table, should they hear about the restaurant from one of the locals. It's worked that way for years so I guess the owner has no plans to advertise.'

'Well, I don't blame him. Maybe it would lose something of the magic otherwise.'

'Exactly,' says Kyros as our drinks arrive. 'So tell me a little more about your family life. I know your uncle Henry, of course, but what about back home? Is there anyone special in your life?' Kyros asks candidly.

'I'm not sure I'd be sitting here in such a romantic location with another man if there was,' I tell him, raising an eyebrow.

'That's good to know.' He nods. 'Sometimes people are just after a little distraction from their everyday life when they come on holiday,' he says as he pours me a glass of white wine from a bottle and himself a small one.

'Are you talking about people who are looking for a holiday romance?' I ask, wondering what he's getting at.

'I suppose I am, yes.' He fixes me with his brown eyes framed by long black eyelashes.

I think of Abby, who will shortly be at the beach party with Paige, no doubting flirting with Jonas and wonder if she is just after a distraction from her life back home, as Kyros suggests people are. 'It's true, people can let their hair down on holiday. But that's usually when they have no ties back home.'

'Well, that's good to know,' he replies, and I can't help wondering whether he has been hurt by a tourist on holiday in the past.

Kyros is right about the kleftiko: the tender lamb melts in my mouth, and the sauce is rich with the taste of tomatoes and oregano. The food is served with delicious, crunchy roast potatoes and green beans. I have a second glass of wine and Kyros opts for a coffee as he is driving. The evening seems to vanish as we chat easily, until we're enjoying a slice of watermelon at the end of the wonderful meal.

The man with the guitar begins to sing a Greek song as he strums, the melodious tone filling the night air, adding to the charm of the evening.

'What's he singing about?' I ask Kyros as I sip the last of my wine.

'It's a song about star-crossed lovers. A bit like Romeo and Juliet, I suppose,' he tells me.

'Do they have a happy ending?' I ask.

'I don't know. The song does not reveal that, so maybe not.' He shrugs. 'Maybe love is not as neatly wrapped up as it is in the movies,' he says, and I wonder if I can detect a hint of cynicism in his voice.

'Maybe not.'

It's a little after ten thirty when we head towards the car, making our way back through the brief darkness of the nature reserve, with silvery moonlight filtering through the branches of the trees. Maybe it's the effect of the wine, but I feel more relaxed as we stroll along. In the distance, what looks like a fire on the beach can be seen, its flames flickering and the faint sound of music in the background as the BBQ party seems to be in full swing. I hope Paige and Abby are having a good time and almost suggest heading off to the beach to join them, before deciding it might be nicer to invite Kyros to the villa for a coffee. All of my apprehension from earlier has completely vanished and I have to admit to myself now, I really do like this man.

'Thank you for this evening,' I say as we drive along, the window open in the warm night air.

We pass a bird that flies in front of the car and startles me for a second, and Kyros smiles.

'You get used to wildlife appearing when you drive in the evening, although it can be a little alarming,' he says.

I study his face in profile, thinking him the most handsome man I have seen in a long time. He's handsome in an old-fashioned, manly way and almost reminds me of a Hollywood film star from days gone by, like a darker-skinned version of a young Sean Connery. To my surprise, for a second I imagine his strong arms around me, playfully throwing me in the water at the beach, before pinning me down on the sand and kissing me like the beach scene from *Dr. No.*

'So you have to watch out for them,' says Kyros, jolting me out of my daydream.

'What? Sorry I was miles away,' I tell him, thankful that it's dark in case I'm blushing.

'Deer. I was just saying that sometimes you spot deer when you are driving in the evening so you have to drive carefully.'

'Oh, yes, of course.'

A short while later we pull up outside the villa and I invite Kyros in for coffee, hoping he knows that I do indeed mean coffee and doesn't think I'm suggesting anything else, before wondering why I am overthinking the situation.

'Henry really does have a beautiful place here,' says Kyros when we are seated on the comfy outdoor sofa on the veranda, watching the twinkling lights from the town below as the nightlife continues and the headlights from cars steadily make their way along the winding road. There's a porch light on at the villa opposite, and I find myself telling Kyros all about Paige flashing the neighbours and he laughs loudly. I like his laugh; it's a throaty, manly laugh, if there is such a thing.

'She is what I suppose you would call a real character,' says Kyros with a smile on his face. 'Have you all been friends for long?' he asks as he sips his coffee.

'Around three years, when I moved to a different area,' I tell him. 'Which doesn't sound that long when you think about it, but we became friends very quickly and have been inseparable ever since.'

I'm grateful that Kyros doesn't probe any further about why I moved to a different part of the country, as I don't feel like bringing Scott's name into the conversation this evening.

We chat about the restaurant and the summer months here in Skiathos, and I tell him how much I am enjoying being here, and resolve to visit Henry a little more in the future.

'I hope you do.' He edges closer to me and I can feel my pulse quicken when he fixes me with his dark eyes. 'Becky, this evening has been such a pleasure for me; I hope you have enjoyed it too.'

He takes my coffee cup from my hand, placing it on the table in front of us, before he moves his face closer to mine, then I hear the shrill sound of my mobile phone coming from my handbag.

'Do you mind if I get that?' I ask, the moment broken.

'Sure.' He leans back on the couch with a smile and laces his arms behind his head.

I answer the phone to the sound of Paige's voice, asking if we are anywhere close by. She gabbles something about Abby.

'Wait, slow down. Yes, we're at the villa. What's up?' I ask, with rising panic.

'I'm so sorry, gosh I hope I'm not interrupting anything. I know you're out with Kyros, it's just that Abby is as drunk as a skunk and I can't get a taxi. I don't think she's fit to go on the bus. Is there any chance you could come and collect us?' she pleads.

'Where are you?'

'At the bus stop near the beach.'

'We could maybe be there in ten minutes.' I glance hopefully at Kyros and he nods, draining his coffee and standing up.

'Thanks. You're a superstar,' she says and I'm sure I can hear Abby singing in the background.

I fill Kyros in on the situation as we hurry to the car.

'I'm so sorry our date has had to end this way, Kyros, but it sounds like we need to get Abby home,' I say as we climb into the car.

'Think nothing of it. I hope your friend is okay,' he replies and starts up the engine.

He puts his foot down and thankfully the roads are empty, so in no time at all we are pulling up at the bus stop, where Abby is seated with her head between her legs.

'Sorry for ruining your evening,' says Paige. 'I wasn't sure what to do next; Abby kept trying to head back to the beach.'

Abby's eyes widen when she sees me striding towards her.

'Becky! What are you doing here?' she slurs. 'And you too, Krypton.' She points drunkenly at Kyros, attempting to stand up, before promptly sitting down again and laughing. 'Are you coming to the party? Paige is being a party pooper and making us go home early.' She pokes her tongue out childishly at Paige.

'Oh no, what's she been drinking?' I ask Paige, looping Abby's arm around my shoulder as she kisses me and tells me she loves me, whilst Paige does the same on the other side.

Kyros is already holding the car door open, chuckling as he watches our attempts to wrangle Abby into the car.

'Tequila shots, followed by some home-made punch, which turned out to be a lethal combination, so she got drunk rather quickly. Jonas was coming on to her quite strong and I was worried she might end up doing something she regretted, so I suggested we leave.'

'You did the right thing,' says Kyros as we chat outside the car, having deposited Abby in the back seat. 'Some of the guys who work the bars are all about having fun, nothing more. At least Abby will regret no more than a hangover in the morning,' he says wisely.

'That's what I thought,' says Paige. 'Hang on a sec.'

She crosses the road to a shop and returns with a bottle of water in a carrier bag.

'Just in case.' She takes the water from the bag. 'I wouldn't want her to throw up in your car.'

The same thought crosses my mind too, especially with all those bends in the road but, thankfully, Abby falls asleep almost immediately and remains so for the rest of the journey.

Kyros helps us get Abby inside and once Paige and I have put her to bed, I say good night to him.

'Thank you so much for this evening, Kyros, I had the most wonderful time. I don't think I'll ever forget the restaurant; you've ruined dining out for me now.' I smile. 'Nothing will be able to compare. And thanks for helping with Abby too.'

'It was no problem. I hope I get to spend another evening with you. In the meantime, I hope Abby is okay. She is lucky to have friends like you and Paige,' he adds, before kissing me gently on the cheek and setting off.

We decide to all bunk in together this evening, to keep an eye on Abby, and have placed a bucket at the side of her bed, just in case.

'My goodness, what a night,' says Paige, climbing into the huge double bed next to me, whilst Abby snoozes in a single bed opposite.

'So, what happened?' I ask. 'She doesn't normally drink much these days since having the twins.'

'I know, but she'd been talking about Joe popping next door again, so things had obviously been playing on her mind,' Paige explains. 'Anyway, she just started knocking back the drinks and enjoying herself. Everything was fine for a few hours, until everyone started dancing and Jonas grabbed her and got up close. A bit too close for my liking.' She takes a long sip of water from a bottle. 'At that point, I told her we ought to get going and Jonas told me to relax, sniggering and asking me if I was her mother. I didn't like the way he spoke to me, to be honest; his mates were laughing so I lost it then and gave him a right mouthful. He's lucky that's all he got. I kept thinking about Abby's kids back home. Somehow, I managed to drag Abby away, even though she wasn't very happy with me.'

'She'll thank you in the morning,' I tell her, glancing at Abby's open-mouthed, mascara-streaked face.

Paige is asleep before I am, and I lie awake for a while thinking about how the evening with Kyros ended and I wonder how things might have turned out had Paige not called and asked for help. I know Kyros was moving in for a kiss and I'm pretty sure I would have responded, as I could feel the heat between us. Would I have been able to resist anything more than a kiss? I wonder. It's been so long since I've been intimate with a man, I'm not sure how I feel about it. Maybe I won't be able to enjoy being so close to someone again. Plus, I'll be heading home soon so I don't want to get too involved with anyone. I feel a sense of confusion as I eventually drift off to sleep, to the gentle sound of Abby's snores in the background.

Chapter Eighteen

I wake Abby the next morning with fresh orange juice and aspirin just as Paige emerges from another shower room that is not over-looked – I'm sure to the disappointment of the guy in the opposite villa who seems to have spent a lot of time on his balcony this morning, I can't help noticing.

'Ugh, I feel as though I've been run over by a bus.' Abby swallows the tablets down and disappears beneath the sheets.

'You nearly were last night,' says Paige as she walks past the bed and yanks the cover from Abby, who is lying in the foetal position wearing last night's outfit of white shorts and a pink top. 'Come on, sleepyhead. We only have two days of our holiday left and you don't want to be wasting it.'

Abby attempts to grab the covers again, but Paige persuades her to sit up and drink some more water.

'What the hell was I drinking last night?' Abby asks as she rubs her temples. 'I don't even remember getting home.'

'Kyros and Becky came to the rescue,' Paige tells Abby as she plugs her hairdryer in ready to dry her hair.

'Oh yes, I vaguely remember seeing you now, but it's all a bit fuzzy. I'm so sorry I ruined your evening out,' she says sheepishly.

'Don't worry about it. Our evening was coming to an end anyway,' I tell her, once again wondering how things might have panned out without the interruption.

Paige begins to dry her hair and I head downstairs. I'm making a pot of coffee when I hear the sound of a car engine approaching the villa and I go to open the front door. It's Kyros.

'Good morning, I just thought I would call in and make sure your friend is okay this morning,' he says, stepping out of the car into the bright sunshine.

'She's just surfaced. Suffering a little, I think. Would you like some coffee?'

'Yes, thanks, a coffee would be good.'

He takes a seat at the breakfast bar and I pour him a coffee from a cafetière.

Kyros is wearing jeans and a white polo shirt, his sunglasses perched on top of his slightly tousled hair, which makes him look ruggedly sexy.

'So what are your plans today?' he asks as he sips his coffee.

'Not too sure. I think it might just be a day of hanging around the pool today and we'll have a think about what to do this evening.'

'I was thinking about that too. I've gone to the liberty of arranging a night out for you and your girlfriends,' he says.

'Really?' I ask, intrigued, yet flattered.

'There is a cinema in Skiathos at the top of the town, on Papadiamantis Street,' Kyros explains. 'It is an open-air cinema. They are screening *Mamma Mia!* this week, which I thought you and your friends might like to watch while you are here.'

'Wow! Thanks, Kyros. I didn't know there was a cinema here and a night out watching *Mamma Mia!* sounds just about perfect,' I tell him gratefully.

'You have to book in advance, so I booked online and printed the tickets out.'

He hands me an envelope with the tickets inside.

'Apparently it is a must-see for visitors to the island, so I thought you might enjoy it.' He smiles and I'm so touched by his thoughtfulness. I see pure kindness in his gesture and nothing remotely controlling, and it shocks me for a second.

'Don't you fancy joining us?' I ask. Although I think I already know the answer.

'Not really, I think it is mainly for ABBA fans. And groups of women. I'm told the staff get the atmosphere going and there is lots of singing and dancing.'

'Sounds amazing.'

I find myself thinking it will be a really fun night out and hope Abby makes a full recovery from her hangover.

'I hope I may get the chance to see you again after your friends leave?' Kyros asks as he sips the last of his coffee and stands up to leave.

'I'd like that. And I can only think of one place we would like to dine for our final night together tomorrow, if you can make a reservation for us,' I ask.

'Consider it done. Any particular time?'

'Maybe seven thirty? The girls have to be at the airport early the following day for a midday flight,' I explain.

Kyros heads off and a short time later, the girls join me in the kitchen. Paige is wearing a sheer, black beach kaftan with a colourful bikini underneath and Abby is hugging her bathrobe around her, looking like death warmed up but at least she's managed to have a shower.

I place tea and a plate of toast in front of Abby, which she once told me is her tried and tested hangover cure and she smiles gratefully, before sipping her tea and tentatively taking a bite of the toast.

'Do you fancy a night at the cinema tonight, ladies?' I ask as I top up the coffee pot.

I tell them all about the showing of *Mamma Mia!* at the open-air cinema in Skiathos.

'Ooh that sound like fun,' says Paige. 'I'd planned a pool day anyway with this one.' She nods at Abby. 'A night at the cinema sounds just about perfect.'

'Sounds good to me,' says Abby. 'I'm sure I'll be fine later after a day lazing around the pool.'

'And drink plenty of water.' Paige leans over precariously on her bar stool, and grabs a bottle of water from the fridge and hands it to Abby. 'Tea and coffee will only dehydrate you even more,' she sensibly advises.

'Yes, Mother,' says Abby, although obediently taking a long glug of water from the bottle.

When we've cleared up, we head outside and take our places around the pool. Abby has reappeared after nipping upstairs to change into a swimsuit and grab her book and Paige has her headphones plugged in listening to some music, while I pile my hair on top of my head with a hair band and decide to go for a swim in the pool.

It's almost eleven o'clock and the sun is already beating down fiercely, so the water in the pool is gloriously cool in contrast. I immerse myself in the water as I concentrate on my breathing and start swimming lengths. It feels strange that in two days' time I'll be waving my friends off at the airport as I continue my stay here alone. I wonder for a moment whether I should be staying here for so long. Should I be heading back home with my friends and concentrating on the shop? Then again, maybe a break is exactly what I need and Mum is more than happy to help out, I tell myself. Besides, once I'm back home, I know I'll be thinking about Scott, and looking over my shoulder, so at least I can have some respite from those thoughts whilst I'm here.

Chapter Nineteen

Just before six, we're showered and dressed. Abby is now fully recovered from the previous evenings overindulgence and we're ready to hit the town for our night out at the cinema.

Paige decides to drive the car down to the harbour this evening and we wind down the mountain road, passing young couples on quad bikes enjoying the freedom, the young women's hair billowing in the wind as they wrap their arms around their drivers' waists. A Jeep safari of four Jeeps in convoy toot their horns as they head in the opposite direction, higher up towards a village and a church high in the hills.

After parking up, we head along the main street leading away from the harbour and passing the familiar shops and cafés, until we walk up a slight incline and locate the cinema that has a *Mamma Mia!* poster displayed on its white rough painted walls. A short walk away we come across a pretty taverna with peach painted walls and dark wooden window boxes spilling over with red flowers. There are several empty tables outside, so we find a seat and a young waiter soon appears.

'I asked Kyros to reserve a table at the Two Brothers' restaurant tomorrow night, if that's okay,' I tell Abby and Paige as we peruse the menu.

'Do you mean Krypton?' Paige glances at Abby with a wicked glint in her eye.

'Why are you looking at me?' asks Abby.

'Oh nothing.'

Abby presses us until we tell her what we are talking about and she is totally mortified.

'Oh no. Maybe we'll find somewhere else to eat tomorrow night; I'm not sure I can look him in the eye.' She cringes.

'Don't worry. At least you didn't puke on his shoes. You managed to make it to a nearby dustbin.'

'I did WHAT? Oh my goodness, that's it, I'm never drinking again. Although in truth, I never even drank that much, I'm just not much of a drinker these days. I blame that rum punch. It tasted like pineapple juice, so it went down a bit too easily.'

'Don't worry, I've spoken to Kyros this morning, he's not a bit bothered. In fact, I think he found it rather amusing.'

'Can you remember dancing with Jonas?' Paige asks Abby.

'Kind of. I think that's when I started feeling the effects of the punch.' She grimaces.

'I think so too. Talking of punch, Jonas and his mates are lucky they didn't get one from me. One of them asked if I was your mother when I decided to drag you away and get you home,' huffs Paige. 'In fact, didn't you say the same thing when I told you to drink more water? Maybe I *am* turning into my mother.' Paige pulls a face. 'Although I don't mind if I do. My mum was great,' she says with affection in her voice.

'I'm grateful you were there to look after me. Sorry if I ruined your evening. Both of you,' Abby says sincerely.

We both tell Abby to forget about it, but Paige digs a little deeper and asks why she felt so flattered by the attention of Jonas.

'Truthfully? I really don't know. Maybe I've been feeling a little insecure about the whole marriage thing and felt flattered that someone was giving me so much attention, and then when I called home Joe always seemed to have nipped next door.'

'I'm sure Joe would never cheat on you, but one thing's for sure, you two need to have a serious chat when you get home,' says Paige, and I agree.

I'm pretty certain Joe would never cheat on Abby, but one thing I've learned is that you never really know what goes on in other people's relationships. I guess me and Scott looked like the perfect couple to the outside world but nothing could have been further from the truth.

An hour and a half later, we have finished a delicious BBQ grill feast of pork chops, calamari, grilled halloumi and shared a Greek salad. We finish up with a glass of *tsipouro*, which is a type of raki. But Abby sticks to mineral water after last night, as well as being our designated driver.

Climbing the stairs to the open-air theatre, we present our tickets to an attendant and notice the space is almost already full and there's the buzz of excited chatter ringing around the auditorium. There are blue camping style chairs set out, some with drinks holders, and we are shown to the latter. A huge drop-down screen is at the front of the cinema, and a bar to the right. Kyros was right about the audience consisting mainly of groups of women, although there are one or two men with family groups.

Paige nips to the bar for some drinks and ten minutes later the familiar ABBA tune strikes up to indicate the start of the film, and the audience begin to stamp their feet in anticipation.

'Isn't this wonderful.' I sigh as the sun begins its descent and I relish the thought of watching the movie beneath the stars.

'Gorgeous. They should have more of these cinemas back home, but I don't suppose we really get the weather,' says Abby.

We spend a fabulous two hours watching the movie and singing along to the songs, encouraged by the staff, who occasionally stand up and join in, rousing the audience as they sing and dance. At the finale when the actors on screen belt out the 'Mamma Mia' theme tune in their sparkly outfits, every single person is on their feet, and would have raised the roof if there was one.

'Oh wow! What an experience,' says Abby as we make our way down the steps of the cinema with the departing crowd.

'I agree, it was fabulous and it was really thoughtful of Kyros to arrange that for us,' agrees Paige. 'It's been ages since I last went to a singalong type event. I got dressed up as a nun and went to watch *The Sound of Music* at the Liverpool Empire. I'd forgotten what fun they could be.'

'What is it with you and nuns? Maybe you have a latent desire to become one after all,' I tease.

'Maybe I do.' She laughs.

'I've never really considered myself a fan of ABBA but I knew every word of their songs. I loved every minute,' I say as we head contentedly towards the harbour to pick up the car, the songs still going around in my head.

Walking through the old town near the harbour, we pass the Two Brothers' restaurant and Kyros is serving a table outside with coffee. He lifts his hand and waves and we head over to say hello, to find the restaurant bouncing to the sound of music. I glance inside to see a floor show of Greek dancing with Alex at the very centre.

'Did you enjoy your evening, ladies?' asks Kyros with a grin, before asking if he can get us anything.

'It was amazing! We can't thank you enough.'

Suddenly there's a loud, 'Oh-pa!' as the Greek music speeds up.

'Excuse me, ladies.'

Kyros heads towards the group of dancers, dressed in traditional Greek costume, and says something to the man who must be his father, who appears to bat him away and continue dancing.

We order some coffee and sip a creamy cappuccino at an outside table and chat for half an hour. Kyros pops over to chat in between serving tables of diners and Abby apologises profusely to him for cutting his evening short with me in order to drive her home.

'Was that your father? Is he okay?' I ask, when Kyros finally persuades Abby it was not a problem.

'I hope so. I was telling him to take things a little slower, but maybe I worry about him a little too much. He will probably outlive all of us,' Kyros says, a half-smile on his face.

When it's time for us to leave, Kyros says good night and places his hand gently on my arm and I get butterflies in my stomach.

'See you tomorrow,' he says and I can feel his eyes on me, watching from the doorway as we walk towards the car park.

We've had a perfectly lovely evening and as Abby isn't in the mood for partying, we head home well before midnight with the welcoming lights of the villa beckoning us towards them as we drive. Once inside, Abby and Paige head straight to bed, whilst I sit outside in the warm evening air with my thoughts. I find myself wondering where Henry is right now on his journey across the water. I hope he and his friends are sitting on deck beneath the stars, laughing and playing poker like they were the last time they called, living life to the full. For a moment I envy his carefree spirit and lust for life. The stars look so much brighter here than they do back home, contrasting with the clear inky sky above. It's just so beautiful.

As I lie in bed thinking about spending the last day with my friends tomorrow, I receive a text from Kyros telling me it was good to see us this evening and he is pleased we enjoyed our evening at the cinema. I thank him again and tell him I'm looking forward to tomorrow evening. He tells me he has reserved the best table for us and I've come to expect nothing less.

Chapter Twenty

'So what do you want to do today then? It's our last day so we'd better make the most of it.' Paige has her head in her little guidebook looking for things to do.

Abby had another Skype call with the kids this morning despite resolving not to and can't wait to be at home with her family, especially after the events at the beach with Jonas, which I think she is bitterly regretting.

'I've missed their smiling faces so much. I hope they're not too upset seeing me on camera; it must be very confusing for them,' she frets.

'Did they look upset?' asks Paige.

'No, they were giggling at the camera and shouting, "Mamma".'

'Ah how cute. Well then, don't worry. They are with their father and sister after all and you'll be back home tomorrow. In the meantime, what do you fancy doing today?' she asks brightly.

'You know, I wouldn't mind just working on my tan for a few hours but maybe later we could head down to the beach and hire a speedboat this afternoon – what do you think?'

'A speedboat? Yeah! That sounds like a great idea. Have you driven one before?' asks Paige.

'I have actually. It was quite a few years ago in Corfu, before the twins were born, but I managed it alright, even managing to moor up successfully at a restaurant for lunch.'

'Brilliant. Do you fancy that too, Becky?' asks Paige.

'That does sound like a lot of fun, yes, I'm in,' I reply enthusiastically. 'In fact, there's a card on the fridge with a number for speedboat hire,' I tell them, remembering that Uncle Henry left some tourist information for us.

An hour or so later, we set off to collect a boat from a man called Kostas, who is meeting us at a beach just up the road.

'I'm glad we didn't have to go to Koukounaries beach,' says Abby. 'I'm not sure I can look Jonas in the eye again.'

'Forget about that now,' says Paige, touching her arm. 'We all do daft things on holiday. I once fell onto the baggage carousel at an airport trying to retrieve my suitcase.'

'You never! What happened?' asks Abby, aghast.

'I actually chugged along with the suitcases for a few seconds, before a man helped me off. The friend I went on holiday with was completely useless; she just stood there laughing hysterically.'

'Oh, Paige, I'm sure I would have laughed too,' I say, picturing the scene.

Out on the open water, we take turns at the wheel, me a little hesitantly at first, but growing in confidence after a while as the boat skims across the water.

'Oh, this really is the life,' says Paige as she takes the wheel wearing designer sunglasses and a white bikini, and looking a bit like a Bond girl. A couple of guys pass us in the opposite direction on jet skis, making a figure of eight shape and showing off before they zoom off into the distance.

After a while, we drop anchor and snorkel in the crystal blue shallow waters – spotting colourful little fish beneath the surface – just relaxing and having the time of our lives. As I lie on my back and gaze at the sky above, I thank God for my friends and know that whatever happens in the future, I will always have them by my side and it fills me with inner strength.

I splutter as Paige swims up close and splashes me with water while I was floating on my back, lost in a daydream.

'According to my little map, there's a café a couple of miles away near a little cove where we could grab a drink,' she says.

'Sounds good,' I say, and we both swim back to the boat in the warm, turquoise water.

Abby is already on board, sitting on the wooden seat of the boat and staring out to sea.

'Are you alright?' I ask her as I dry myself off with a towel.

'I'm fine, just thinking about my family. I can't wait to see them but I'll really miss this place,' she says, gazing out past the hills rising up from the beaches. 'I can't thank you enough for asking me.' She turns and wraps me in a hug. 'I feel like I'm ready for anything when I get home; I feel completely energised having a few undisturbed nights' sleep.'

'I'm glad it's done you good.' I smile.

'I can't help feeling a little selfish though as Joe hasn't had a break this year.' She sighs. 'I think we need to book a family holiday at the end of August before Heather goes back to school.'

'He was fine about you coming away, remember, although a family holiday might be just the thing,' I tell her, thinking about her recent self doubt and how some quality time together as a family might do them the world of good.

Abby takes the wheel and we head off around a cliff that juts out into the sea, and a short while later we've moored the boat up near a waterside restaurant, with bamboo furniture and white painted floorboards. The walls are painted a soft green with ceiling fans above, and the place has a Caribbean feel. We are shown to a table overlooking the crystal-clear water, where shoals of silver fish are hovering just below the surface. As we're taking turns driving the boat, we all opt for delicious mocktails that arrive with straws and fruit poking from the top.

Chatting in the restaurant, talk turns to how I'll spend my time when the girls head home tomorrow.

'Well, there's a stack of books in Henry's library for a start and I might go off and do a bit of walking. There's a lot of footpaths in the nearby hills.'

'Won't you be lonely in that big villa all on your own?' asks Paige, and her and Abby exchange a look and smile.

'Not really. Although I know what you're thinking and, yes, Kyros has said he'd like to take me out again. It doesn't mean I'm going to jump into bed with him,' I protest.

'Who said anything about jumping into bed? Although come to think of it, what's stopping you?' asks Abby, taking a sip of her drink.

'I'm not sure.' I shrug. 'There's no doubt Kyros is very attractive.'

'No doubt at all.' Paige winks.

'It's just that, well, I'm not sure I'm ready for a relationship. And Kyros might not be either, for all I know; we barely know each other.'

'I'm sure you'll get to know each other a little more when we leave. You should let your hair down and enjoy yourself; you deserve it after everything you've been through,' adds Abby.

Which I suppose is true. And one thing I don't need to worry about is the shop, so I should be switching off and relaxing a little more. Mum is having the time of her life looking after the shop, sending me regular updates and photos of the interior, which she has been adding little touches to and I have to admit it looks rather good. She's added strands of fake white trailing roses to some of the shelves, which really add a special touch, and with Dad's chalkboard outside gives a it an edgy, vintage feel. It's the kind of look I was originally hoping to achieve for the shop but maybe a bit of apathy had set in. It turns out a pair of fresh eyes have been marvellous, and I guess I should have allowed her to help out more before, instead of feeling suffocated by the fact that she had moved to be so close to me.

We finish our lunch and before we head back to the beach we stop for another swim, all of us dreaming about having a holiday home here, with a little speedboat near a jetty to zip out across the water whenever we felt like it. We drop the boat off with Kostas feeling refreshed and energised.

Paige heads upstairs to call Rob when we arrive back at the villa and I give Mum a quick call and I'm surprised to hear Dad answer the phone in the shop.

'Oh hi, love, your mum has just popped next door to get her hair trimmed. She should be back in half an hour. Hang on a minute.'

I can hear him passing change to a customer and saying goodbye to them.

'She's left you in charge?' I ask in surprise.

'Yeah, and I've enjoyed myself, to be honest. I was talking to a bloke earlier who was in with his wife and he asked if we had any shaving soap. He told me it's hard to get any organic soap around here. It might be something you could add to your range.'

'It might indeed, Dad,' I say with interest. I suppose I should include men's products a little more as male grooming is a big thing.

I'm thrilled Mum and Dad are enjoying being in the shop and I'm grateful they are injecting fresh ideas. A new broom sweeps clean, as they say. I step out onto the terrace and as I take in the breathtaking view, for a minute I dream about staying here a while longer. Before recognising the thought as precisely that. A dream.

Chapter Twenty-One

I dress carefully for dinner, choosing a white knee-length strapless dress that shows off my tan perfectly. I decide to wear my curly hair down today and let it dry naturally, after I've scrunched some hair mousse through it. I complete my outfit with the pair of gold strappy wedges that I bagged in the sale back home.

'You look lovely,' says Paige, when I appear on the terrace.

'Thanks, so do you,' I reply. 'You both do.'

Paige is wearing fashionable jeans and a white, slightly low-cut top and high heels, whilst Abby is wearing a pretty, fitted, floral dress.

'I can't believe it's our last evening together,' says Abby as we walk down the driveway, ready to climb into the car.

'Actually, I'll drive,' says Paige. 'I know it's our last evening but we have to be up early. Besides, the last time I went on holiday abroad a couple of years ago, I celebrated the last evening with a few cocktails and ended up with my head out of the taxi window all the way to the airport, willing myself not to throw up.' She grimaces at the thought.

'So you've matured a bit since then,' I tease.

The harbour is busy with tourists, some strolling along dressed casually in shorts and T-shirts, others dressed smartly and sipping drinks outside restaurants. Others line the benches near the Bourtzi, watching the sun begin its descent towards the sea as dusk draws in.

Kyros is standing near the entrance to the restaurant when we arrive, and he looks me up and down as I walk closer.

'Ladies, good evening and welcome. You all look beautiful.'

He guides us to our table and whispers in my ear, 'And you look sensational.' His comment thrills me.

At the centre of the table is a bucket of ice with a bottle of champagne nestled in it.

'Compliments of the house,' says Kyros as he pops the cork and pours us each a glass. 'I hope you have enjoyed your holiday here in Skiathos and I hope you will return. *Ya mas.*'

'How very kind,' says Paige, taking a sip of the fizz and we all clink our glasses together.

'Thank you, Kyros, I'll be sure to tell everyone about your restaurant. I'll do a little write-up about it,' says Abby.

She tells Kyros all about her blog and her work as a freelance writer.

'I would really appreciate that, thank you,' he tells her.

'Maybe it's my way of an apology for ruining your date the other night. I'd be happy to recommend your restaurant; the food here is fantastic,' she says.

'I'm glad you think so. Enjoy your evening, ladies. I will see you later.'

Kyros smiles and beckons a waiter to take our order, before disappearing to the bar to serve a trio of young men who have just arrived.

'He's so lovely,' says Abby, snapping a breadstick. 'I bet you can't wait to get him alone once we've gone.'

If I'm honest the thought scares me a bit, but it's true, the idea of spending time alone with him is appealing, as I enjoyed our date together so much when we dined out near the nature reserve. 'I'd like to learn a lot more about him.'

We dine on delicious seafood and risotto dishes, lingering over our meal, appreciating the feeling of not being rushed in the restaurants here, savouring the food and the atmosphere.

All too soon it's time to leave, and it's around ten o'clock when we say good night to Kyros. His brother Linus appears from the bar and kitchen area and Kyros wishes Abby and Paige a safe journey home.

'I have heard a lot about you all,' says Linus, who has a tea towel draped over his shoulder and is smiling broadly. He's doesn't look much like Kyros, apart from his dark hair and physique, although I recall Kyros saying he looked more like their mother. 'I hope you have a safe journey home,' he says, before he heads back to the kitchen.

'I will call you tomorrow morning,' says Kyros when we depart.

Wandering the cobbled streets in the dark, the lights twinkling from restaurants and bustling shops, the girls pick up some last souvenirs of their visit. Abby buys the twins a cuddly lion and tiger that have an accompanying picture book, saying she will treat Heather to her favourite perfume from the airport and Joe some of his favourite bourbon.

'I don't know what to buy for Rob,' says Paige, browsing shops and rails on a small street market. 'He's a bit fussy with his clothes and he's already got tons of aftershave.'

'Isn't it funny how women can buy men clothes, but if it's the other way round, it can be seen as a bit controlling.' I say this out loud without even realising it, recalling a time Scott bought me a very short dress that wasn't my style at all.

'I suppose that's true,' says Paige, unoffended. 'But if I didn't buy Rob's underwear, he'd still be walking round in the same ones he's had since we met.' She laughs.

We pass a shop with a multicoloured designer shirt in the window, and it's in a sale.

'That's it,' says Paige when she spots it. 'Rob would look fantastic in that.'

She nips inside to buy the shirt and Abby and I wait outside chatting.

'I hope everything works out with you and Joe when you get home,' I tell her. 'Maybe there's a simple explanation why he was spending time with Priya. You have to trust him.'

'I know, you're right. I have to, don't I? Without trust, what's the point?'

'That's the spirit. You must communicate, though, don't let things fester in your imagination.'

'I won't. I just hope the feelings I have are only in my imagination.' She sighs just as Paige appears from the shop.

'There was a further ten per cent off the sale price. What a bargain.' She lifts the paper bag, a huge grin on her face.

Walking along the dusty road, the smell of pancakes from a nearby stall fills my nostrils. Two teenage girls are watching the vendor spread the mixture over a large pan, and pointing to Nutella and banana as fillings.

The shops are bustling with tourists, and bars in side streets are full of customers sitting outside the ancient stone buildings, chatting and talking. The atmosphere is so good it's difficult to tear ourselves away and head for the car. There's something about shopping after dark, the buzz of shops and market stalls that makes it seem more exciting somehow. Before we head to the car, I spot an attractive ship in a bottle in a gift shop window, which I think will make a lovely present for Henry, so I nip inside to purchase it and the girls insist on making a contribution towards it.

Eventually, we weave our way through the streets until we finally arrive at the car park.

'Gosh I'm really going to miss this place,' Paige says with a deep sigh.

We're all in bed before midnight, including myself as I want to be up to make the girls breakfast before driving them to the airport. The thought of being here alone when my friends head off feels a little strange. Yet, if I'm honest, also a little bit exciting.

Chapter Twenty-Two

We enjoy a final breakfast together on the terrace and Abby and Paige have left an envelope on the kitchen counter containing money for me to go shopping and replenish the contents of the fridge, which is finally looking a little empty. They'd offered to come with me to a supermarket yesterday, but I wanted them to make the most of everything Skiathos has to offer before they leave.

'You enjoy the rest of your time here.' Paige squeezes me in a hug, quickly followed by Abby at the airport.

'And don't be thinking about the shop, it sounds like your mum and dad are doing a fine job,' says Paige.

'Well, I wasn't thinking about the shop but I am now,' I say jokingly. 'Oh, and watch out for that baggage carousel,' I tell Paige and she rolls her eyes and laughs.

The truth is, it's not the shop I occasionally think of; I know it's well stocked and Mum sends me regular updates by text, but thoughts of Scott and his release from prison have regularly popped into my mind, despite being here with my friends and having a great time.

I wave the girls off as they head towards the departure lounge and climb back into the car for the journey to the villa. I think about calling in to the Two Brothers' restaurant for a coffee, but don't want to seem too keen, as my friends have only just left. I'm sure Kyros will be in touch soon. At least I hope he will.

I decide to take a drive along the road alongside the harbour, staking out little restaurants and footpaths for walking, as well as smaller, less populated beaches. On the way back to the villa, I glance at my watch as I find myself driving along the port in the direction of the airport runway. There's a little restaurant bar there set back just off the runway, nestled amongst some trees. I've read this is where the plane spotters congregate waiting for the perfect photo of the low-flying planes. I'd like to take a photo too, and send it to the girls later. They will probably think I'm crazy, given the comments they made about the plane spotters when we first arrived. I head inside the restaurant and order a frappé, which I take to an outside table.

'Are you here for the next plane?' A middle-aged man wearing glasses and a camera around his neck is beaming at me.

'Yes, actually. My friends are on the next plane. I wouldn't mind taking a photo,' I reply.

'Is it your first time?' he asks.

'What. Oh, yes, it is.'

'You might want to stand back a bit then, but if you want to feel the breeze from the plane and get as close as possible, stand over there.' He points to a fence, where a group of enthusiasts have already gathered, cameras at the ready.

An hour later, I hear the unmistakeable rumble of the plane and a feeling of excitement filters through the assembled crowd. I plan to stand back across the car park when a sudden urge to be closer overtakes me.

The plane zooms closer, like a huge flying bird, and as the anticipation of the crowd grows, I can feel the adrenalin shooting through my body. A few minutes later, the plane flies so low above me, I can almost touch it. I snap a photo before I have to steady myself against the fence as a great gust of wind ruses through my hair and I catch my breath. It's completely exhilarating and like nothing I've experienced before.

'You joined us then.' The guy with the camera is beaming at me as the plane disappears into the distance, and I wonder if my friends caught a glimpse of me.

'Yes, it was fantastic. I'm surprised by how much I enjoyed it,' I tell him.

'I'm glad you enjoyed it. It's good to try new experiences every now and then.' He beams as he joins his friends to discuss the finer points of the giant airbus.

It certainly is, I think to myself as I fire up the engine of the car and head off, wondering what I'll discover next!

Back at the villa, I have a swim in the pool and must have dozed off as I lay sunbathing, as a while later, I'm awakened by the sound of my phone ringing.

'Kyros, hi.' I'm delighted to hear the sound of his delicious voice on the other end of the phone.

'Hi, Becky. I hope your friends got away okay?'

'Yes, thanks. Would you believe, I actually waved them off from the runway, although I'm not sure if they saw me. It feels a bit strange being here alone.' I bite my lip, wondering why I said that, hoping he doesn't think I'm hinting for him to join me.

'Hopefully you will not be alone all of the time. I have a very busy evening at the restaurant tonight, but I wondered, are you free tomorrow for a day out?' he asks.

'Yes, of course.' I feel relieved that he didn't suggest calling over after work late this evening, proving he is a gentleman.

'Wonderful. I will collect you at ten o'clock. Oh and wear a pair of trainers, if you have any.'

Luckily I'd packed some trainers as I planned to do a little walking and exploring myself.

'Where are we going?' I ask, intrigued.

'Somewhere I think is very special. I will bring the water,' he says, not giving too much away.

'Okay, I'll see you tomorrow then. Have a good evening at the restaurant.' When I finish the call I realise I'm looking forward to tomorrow already.

I prepare a salad from the fridge and enjoy it outside as I watch the sun go down. The sky is a glorious mix of orange and pink this evening, and I stay outdoors until it turns indigo, studded with bright stars. It's still so warm, I could happily lie on the sunbed near the pool and snooze beneath the stars all night but eventually I head to bed, as I suppose I had better get a good night's sleep. I have no idea what Kyros has planned for tomorrow, although I know it does involve some walking. I can hardly wait to see him again.

Chapter Twenty-Three

Kyros arrives just after ten o'clock the next morning.

'Good morning.' He kisses me lightly on the cheek in greeting and it gives me a warm glow.

'How are you today?' he asks.

'I'm well, thanks, Kyros. How are you?'

'Good. I've been looking forward to spending the day with you,' he tells me. 'It got me through a very busy service last night.'

I'm flattered by his comment and as he meets my gaze, I feel a flush of happiness as I climb into his silver car and we drive off down the mountain road. Kyros tells me the restaurant was so busy last night that he only got to bed at two in the morning.

'Don't get me wrong, it is a blessing when things are so busy, but I must admit I am looking forward to a break in the winter months. Maybe I will take that trip to England that I always promised myself.'

He casts a sideways glance at me as he drives.

'It's not the warmest of places in the winter,' I remind him, thinking of Renos on the boat saying how cold he found Scotland in the winter, although I suppose it is further north than where I live. 'Although I imagine you'd want to visit London and the weather is usually a little better down south,' I tell him.

'It depends where the attraction is for me.' He keeps his eyes on the road ahead this time and I feel the heat rush to my cheeks. Is Kyros trying to tell me he would like to visit me in England over the winter?

He says no more on the subject, and we drive through forest along dry, dusty roads until eventually the road begins to narrow. It looks abandoned and barren and eventually the road becomes so narrow, only one car can drive through. Eventually, when it seems we can go no further, Kyros parks the car and we step out into the bright sunshine.

At the end of the footpath, Kyros point up to the ruins of a castle, high upon a headland.

'We're going up there?' I ask in surprise, looking up at the wild, overgrown terrain that seems to reach to the sky. 'Are you sure my trainers will be up to the job?'

'I will guide you along; I know the best paths. The view from the top will be worth it, I promise you.' He smiles in reassurance.

We begin climbing, slowly at first until the path levels out and we make our way along the rocky ground that is flanked by wild grasses, and thistles. There are even cacti dotted about, which give it a remote, desolate feel. The ruins of the Venetian fort can be seen above like a place lost in time.

'What happened to the castle?' I ask him.

Kyros gives me a little history lesson as we stroll along.

'Kastro was once the capital of Skiathos," he informs me. 'The castle, as you can see, was well placed at the top of the fortress to keep invaders away. Pirates too, I believe. A whole settlement of people once lived here before it was abandoned.'

'Really? Why was it abandoned then?' I ask.

'Invaders. The Venetians took over, amongst others, including the Turks. It was finally abandoned in the early eighteen hundreds, I believe.'

After a fairly strenuous walk, precarious in places, we're almost at the top when I stumble on a rock and Kyros catches me, his strong arms around my waist steadying me. I thank him and once I'm upright, he takes me by the hand and guides me along.

With every step, the ruins of the castle grow closer, until we finally reach the top, where I glimpse the blue and white Greek flag placed in the ground and gently fluttering in the breeze.

The view from the summit takes my breath away, as the sparkling blue Aegean Sea can be viewed on all sides as far as the eye can see. I almost feel as though I'm standing on top the world.

'Wow, what a view.'

Kyros comes and stands next to me and together we gaze out to sea, silent for a few moments as we take it all in. He hands me a bottle of water and I take a long sip and wipe my brow, whilst Kyros has hardly broken a sweat, I can't help noticing.

'Come, let's explore,' he says after a few minutes, and when he takes my hand again as we walk, it feels like the most natural thing in the world.

Treading the ancient cobbled path, it's easy to be transported back in time, and passing a rusty old cannon I imagine a lookout watching an approaching pirate ship from the tower. We continue our path and pass a row of house ruins, which Kyros informs me were built in the fifteenth century. I peep through the tiny window of a church, slightly disappointed that the door is locked.

'Don't worry, there is a bigger church further along, which is open for visitors,' Kyros informs me.

He lets go of my hand and for a second I feel a little disheartened, as I'd been enjoying the feeling so much.

As we walk, I find myself wondering if Kyros has brought anyone else to this place. Does he offer this service to other women who have dined at the restaurant?

'I was relieved when you told me you were interested in history,' Kyros says as we walk along. 'This is one of my favourite places to visit.'

A short while later, we arrive at the church of St Nikolas, a large, white, round-shaped building. Tourists are gathered outside, some sitting on a bench beneath a tree enjoying the shade, others taking photographs.

Kyros pushes open the heavy door of the church and we step onto a cool flagstoned floor. A wooden altar is intricately carved and decorated with gold leaf, and murals of Jesus and the apostles adorn the white painted walls.

'It's beautiful,' I whisper as I walk around, slowly taking it all in. It feels a little sad, to be standing in the church where the local people would have stood and have long since fled.

As we continue our walk, we pass the ruins of an old synagogue from the Turkish occupation and several more ruins including a water tower.

'That was such an interesting walk, thank you for bringing me here, Kyros,' I tell him as we take one last look around at the panoramic views.

'I'm glad you liked it. Was it worth the walk up?' he enquires, taking his sunglasses off and turning to face me.

'It certainly was.' I breathe deep, intoxicated by the striking views from every angle. Including the one standing next to me.

'So now, if you like, I will take you for a drink,' he offers.

We head downhill, which is far easier, Kyros offering his hand when we hit a difficult part of the path, until soon enough we are heading towards the car.

As we navigate the narrow road once more, I tell Kyros he would make a good tour guide.

'I think you are right as I am passionate about Greek history. Maybe if I wasn't involved in the family business, I would have considered doing just that,' he reveals. 'How about you?'

'Gosh, I'm not sure. I've always made lotions and soaps since I was a child,' I tell him, recalling the times I spent as a child gathering rose petals. 'Perhaps I might have developed my yoga a little more and maybe become a teacher.'

'Oh, so you like yoga, that is… good to know.' Kyros winks at me playfully and I feel a slight blush on my cheeks.

We park up at a restaurant that has a dramatic view of the sea and are shown to an outside table on a terrace. We sip an ice-cold beer and pick at some nuts from a bowl that a waiter has presented to us.

'So what are you planning to do with your next few days?' Kyros asks.

'Not much, really. I had planned to do a little walking and exploring, but I think I've definitely ticked that box today,' I say, taking a sip of iced water. 'Tomorrow, I might just relax around the pool. Maybe I'll head down near the Bourtzi and watch the world go by.'

'I could come and say hello when I have a break,' suggests Kyros. 'Or maybe you could call in at the restaurant for a drink.'

'Maybe I will.' I smile at him.

I think back to the very first time we met, when I was sitting on the bench watching the boats in the harbour and how I was immediately taken with his looks and easy manner, once his bad mood had blown away.

'So as you have learned a little about where I live, tell me something about your home town,' says Kyros as we enjoy our drinks.

'Actually it's very pretty. I live in Lancashire, which is also very rich in history. There's also plenty of rolling hills to climb, but the sky is hardly ever as blue as this.'

I don't tell Kyros that I've only lived in Lancashire for three years, packing up my old life and creating a new one hundreds of miles away.

'It sounds nice. Do you have a favourite place?' he asks.

'It's hard to choose, as I love many places, especially the canal footpaths that have some beautiful walks through the countryside. I once went on a walk up Pendle Hill, which I enjoyed. I love walks with a bit of history.'

I tell Kyros all about the village of Pendle and how the last witch trial in England took place there and he listens with interest.

'It's so sad really. The women involved in the trials lived in the woods, foraging and living off the land and that, along with the fact that they lived far longer than the average age back then, made people consider them to be witches.'

'That is a sad tale,' agrees Kyros.

'It's funny how times change. These days they would probably be applauded as eco-warriors. Oh, talking of favourite places, there's a fabulous Greek restaurant a few miles from my home. Although I guess you'd have to be the judge of that.'

'Maybe I need to come over and check it out then,' he says and I dare to dream that maybe one day he will.

We arrive back at the villa a little after three thirty and I wonder whether he would like to stay for a while.

'That pool looks inviting,' says Kyros. 'I might have been tempted to take a dip if I'd brought my swimming things.'

The thought of wearing my bikini in front of Kyros fills me with anxiety, even though I've decided I won't hide myself away on the beach. Being intimate with someone is another matter, though.

'Maybe another day then,' I tell him.

Kyros glances at his watch and tells me that he has to leave to prepare for this evening's service at the restaurant.

'I must work again this evening, but tomorrow I have the evening off if you would like to do something? Maybe even a moonlight boat trip around the bay?'

'That sounds wonderful. Thanks again for today, Kyros. I don't think it's something I would have considered doing on my own,' I tell him gratefully.

'And I could reserve you a table at the restaurant this evening, if you like?' he offers.

I feel tired after my climb and I know Kyros will be busy all evening, so I politely decline.

Part of me wants to ask him not to go yet, to stay with me, but I can't find the confidence to say it out loud.

I expect him to turn and leave, but he steps towards me slowly, circling his arms around my waist and drawing me closer to him. He presses his lips down on mine and kisses me, and fireworks appear to suddenly explode all around me.

'You are welcome,' he says. 'I enjoyed it too.'

He waves from the bottom of the driveway before he turns onto the road and I float off inside the villa touching my lips, which are tingling. Once inside, I close my eyes and relive that wonderful kiss that took me completely by surprise and wonder what on earth is happening here. I seem to be quickly falling under the spell of a man I haven't known for very long, which is something I swore I would never do again.

I decide to make a shopping list before I head to the supermarket to stock up on food. Maybe tomorrow I will offer to cook one evening, although I'm frightened by what it could lead to. My hand touches my scar, and I wonder if I am always going to feel this way when I meet someone new. Maybe if I got to know someone over a long period of time it wouldn't matter so much, but I'm not going to be here for much longer. Would Kyros be repulsed by my scar? Would he even care, if it was only a holiday romance he was after? Or am I overthinking things? He knows I'm going home in a few days, so maybe he doesn't want things to even move to that level. I head inside to freshen up before deciding I guess I'll find out tomorrow.

Chapter Twenty-Four

'Mum. Hi, I was just thinking about ringing you, is all well?' I ask brightly.

It's the following morning and I'm listening to some music on the surround sound in the villa as I read, only alerted to the call as my phone flashed on the table beside me.

'Hi, love, yes, everything's okay. Well, it is now,' she says quietly.

My heart sinks, remembering the last news she delivered.

'What does that mean?' I ask, already dreading the answer.

'Well, I'm afraid there's been a break-in at the shop.'

'What? Oh no, when?' I ask, panicked.

'Last night. The police think it might have been kids, as hardly anything was taken. Just some of those basil and lime candles and a few bits. In fact, it was probably the girls who were eyeing them up the other day. It's a pity you don't have CCTV.'

'I know, Mum, but it costs a lot of money,' I say, suddenly feeling stressed.

For a split second, I wonder whether it could be Scott sending me a message, before reassuring myself that he can't possibly know of my whereabouts. Even the magazine article won't be out yet.

Thank goodness I have insurance, I think to myself. I'll need to get the little window repaired and maybe some new locks for the front door, as Mum told me that both are broken. 'Your dad says he will sort it out and you can reimburse him when the insurance money comes through. You do have insurance?' asks Mum.

'Yes, of course I do,' I tell her, feeling slightly better that the repairs will be carried out today. Many of the shops don't have shutters, as crime is fairly low in the area, but maybe I do need to think about an alarm system.

'Anyway, how's the holiday going?' Mum asks.

'It's lovely, Mum. The girls have gone home now but I'm enjoying the time here alone, doing a little exploring.'

'I wish I was there with you.' Mum sighs. 'I really ought to pluck up the courage to fly again. In fact, I might even consult a hypnotherapist as I've heard they can work wonders. Evelyn was telling me about one of her customers in the salon who had the same issues with flying. She saw this therapist and flew all the way to America. The only problem was, by the time she got on the return flight, it had worn off and she had to be practically dragged on the plane kicking and screaming.'

'Oh no, that sounds awful.'

I find myself telling her a little bit about spending time with Kyros. If only to stop her worrying about me being lonely.

'Ooh are you having a little bit of a holiday romance? That might do you the world of good,' Mum enthuses. 'You're a young woman; you don't want to let one bad experience put you off men for life,' she advises.

'Who said anything about me being off men for life?' I laugh.

'But it's been such a long time since you've had a boyfriend. I don't want that Scott to put you off meeting someone else,' she says gently.

'Don't worry, Mum, he won't. It's just that I don't want to be rushing into anything, that's all. Things got intense and serious too quickly with him and look how that turned out.'

Thinking about it, I haven't really felt attracted to anyone in a long while, so maybe Mum's right. Perhaps I ought to let my defences down a little, but then I haven't really had the opportunity to meet anyone. I work in the shop alone and any male customers are usually buying gifts for their other halves. Admittedly when I've been on nights out with the girls, they have alerted me to men who seem to be casting admiring glances my way, but I guess I've avoided their interest. For the first time, I feel an attraction towards Kyros and maybe a casual romance is just what I need.

I'm just pottering about the villa, thinking about going shopping for some food, when Paige calls.

'Hiya, I'm just on my lunch break,' she tells me. 'How's things?'

'Good, thanks. You're not splashing the cash in town, are you? Remember that weekend in the Lake District with Rob,' I remind her.

'I'm not, as it happens.' She goes on to tell me all about a story involving a recent house sale.

'Would you believe I was showing someone around a house belonging to an old couple who are moving into a small flat. I got chatting to the sellers and they told me they were getting rid of a load of old "junk" from the attic, which was in some boxes in the lounge. I spied a vase that I thought I recognised from one of those antiques programmes on the telly. I had a look, and sure enough, there was a designer's mark on the bottom. It was only a flipping Lalique vase that could be worth a fortune.'

'Wow. No way. Really? Maybe I'd better get up into the attic at home and see if the previous tenants have left anything of value.'

'Maybe you should. The old couple said they would sort me out with some money after they've put it in an auction, but I told them I would rather they spent it on some fancy furniture for their new place or a Caribbean cruise. Maybe both, depending on how much it is worth.'

I tell her all about my date later with Kyros and she says she hopes it goes well and that I deserve to be treated well by a nice bloke like Kyros.

A while later, I get ready and head out to take a drive along the coast road and stop at a beach café for a coffee. In the distance, I spy the dome-shaped islet of Troulos, which I read is a favourite destination for kayakers when the sea is calm enough. As I sit taking in the views around me, I think of Kyros and that kiss. Despite trying to resist my feelings, being with him thrills me so much. I wonder where this might be leading, although we haven't actually arranged the details of our date yet for this evening. I'm glancing out to sea, when, as if tapping into my thoughts, Kyros rings.

'Hi, Kyros, how are you?' I ask, elated that he's got in touch.

'Busy. It's been crazy here since breakfast. I've just taken a minute to ask if I can take you out this evening.'

'That would be lovely,' I tell him, feeling a jolt of excitement at the thought.

'Wonderful. I will collect you at seven thirty, if that's okay? That evening cruise around the harbour leaves at eight o'clock, if you would like to go on it?' he asks.

'That sounds really lovely,' I reply, imagining sailing around the harbour and returning as the night draws in. I can't think of anything more romantic. For a second, I feel a little guilty being here, especially after the break-in at the shop, but Mum assured me everything was in good hands and not to hurry back. Besides, I know Uncle Henry isn't keen on the villa standing empty, so I guess I'm doing him a favour too.

I finish my coffee and head off to a local store where I purchase a bottle of champagne to round off the evening later. If Kyros wants to stay and have a nightcap, that is.

When I return, I spend the rest of the afternoon doing some tidying up, even though Henry's cleaner is due tomorrow.

As I lift a photograph in a frame from a white display cabinet, I can't help noticing there aren't a lot of pictures of Aunt Bea and I wonder if it's too painful for Henry to have them on display.

The photo I'm holding shows Henry and his pals standing on the deck of a boat on one of their trips. I guess people deal with their grief in different ways, some wiping away any visible traces of loved ones in an attempt to try and move on, whilst others never want to forget times spent with loved ones and find comfort in seeing constant reminders of them. It makes me realise I don't have a photo of a significant other displayed in my home, just friends and family. I used to think being in a relationship caused more heartache than it was worth, but I'm slowly learning that perhaps it's a cynical view to have, based on one bad experience.

I spend the remainder of the afternoon listening to some music outdoors on the terrace, where the guy in the villa opposite lifts his hand and waves and I wave back, remembering how I teased Paige about her naked dancing in the bathroom above that faces his balcony. I suddenly hope he doesn't think it was me doing the dancing and wish I hadn't waved back quite so fervently.

I head off to shower and just after seven thirty Kyros arrives to collect me for our date.

'Hello, beautiful,' he says as he steps out of the car. 'Have you had a good day?'

'It's been lovely actually. I'm quite enjoying spending some time alone.'

He pretends to get back in the car and drive away and I let out a laugh.

'It doesn't mean I don't want other people's company,' I tell him, before stopping myself from adding, 'Especially yours.'

'Thank goodness for that.' He opens the car door for me and I climb in, feeling a bit excited when he sits beside me in the driver's seat and I can smell his citrusy aftershave.

'So, how has your day been?' I ask as we drive downhill towards the harbour.

'Eventful. I was witness to what you might call a love triangle at the restaurant,' he reveals.

'Oh no really? What happened?' I ask, intrigued.

'A lady and a man were enjoying a romantic lunch, holding hands the whole time, when a guy storms into the restaurant with a look of fury on his face. He looks around before striding towards their table. Linus and I exchanged glances, anticipating trouble, when the guy who was seated stands up. A punch was thrown, but luckily we managed to get them outside the restaurant.'

'Oh my goodness, I hope no one got hurt.'

'The two of them scrambled around for a while, before the guy who caught the couple in the act punched the other bloke and he landed on a chair and broke it clean in two.'

I clasp my hand over my mouth.

'What happened to the woman?' I ask, curious as to how she must have felt watching two men fighting.

'She stood there screaming the whole time until it was all over, before leaving with the injured guy who broke the chair.'

'So he was alright then?'

'Yes, I think his ego was more injured than anything, although he did limp along a little. I was worried that the whole thing would ruin the other diners' lunch, but hearing some of their comments, I got the feeling some of them enjoyed the drama.' He shakes his head and smiles.

'Some people are like that,' I say, recalling a shoplifter being chased through the market, and Sheila from the wool stall sticking her leg out and tripping him up before a policeman handcuffed him. The stallholders gossiped about it for the rest of the day, although I think they were more shocked by Sheila's part in having the criminal apprehended.

'I felt a little sorry for the scorned man,' he says thoughtfully. 'Even though I am going to have to buy another chair.' He turns and gives a wry smile.

It's just after eight o'clock when we take our seats on the sailing boat and the captain welcomes us all aboard. A table is set at the front of the boat with nibbles and wine and lights are strung along the deck.

We chat to some of the passengers, one couple celebrating their tenth wedding anniversary this week and have booked dinner tomorrow evening at the Two Brothers' restaurant.

'Congratulations. I will make sure you have a bottle of something to celebrate, courtesy of the restaurant,' Kyros tells them and they thank him in surprise when they realise he is the owner.

Sailing around the headland, it feels far more romantic than it does during the day as dusk begins to appear and the lights that are strung around the boat begin to gently glow. During our sail, a waiter passes drinks around on a tray whilst we help ourselves from the food table groaning with breads and dips. Kyros dips some bread into an aubergine dip.

'Is it as good as yours?' I ask, already knowing the answer.

'Not quite. Although it is pretty good,' he concedes.

I feel soothed by the wine and the gentle motion of the boat gliding across the sea, which is becoming darker, and fully immerse myself in the experience. I've never been sailing in the evening before, and as the sun begins to vanish behind the mountains, I feel gloriously relaxed and happy.

By the time we return to the harbour it is illuminated by the lights from the bars and restaurants as the evening is in full swing. 'Would you like to go for a walk?' Kyros offers when we disembark. 'The night is still young.'

'Yes, I think I'd like that,' I tell him, thinking it will be good to stretch my legs, rather than sitting at a bar somewhere.

We take the path towards the top of the town, eventually passing the open-air cinema where the sound of foot stomping and singing can be heard and I recall the wonderful evening I spent there with the girls and how thoughtful it was of Kyros to purchase the tickets.

'You don't know what you're missing,' I tell Kyros, nodding towards the cinema and he laughs and tells me he will take my word for it.

Walking on, we thread through narrow streets of houses, where women are sitting outside on chairs chatting to each other, whilst two men are facing each other across a small table playing dominoes. A smell of something tantalising drifts into the warm night air from one of the houses that has its front door flung open.

'Do you live above the restaurant?' I ask Kyros as we walk along.

'Yes. There is a two-bedroomed apartment above. The front bedroom gives quite a view of the harbour that would be hard to find anywhere else. I shared the space with my brother before he married.'

Kyros tells me that his brother now lives in a house across town that has a garden for his son.

'I've suggested to my father that he should come and live with me but he tells me not to fuss. Besides, I know he would never leave the family home he shared with my mother. All his memories are there.'

I find myself wondering if Kyros has ever lived with a woman. It's hard to gauge his age, but I think he is probably a couple of years younger than me. As we head away from the houses, to complete a circular walk towards the harbour again, we pass a small children's park that has a few swings and a bench. A teenage couple entwined in each other's arms get up and walk out of the park when we arrive, obviously disturbed by our presence, and Kyros heads to one of the swings and sits down.

'Are you sure it will take your weight?' I ask doubtfully as he beckons me to join him on the swing next to him.

'What are you trying to say? That I am overweight.' He feigns a frown.

'Not at all, but the swings are made for children. I'm not even sure I should sit down myself.'

He begins to swing to and fro, slowly at first before swinging higher, demonstrating that it's okay and I hope to goodness he doesn't fall from a great height.

'Okay, well maybe I'll take it easy,' I say, sitting down and gently swinging back and forth. Kyros is grinning and urging me to go higher, so a few minutes later, we're swinging through the air laughing and giggling like a pair of kids and I find myself having a whale of a time.

'Who knew that could be so much fun,' I tell him when we've stopped swinging and are sitting on the bench.

'Sometimes we forget what it's like to have fun. We should never stop remembering the child in us. I like to remember how it feels to be a young boy now and then, although maybe a boy would not do this.'

He takes me by surprise by pulling me towards him and kissing me so intensely my head spins. There was certainly nothing boyish about that.

We sit on the bench beneath the light of a full moon, the park trees bathed in the moonlight as he curls his hand around mine.

'Would you like to go somewhere else?' Kyros asks in a breathless whisper, after he has kissed me again and I find myself suggesting we head back to the villa. We walk downhill almost wordlessly, his hand in mine and every now and then he gives it a little squeeze as he casts a glance at me. We're barely out of the car and inside the villa, when Kyros presses me up against a wall and begins kissing me and running his hands over my body. I'm completely lost in the moment, until he begins to unbutton my shirt dress and I suddenly freeze.

'Is something wrong?' He pulls away from me. My hand touches my stomach and I can feel the bumpy skin beneath the fabric of my dress.

'Kyros. I... I feel a little embarrassed about something. There's something I haven't told you.'

A look of confusion crosses his face. 'I hope I have not done the wrong thing,' he says anxiously. 'I thought you wanted the same thing.'

'No, it isn't that. Of course I do.' I lead him to a couch and we sit down. I take a deep breath and tell him all about Scott and about the scarring on my body.

'I am sorry you have been through such a terrible time.' He says something that sounds like a swear word in Greek and draws me close to him, almost protectively.

'I've moved on with my life, well most of the time anyway, it's just that I haven't been intimate with anyone since,' I reveal, feeling remarkably calm.

'I understand. But do not feel ashamed of your body. It is something that happened in your past; you can't erase it,' he says gently.

We kiss again and Kyros asks if I would still like him to stay this evening, but I gently decline and we agree to talk tomorrow. Henry is arriving back the day after tomorrow so I ask Kyros if he is available to join us for dinner, as I would like to cook a welcome home meal for Henry.

'I would like that very much,' he says. 'Our new chef is very competent in the kitchen now thankfully, so I am able to take time away.'

'Actually, would you like to invite your father too? If he would care to join us.'

'My father? Well, yes, if you are sure. He likes Henry. Thank you, I am sure he will enjoy that very much.'

As Kyros drives away, I wonder whether I should have completely abandoned my fears and headed to the bedroom with him and I spend the rest of the evening dwelling on it, tossing and turning restlessly, unable to sleep. I wonder if my physical and emotional scars are going to stop me from enjoying a relationship with another man for the rest of my life? Maybe a holiday romance would have been just the thing for me to regain a little confidence, but then what of the future? My life is back home and I feel happy and secure with my friends that I have made a new life with. And, of course, there's my business to think of although Mum is doing rather well looking after that, I suppose.

Chapter Twenty-Five

Kyros phones the next morning to ask if I am okay and tells me his father is looking forward to dining with us and hearing all about Henry's latest trip.

Over breakfast, I'd been looking at a map of the island and on impulse I decide to drive down into town to hire a quad bike and explore the island on my own. An hour later, I've taken possession of a blue quad bike at a hire place near the harbour and am driving off along the coast road.

I pass Jimmy's Taverna, where Henry took us the first evening we arrived before he went off on his sailing trip and recall the pleasant evening we all spent together sitting beneath the stars. Soon, I'm zipping along the coast road, passing signs for beaches and small cafés, wind billowing beneath my safety helmet. I can feel the rush of the wind cooling my skin as the midday sun approaches and feel exhilarated by the thought of not knowing exactly where I am heading. Eventually, I end up near the nature reserve at the rear of Koukounaries beach and I stop to look out over the lake, where a family of geese are together in a group. A goose swoops down, splashing into the water, casting far-reaching ripples. I drive along a dusty bike track, ducking below some low-hanging tree branches before I'm out on the open road again, as a blue bus is dropping people off at the beach. Being here makes me think of Abby and how she was flattered by the attentions of Jonas. I hope things are okay with her and Joe back home and decide I'll ring her when I get back. I still find it hard to believe that Joe could be up to no good, as from what I have observed he dotes on her and the children.

Half an hour later, I've pulled up at a beach café and ordered a frappé. The café overlooks some rocks with steps that lead down to a small stretch of sandy beach that belongs to a hotel. The sparkling blue-green sea stretches out as far as the eye can see.

'It's lovely here, isn't?'

It takes me a minute to realise that someone is speaking to me.

'What? Oh sorry, I was miles away. Yes, it's gorgeous,' I agree.

The woman, who looks to be in her fifties, is sitting with her partner nursing a beer.

'Are you on holiday?' asks the lady, who has blonde curly hair and a friendly face.

'I am actually. I'm staying at my uncle's villa in the hills.'

'Ooh that sounds lovely. I wasn't sure if you were English actually, you look a bit Greek,' she tells me.

Looking at my now deeply tanned skin, coupled with my dark hair and eyes, I'm not surprised. I do look a little like a local.

We chat and the couple tell me it's only their second day of their holiday so I give them a few recommendations for restaurants, as well a visit to the monastery.

'Ooh yes, that's on my to-do list. Bob's not so keen, are you, love?' She turns to her husband and he shrugs.

'I'll go if you like, but I'd rather be out on a boat,' he reveals.

'And wouldn't you know it, I hate boats. I get seasick,' she explains.

'I'm sure there's a coach trip of the island that visits the monastery,' I tell the woman, who has introduced herself as Carol. 'The hotel reception might be able to tell you about that.'

'Now that's a good idea. I could go off for the day whilst you go on your boat trip,' she tells her husband, who agrees it's a good idea.

We chat for a while longer, before I ride off downhill as the sparkling sea draws closer. I think about calling into the Two Brothers' restaurant for lunch, before deciding against it. I only have today to enjoy my own company before Henry arrives back tomorrow afternoon and then I'll be hosting a dinner party.

Spotting a wooden sign for a beach, I pull in to find tables set up around a beach bar and a small crowd who seem to be sampling the food. A couple of people are standing with a board, and one of them whispers to the other when he sees me.

It seems I have stumbled across a cookery competition, the winner's recipe to be featured in the owner's restaurant on the beach along with a cash prize. A slightly rotund man with a moustache and wearing a white shirt and a pair of dark trousers approaches me.

'Excuse me, are you English?' he asks, looking a little unsure, just like the couple I chatted to earlier.

'Yes, I am,' I reply and a smile spreads across his face.

'Excellent. Then I wonder, could you be one of our judges? I have just been informed that one of our judges has been taken ill.'

The man explains the competition is taken very seriously as to who has the best moussaka and it would be good to have a non-Greek to give an honest opinion. I feel the weight of responsibility on my shoulders as the eyes of some Greek people seem to bore into me. My stomach gives a little growl when I approach the tables, and the delicious aromas of the moussakas fill the air. I can think of worse ways to spend an afternoon as I sample mouthful after mouthful of wonderful tasty food. But there is one that's head and shoulders above the others, in my view at least. I consult with the other Greek judge, who agrees with me. It seems they were torn between two entrants and I gave the casting vote.

There is a big build-up before the announcement and before the judge finally approaches the winning plate of food.

'Ladies and gentlemen. It is this one.' The winner is thrilled because there is also a prize of a hundred euros, as well as the dish being put on the restaurant menu.

'Thank you so much for helping to reach the decision.' A young Greek man with tousled black hair jogs towards me as I'm about to climb onto the bike and leave. 'Winning this competition may help me to get a job in a restaurant. And this will help me buy some more kitchen equipment.' He lifts the hundred euros and kisses them. 'I practise my recipes in my mother's kitchen, but one day, I dream of having my own beach restaurant, just like this.'

'Keep hold of those dreams,' I tell him. 'And good luck. Are you local?'

'Yes, my name is Nicos, I live at the blue house across the road, near the bend.'

I remember driving past the small house and feel thrilled that I may have played a tiny part of helping someone's dream come true. Nicos from the blue house, I hope it isn't long before you get the chance to shine.

*

It's just after seven when I arrive back at the villa, and after shower-
ing and changing I sit outside with a gin and tonic, enjoying the
solitude, when Abby calls.

'Abby, hi! How are you?' I ask, pleased to hear her voice.

'I'm fine, thanks. How's it going there?'

'It's wonderful. I've just spent the whole day alone exploring
on a quad bike.'

'Alone. Really?'

'Yes, really. Kyros has a restaurant to run; I can't spend every
minute with him.'

As I tell her this, I remember how worried I was about travelling
alone here to Greece originally, yet here I am exploring the island on
my own. No wonder she's a little surprised. I tell her all about my day
and how I stumbled upon the cookery competition on the beach.

'Wait until I tell Paige that she's missed out on a food-eating
contest,' she says and we both giggle.

'So what have you been up to since you got home?' I ask.

'Enjoying some family time. The twins covered my face with
kisses when I got back,' she tells me, and I find myself wondering
if Joe did the same.

'I've secured a travel piece with a magazine to review Skiathos.
I'm going to give the Two Brothers' restaurant a mention.'

'That's brilliant, Abby. I'm sure Kyros and his family will be
grateful for that. So how's things with Joe?' I ask tentatively.

'Okay actually, but he's still acting a little strangely.' She sighs.
'I nipped to the local shop yesterday and when I returned, I found

him rooting through my wardrobe. He mumbled something about looking for spare coat hangers because he was running low. I don't know, maybe I'm becoming paranoid.' She attempts a laugh. 'Because actually, things are fine. He welcomed me home with a nice steak dinner and a good bottle of red.'

'I'm glad things are good,' I tell her, feeling relieved. 'And don't forget to book a restaurant for a night out together, like we discussed,' I remind her.

'We definitely will in a week or two. I don't want to abuse my babysitters so soon after being away on holiday.'

When we've finished talking, it's around eight o'clock. I decide to head inside and draw the curtains, and watch a film on the huge wall-mounted television screen with surround sound. I settle with some snacks in the huge sofa. I find a romantic comedy on Netflix and sit down with my snacks, feeling completely relaxed. As I enjoy the moment, home feels like a million miles away, but not for long. I'll be leaving here soon and the thought fills me with feelings of conflict.

Chapter Twenty-Six

Henry's tan is even deeper as he steps off the yacht.

I'm waving furiously on the harbour front and he strolls towards me and wraps me in a hug.

'You look amazing,' I tell him as we drive home.

'I feel great. There's nothing I love more than getting out on the open sea. I should have joined the navy instead of being a businessman.' He chuckles.

I'm wondering whether Henry might be tired after his sailing jaunt and hope I haven't done the wrong thing in inviting Kyros and Alex to dinner this evening.

'That's a wonderful idea!' he says when I tell him, putting my doubts to rest. 'Alex is a good bloke and so is Kyros, but won't he be busy at the restaurant, though?' he asks.

'They have a new chef and I think Kyros has worked flat out this past year when Linus took time off, so he's easing back a little this summer,' I tell him.

'I bet that's only while you're around,' says Henry, with a twinkle in his eye.

Maybe that's true and as soon as I leave he'll be working full-time in the restaurant. Until the next holidaymaker who comes along takes his eye, I can't help thinking.

Back at the villa, Henry and I sip drinks and munch on some snacks while he tells me all about his trip.

'Did you have a favourite place?' I ask him.

'Not really, everywhere was amazing, although I do love Skopelos, not to mention all that delicious food.' He pats his stomach. 'I'm afraid I always gain a few pounds when I go off on these trips. I'll have to get some lengths in in the pool.'

Henry tells me more about the places he visited, and I listen with great interest, as he is a good storyteller, injecting everyday stories with colour and humour.

'Did Bea like the water?' I ask, wondering if she ever went out sailing with him.

'No, not really. She wasn't keen on sailing, but she never liked being left alone either,' he tells me candidly.

'Did she make any friends here?' I ask.

'A few, yes, but she never mixed much. It was her idea to sell up and live in the sun but truthfully, I don't think she really took to it,' he says, with a hint of regret in his voice. 'She said she missed her friends back home and at the height of summer, she found the heat a little difficult.'

I can imagine that being the case as Bea was pale skinned with reddish coloured hair.

Henry swirls some ice around in his drink. 'It was a real shame,' he continues, 'as I felt like I'd come home when I first arrived here in Greece. I've always loved the sunshine and the Greek way of life, ever since I first visited Crete in the mid-eighties. Skiathos being a smaller island, it felt like a perfect place to live. Somewhere you could really get to know the locals. Anyway, I tried my best to make her happy, and at one point even considered selling up and moving back to England. We compromised with regular visits back home. She would sometimes stay on for longer with her sister when I headed back here,' he reveals.

I remember when I first met Kyros and he'd commented that Henry often went into the restaurant alone. It makes me sad to think they were living slightly separate lives here and may have even been unhappy. Maybe there are things I didn't know about their marriage and again it illustrates that we don't know what goes on behind closed doors. How many marriages just amble along, without being truly happy? I can't help wondering. Perhaps that's why he revamped the villa and doesn't display her photographs, in an attempt to move on and make a new life for himself. Thinking of my own situation with Scott, I can certainly relate to that.

'Right. I'm off to buy the ingredients for tonight's dinner,' I tell Henry. 'Maybe you could take the opportunity to get those lengths in,' I say, glancing at the swimming pool.

'Maybe I will,' he says, stretching his arms above his head. 'After I've had a little siesta, that is. All that sailing has left me feeling exhausted.' He winks.

Henry has told me about a man who sells fresh fruit and vegetables from a van at a small outdoor market a couple of miles away, close to Papadiamantis Street, where there is also a fish van, selling freshly caught fish of the day. I'm hoping I can get a sea bass to cook on the BBQ this evening, as I'm worried about cooking traditional Greek food for a restaurateur.

As I drive along my thoughts return to Henry and Bea's marriage, which it seems was not particularly happy, despite having a lot of material wealth. Thinking about it, maybe the clues were there, as Bea never visited our home with him and he never spoke of her much, so maybe they did their own thing. I think of my own parents' marriage, which despite their different personalities has survived for almost fifty years and I know they would be completely lost without each other.

Having parked the car and followed Uncle Henry's directions, I'm soon stood at the fruit and vegetable van, piled high with crates of ripe, juicy fruit and vegetables. Fat, red tomatoes sit beside smooth purple aubergines and outsized peaches, watermelons and grapes jostle for space. I fill a hessian bag with tomatoes, fennel and aubergines and the old man on the stall, who is wearing a flat cap, tells me he will find me 'the best watermelon' before he places one into a carrier bag with a toothless smile. His eyes crinkle at the corners when he smiles, his leathery brown skin the result of a lifetime working outdoors.

Heading back towards the car, I spot a bakery with sweet delights in the window, so head inside to buy a custard tart called *galakto-boureko*, having decided watermelon may be a bit too simple. But on the other hand, I don't want Kyros to think I'm trying too hard, before wondering why I am overthinking this. It's just a casual dinner with new friends after all, and they both know Henry very well, so why am I fussing? All the same, I can't seem to quell the nerves that have suddenly appeared and the butterflies in my stomach.

By the time I arrive home, I'm feeling so anxious I drop an aubergine from my shopping bag and it rolls along the floor.

'Are you alright?' asks Henry, retrieving the aubergine and placing it on the kitchen counter. 'You're not nervous about this dinner, are you? Or maybe you are trying to impress someone?' He smiles at me with a mischievous glint in his eye.

'Whatever gave you that impression?' I smile back at him as I place the fish in the fridge and the rest of the food on the side. 'Although I have to confess, maybe I am a little nervous. Kyros is a restauranteur after all.'

'And one of the nicest guys you will meet.'

'Is he really?' I ask Henry, wondering how well he really knows him. 'He seems perfectly charming, of course, but I can't possibly know him well, after such a short time.'

'I'm sure of it. He's a really genuine guy. The family were very close and it was tragic when his mother died but Kyros and Linus looked after their father. He has friends that he spends time with, everyone in town knows him and his family, but he is usually at the restaurant, or sitting down by the Bourtzi.'

I dress casually in smart shorts and a vest top with a few sparkles around the neckline, and my hair piled on top of my head. I've stuffed the sea bass with fennel and garlic; later I'll cook it on the BBQ along with some charred aubergine, along with breads, dips and my special potato salad I like to make back home.

As I lay the table carefully outside, setting it with candles ready to light when my guests arrive, I find I have mixed feelings about returning home. Obviously, I am looking forward to seeing my family and friends, but I know I will miss this place so much. It would be so tempting to up sticks and stay with Henry and maybe look for a shop to rent and sell my soaps in the sunshine here. But then again, Henry may not even want someone living with him here permanently, cramping his single lifestyle. Perhaps I could stay with him until I built up my business and looked for a place of my own. I smile to myself and shake my head, realising most people probably feel exactly the same way when they have had a wonderful holiday somewhere and tell myself to stop daydreaming.

Half an hour later, a taxi has pulled up outside the villa and out step Kyros and Alex.

Kyros looks handsome in a black shirt and jeans, his hair slightly damp and tousled as though he has just stepped out of the shower.

'*Kalispera*, welcome,' I say greeting them both and Alex hands me a bottle of Greek brandy.

'That will go down very nicely,' says Henry, shaking both men warmly by the hands.

'Good to see you, Henry. I'm looking forward to hearing all about your sailing trip,' says Kyros.

'Don't encourage him,' I tease, and Henry shoots me a playful scowl.

Henry dispenses beers to our guests and Alex thanks me for inviting him for dinner.

'You would like some help?' Alex asks in his heavy Greek accent, his English not as fluent as Kyros's. He approaches the BBQ where the fragrant scent of fennel fills the air. He is standing next to me, smiling, a beer in his hand.

'Actually, would you mind turning the fish, whilst I just check on the potatoes?' I ask and he nods cheerfully. I leave the cooked potatoes to cool before I head back outside. Alex is gently turning the fish over and I think that he must miss cooking at the restaurant and how important it is to make older people feel useful.

Soon enough, dinner is served around the huge table and as the drinks flow, everyone is in a relaxed mood. The fish, thankfully, is delicious and melts in the mouth and my home-made potato salad goes down a treat. Alex speaks to Kyros in Greek, and Kyros tells me that he is asking what is the flavour in the potatoes.

'Ah, that is my secret ingredient,' I tell him. 'It's actually a dash of Worcestershire sauce.'

'So it's not really a secret.' Kyros smiles as he tells his father.

Alex nods as he tucks into the food appreciatively.

Henry is a great host and has us all entertained with his stories.

'I bet you have some stories to tell too, Alex,' he says, inviting him into the conversation. . 'Especially running the restaurant in the eighties.'

Alex's eyes suddenly light up as he talks of the booming years of the restaurant.

'Yes, yes, it was my whole life.' He nods and his eyes mist over a little. 'There are so many memories, so many.'

Kyros tells his father about my idea to display some photographs in the restaurant.

'Please, are you free some time before you leave?' he enquires. 'I have many photographs. Maybe you could help to choose some for the walls.'

'I would be glad to,' I tell him. Alex seems to have perked up at the thought of displaying the photos and doing something to help the restaurant again.

A short while later, we've finished eating and, if I say so myself, the food has gone down a treat. Henry has opened the brandy and he and Alex enjoy a game of cards and a cigar, while Kyros and I sit beside each other on the sofa.

'Thank you,' Kyros says to me. 'You have made an old man very happy, maybe given him a little project. As long as he doesn't try to revamp the restaurant.' He pulls a face.

'It's my pleasure. He comes alive when he talks of the busy years in the restaurant, doesn't he?'

'He does. And, of course, we do try to involve him, but he is supposed to be taking things easy.'

I know Linus and Kyros are trying to include their father in the running of the restaurant, although Alex does seem perfectly happy just chatting to people, but who knows how he really feels? How would any of us feel when we are no longer able to do the things that drive us? The things we love.

When the evening finally draws to an end, I agree to meet Alex tomorrow morning at the restaurant for coffee, so I can have a look at his old photographs. Alex steps in to the kitchen for a moment with Henry to take their glasses to the sink and Kyros takes the opportunity to kiss me.

'I am going to miss you,' he tells me, with real feeling in his voice.

'I haven't gone yet. I'll see you in the morning,' I tell him as Alex appears outside ready to leave.

'Thank you for this evening.' Alex shakes my hand courteously. 'I have enjoyed myself.'

'That was a great evening, Becky, I'd forgotten how good Alex's company can be,' Henry tells me when they leave.

I had been surprised to learn that when he first arrived here, Henry and Bea became friends with Alex and his wife Rhea, and despite Bea's initial reluctance to mingle, Henry tells me she liked Rhea's company.

'Strangely enough, the two women died around the same time,' Henry reveals. 'Tonight has reminded me what good friends Alex and I once were. I really ought to make an effort to spend some time with him.'

'I'm sure he'd enjoy that,' I tell him.

It's just before midnight when I head to bed, the night still and warm. I imagine living here must feel a little bit like living in paradise. I'd better make the most of the time I have left here.

Chapter Twenty-Seven

I arrive at the restaurant just after ten o'clock the next morning, having left Henry hosing down the tiled area around the pool.

Alex is sitting outside when I arrive, enjoying a cappuccino in a quiet area of the restaurant.

'*Kalimera!*' He stands to greet me. Kyros is chatting to a couple of women who are eating breakfast and I watch him throw his head back and laugh at something they say and, to my surprise, I feel a little pang of jealousy.

Kyros excuses himself from the ladies when he notices me, and heads over.

'*Kalimera*, how are you this morning?'

I study his face and know that I'm going to miss that smile when I head home.

My eyes roam over the photographs in front of me; the old port in black and white looks beguiling with a grey sky above. There's a gorgeous family photo of Alex and his wife, with Linus and Kyros as children, leaning against a beach wall and several more pictures show the town in years gone by. The photographs are all in black and white and an hour later we've agreed on the ones that should be displayed on the walls of the restaurant.

'Wonderful. It has brought back memories, so many memories,' says Alex, his eyes full of nostalgia as he strokes a picture of his wife and sons when they were young. 'Tomorrow, I shop for photo frames.'

Kyros glances at his watch.

'Do you want to go for a walk in between the breakfast and dinner service?' he asks.

'Yes, I'd like that,' I tell him.

We head towards the new port, passing the Bourtzi as a man is unloading a van with urns and huge displays of flowers. So it seems a wedding will be taking place at the Bourtzi. It's a beautiful venue for a wedding with such spectacular vistas all around.

'I wonder what time the wedding will be taking place?' I ask Kyros, thinking I might stick around and watch it.

Kyros speaks to one of the men unloading the van before he turns to me.

'One o'clock. Although maybe you should come a little earlier if you want a good place to view,' he advises. 'The local people love to watch a wedding.'

'Thanks, I'll bear that in mind.'

I glance at my watch that shows it is just before eleven o'clock.

Sitting on a bench near the port, we watch a ferry arrive and it reminds me of the day I was here with my friends, chatting about the boat scene in the movie. I know I will remember this holiday for a long time and hope my friends feel the same. I tell Kyros all about our *Mamma Mia!* day out.

'Did you enjoy the trip?' he asks.

'It was a lot of fun, yes, we had a great time. It was slightly disappointing that we didn't sail through the caves, as we thought we might do. The colours of the water near the entrance looked amazing.'

'You want to sail through some caves?' He looks at me and smiles.

'Yes, I've done it before, I find it really soothing and beautiful.'

'Then tomorrow I will hire a small boat and take you on a journey through a cave.'

'Really? Are you sure you won't be missed in the restaurant?' I ask as we sit on the bench and gaze out across the water.

'It will be fine. We have one or two extra staff for the summer season,' he tells me. 'Although I imagine I'll have to put in some extra hours when you go home.'

'How is your new chef shaping up?' I ask.

'He is very good. In fact, I think it might be time for him to take on an assistant.'

'So you can skive off even more?' I tease.

'Skive?' He looks puzzled.

'Disappear, avoid work.'

'Me? Never.' A smile plays around his mouth.

'Actually, if you're really thinking about hiring a sous-chef, I might be able to suggest someone,' I tell him.

'You know someone, here in Greece?' He looks puzzled once again.

I tell Kyros all about the young man who won the cookery competition at the beach.

'Honestly, his moussaka was to die for,' I tell him. I can almost taste the delicious flavours in my mouth when I think about it.

'Hmm. Did you say you know where this boy lives?' Kyros asks, with interest.

'Yes I do, why?'

'Then let us go and pay him a visit,' Kyros says decisively, getting to his feet.

'What, you mean right now?'

'Why not? There is no time like the present and I don't want to let a promising young talent slip through my fingers.'

After collecting his car, we set off along the coast road, glimpsing the beaches shrouded by trees, and presently we pull up outside the house with the blue front door and a small front garden with a wooden fence.

'Hello,' I say, when Nicos opens the door. I remind him of our meeting at the beach and he nods, his face breaking into a smile as recognition dawns. I introduce him to Kyros, who begins a conversation with him in Greek. After a few seconds he calls his mother to the front door and a small woman with her dark hair tied up in a bun appears, wiping her hands on a black pinny she is wearing. The boy talks to his mother in Greek and she clasps her hands together joyfully, before beckoning us inside.

We follow her to a small, but immaculate, kitchen and she offers us some home-made lemon cake, which we politely decline, as it is not long since breakfast, but do accept a drink of lemonade from the fridge. I spotted the lemon tree in the front garden and think it's wonderful how you can pick your own fruit and turn it into something delicious.

'So you learn how to cook from your mother?' Kyros asks, speaking in English, probably not wishing to exclude me from their conversation any further.

'Yes, my mother and grandmother,' he says. At the mention of the word 'grandmother', his mother crosses herself and raises her eyes upwards.

'I am so happy for this opportunity,' he tells Kyros. 'I hear of jobs as a waiter, but it is hard to find jobs in restaurant kitchen. It is usually family.' He speaks slowly, his English not as fluent as Kyros's.

'That is true.' Kyros nods. 'But I would like to give you a chance. I am being selfish, of course. If your moussaka is as good as Becky says it is, then I expect the restaurant to be fully booked every day.'

When we depart, Kyros shakes him by the hand firmly and his mother kisses us on both cheeks.

'I will expect you tomorrow morning at eight o'clock sharp,' Kyros tells him as he closes the gate behind us.

Back at the harbour front, Kyros heads into the restaurant, while I decide to have a wander around the shops before I head back to watch the wedding at the Bourtzi.

After an hour window shopping and strolling the backstreets, I stumble upon a small church and head inside. The cool interior is a welcome respite from the sun that is really getting up outside. The church has the familiar white painted walls and dark wooden pews, with a beautiful decorated altar of golds, reds and blues. I sit for a little while quietly, contemplating life and giving thanks in the empty church, alone with my thoughts. Ten minutes later, a lady wearing a black lace veil enters and heads to a pew at the front of the altar. She prays loudly in Greek, so I quietly leave the church and head out into the blazing sunshine.

I make my way back towards the Bourtzi and I'm lucky enough to find a space on a bench as a couple with a young child move along to make room for me. A short while later, a wedding car arrives, adorned with cream ribbons, and everyone makes their way along the path that leads to the restaurant at the top, some carrying small posies of flowers or simply handfuls of flower petals.

A stunning bride steps out of the car, dressed in cream lace, her dark hair pinned up, with soft tendrils curling around her face. A man, who I assume to be her father, walks beside her, smiling proudly as they make their way slowly along the path. As she makes her way upwards, smiling, the people throw the flowers in her path and break into applause as they shout '*Kali tychi*,' which means 'good luck'.

I head back to the villa to spend the afternoon and evening with Henry, and find him snoozing beneath his straw hat on a sunlounger, with a book at his side. I change into my bikini and have a swim, before I settle down on a bed beside him. Half an hour later he stirs.

'Becky, when did you get back? You should have woken me.' He stretches his arms over his head.

'Why would I do that? You looked perfectly comfortable there.'

'I thought you might be spending the rest of the day with Kyros,' he says.

'He has to work occasionally. And besides, I want to spend some time with you, Uncle Henry, before I go home. What would you like to do today?'

'Not a lot, to be honest.' He stretches out again. 'I think I'm still recovering from my overindulgence on the sailing trip. But, of course, I'd be happy to accompany you, if you wish to go somewhere,' he adds.

'No, of course not. I'm perfectly happy here for the rest of the day.'

'Actually,' says Henry. 'There is something I would love to do. Do you still play chess?'

Three hours later, Henry has checkmate and has completely reawakened my desire to play chess. I was in a chess club at high school and thoroughly enjoyed it, but never had much opportunity to practise outside school, as no one in the family played. Apart from Uncle Henry, that is.

'I really enjoyed that,' says Henry as we sip a late afternoon gin and tonic on the terrace.

'You should teach Alex to play, unless he already does, of course.'

'You know, that's not a bad idea,' he says, his eyes lighting up. 'In fact, talking of Alex, he's asked me to go fishing with him tomorrow.'

'Really? That's nice. I'm glad you two have decided to spend some more time together.'

'I've told him I'll think about it. It's your last day tomorrow, after all.'

'Which is why it's been lovely spending time with you today and, of course, this evening. Actually, Kyros has offered to hire a boat and take me to some caves tomorrow,' I tell him.

'Then you should go!' he says adamantly.

We both agree to do our own thing tomorrow before having dinner at the Two Brothers' restaurant for my final evening here.

Later, we have a BBQ and a game of cards, enjoying each other's company, and I head to bed feeling contented. My thoughts turn to Kyros, and how tomorrow will be the last time I see him in a long time. I can't imagine I'll be retuning here any time soon as I will have to concentrate on my business and my life when I arrive home. So tomorrow, I'm going to make the most of every single minute.

Chapter Twenty-Eight

Henry headed off for his fishing trip with Alex straight after breakfast and I sit on the terrace to wait for Kyros, who is collecting me around eleven after the breakfast service at the restaurant. I feel excited about our day out today exploring the caves and, not for the first time, wish I was staying here for a little longer.

I'm reading my book and enjoying the morning sun, when I get a call from Paige.

'How's it going?' she asks. 'Are you ready to come home yet? Although I think I know the answer.'

'I've mixed feelings, to be truthful, but all good things must come to an end.'

'Anyway, I just ringing to tell you about a surprise I received this morning,' she says excitedly.

'A surprise? Ooh go on.'

'Remember the old couple who had the Lalique vase? Well, they managed to get it into an auction at the very last minute as there was a lot of interest in it. Apparently, it was a one-off and it only went and sold for ten thousand pounds, didn't it? They called into the office this morning and handed me an envelope with a thousand pounds inside! I declined it, of course, but the man, Mr Brookes, insisted. He said they would never have known its value in a million years. He was adamant I took the money.'

'Oh wow, how generous. I have to say I agree with him actually, you deserve a reward for making them aware of the vase's value, or it might have ended up in the wrong hands.'

'Maybe you're right. I would never have accepted it had they not been so insistent, and I suppose they have come into quite a windfall,' she concedes.

'What will you do with the money?' I ask.

'I think I'll book a winter holiday to somewhere sunny. Forget the Lake District, pretty as it is in the autumn.'

I tell her about Henry and Alex rekindling their friendship, and how I'm heading off for the day with Kyros shortly.

'Well, have a great time. Give him my regards. Right, gotta go, I'm showing a student a flat share in five minutes and I'm waiting in the car outside the property.'

I'm smiling to myself and thinking no one deserves a reward more than Paige, when I hear the sound of a car approaching the villa. Kyros steps out and I can feel my pulse quicken when I see him. Which makes me realise he's really got under my skin. I'd vowed not to let that happen, but it seems nature has other ideas.

'Good morning, are you ready?' he asks, before adding, 'Oh and make sure you have your swimming things.'

I head upstairs to change into a bikini. I look in the mirror at my raised scar across my stomach, before taking a deep breath and slipping into it. This is who I am and I can't change things. I slip a sundress on top and grab a beach bag with a few things in, before heading back downstairs.

Driving along the beach road, I feel a sense of contentment as we chat easily about things, including Nicos, who turned up promptly for work this morning at the restaurant.

'He was very fast and efficient at breakfast,' Kyros tells me. 'And Linus was impressed too. He made eggs Florentine, which his mother taught him how to make, and it was delicious. It's going on the menu.'

'I'm pleased he's made such a good start,' I say, thrilled that I stumbled upon the young man at the beach that day.

Twenty minutes later, we have taken charge of a speedboat, which is slightly larger and newer than the one I took out with the girls, with a comfortable seating area. Kyros takes a cooler bag from the back seat of his car and carries it onto the boat.

'I've brought us a picnic for later.' He smiles.

Soon enough, we're skimming the glorious blue sea and I enjoy the rush of wind on my tanned skin as my hair billows in the wind. We take turns at the wheel, Kyros snapping away with his camera phone as I steer the boat. We take selfies, the pair of us smiling into the camera, looking as though we don't have a care in the world.

Presently, we pull up at the mouth of a cave. The water below us is shades of blue and indigo, giving it a magical feel. There's a narrow entrance that's not wide enough for a boat to pass, and Kyros drops the anchor.

'So now, we swim.' Kyros removes his T-shirt, revealing his muscular tanned body and I barely know where to look.

For a second, I feel nervous as I peel off my dress, to reveal my black bikini underneath. Kyros takes my hand and we jump into the water together. I gasp at the sight of the tall, shimmering caves, in shades of grey and silver, reaching up towards the sky. It's so beautiful I feel like I'm swimming in a lake beside a castle. We swim apart at first, then closer together, and when Kyros pulls me to him and kisses me, it feels like the most natural thing in the world.

'How did you find this place?' I say breathlessly, after he's kissed me again. I notice there isn't another soul around.

'Days out exploring with Linus as kids. The entrance is so narrow, many people drive straight past without discovering it.'

'So it's like a secret cave,' I say as he nuzzles my ear and sends my head into a spin.

'Maybe it is. We used to come and swim here when we were younger.'

We swim some more, in between laughing, and splashing each other with water, and I want to stay in this moment forever.

Climbing back into the boat, I feel we've shared something I will find hard to forget and I wonder if Kyros feels the same. A while later, we've moored up at a tiny cove and Kyros unpacks a picnic of meats, breads and cheeses along with bottles of mineral water. Later, as we lie on a blanket on the soft sand, he pulls me to him. He runs his hand over my scar, before looking me in the eyes and kissing me.

'You are beautiful,' he whispers, and as I respond to his kisses, I find that I actually believe it to be true.

We arrive back at the harbour late in the afternoon, and Kyros drops me at the villa, before heading to the restaurant. I tell him I will see him later with Uncle Henry, and my heart feels heavy at the thought of this being my last evening here in Skiathos. I never imagined I would come here and find love when Henry offered me the chance of coming here with my friends to look after his villa. It shocks me to realise that I have fallen for Kyros so quickly and I feel so confused and conflicted.

I'm in the kitchen putting some dishes away in the cupboards when I hear the sound of men's laughter.

It's Henry and Alex, who have returned from their fishing trip.

'Hi, guys, would you like some coffee? I'm just about to make a pot,' I ask.

'Yes, thanks, Becky, that would be lovely. Then we can tell you all about our trip.'

Settled on the sofas outside, drinking coffee, Henry tells me about the one that got away.

'It was the length of this room,' he says, stretching his arms out and Alex laughs loudly.

'Your uncle, he have a good imagination.' Alex shakes his head. 'It was a swordfish. No bigger than this.' He extends his arms to their full width.

'That was almost the size of his head,' insists Henry. 'You never saw it properly.'

Alex is laughing good-naturedly.

It's so good to hear them laughing and joking together and rekindling their friendship. Perhaps they just needed time to mourn their respective wives before getting on with their lives. Regardless of whether a marriage is completely happy or not, I guess it takes time to adjust to your new situation.

Alex drains his coffee before heading off.

'I will see you this evening at the restaurant. Maybe I do a little dancing.' He winks.

'Only if you want to raise your son's blood pressure,' I tease.

'Pah. He worry too much. I am as strong as an ox.' He flexes an arm muscle and I laugh.

He walks off with a spring in his step, and I can't help wondering whether Kyros is a tiny bit overprotective.

I spend the afternoon taking a swim and doing a little packing, as well as trying to decide what to wear this evening. I hold up two dresses, one casual, the other one a little more formal and ask Henry for his opinion.

'Depends what impression you want to make,' he says thoughtfully. He points to the red and white cotton knee-length dress, cinched in at the waist. 'I like that one. It goes well with your colouring.'

It's funny, because I prefer the one I'm holding in my right hand, which is a navy sleeveless shift, with a slightly low-cut neckline.

'So what impression does the red and white dress make?' I ask.

'I'm not sure. Fun, fresh, young?'

That's decided it for me. I opt for the navy dress, which I'll wear with a statement necklace.

I'm not sure I want Kyros to remember me looking like the girl next door, wearing a wholesome cotton dress. That's not the impression I want to leave him with.

I hang the red dress back in the wardrobe and sigh. What am I even thinking? What does it matter what I wear for dinner this evening? Tomorrow, I'll be on a three p.m. flight back to my life in England and memories of us spending time together will fade, as I'm sure will be the case for him.

The summer season is in full swing so he'll probably barely register my absence. Besides, I'm sure there will be plenty of other female tourists who will catch his eye, I tell myself miserably.

In the end, I throw both dresses into my suitcase, and opt for a floral wraparound skirt and a plain black vest. I'll add a necklace to dress it up a little, but for some reason, I don't want Kyros to think I've gone to an extra special effort this evening.

'Are you ready?' Henry appears in the kitchen wearing a pair of navy chinos and a slightly garish short-sleeved shirt in shades of red, white and blue.

'Are you feeling a bit patriotic?' I ask.

Henry frowns for a second, before bursting into laughter. 'Ah, you mean the colours of the British flag? I never thought about that actually, I was just rather taken by the pattern.'

'Well, you look very handsome,' I tell him and he returns the compliment and tells me I look nice too, before adding truthfully that he preferred the red dress. For a second, I wonder whether I ought to go and change, before deciding I look perfectly fine as I am.

Henry is driving us down to the port this evening, saying he will park up and order us a taxi home later. As we head down towards the harbour, my stomach flips over and I don't think it's due to the bends in the road. I can't believe how quickly I've developed feelings for Kyros, although maybe it's easy to be seduced in such glorious surroundings. I wonder if Kyros will still be single the next time I come and visit Uncle Henry? Even if he feels as I do, we live thousands of miles away from each other. It feels so hopeless, so I mustn't let Kyros know how I really feel as it wouldn't be fair.

Kyros is waiting outside to greet us when we arrive and a waiter shows us to a table. To my surprise, a few minutes later, Linus joins us accompanied by a pretty woman who he introduces as his wife, Alana.

'Tonight, we leave our chef and sous-chef in the kitchen so we can join you in a farewell meal,' explains Linus.

We're sitting close to a wall displaying the photographs that Alex and I looked through yesterday.

'You've done a great job there, they look fantastic,' I tell Alex as I admire the black and white photos, mixed with one or two more recent coloured ones.

'Thank you. I'm happy you thought of the idea.'

'Gosh, the chefs must be feeling nervous having to serve their bosses dinner,' I remark and Alex laughs.

'Maybe I will tell them I find a slug in my salad,' he says, with a mischievous glint in his eye.

'Don't you dare,' says Kyros.

'Relax, I joke.' Alex winks at me and I can't help smiling.

We enjoy a wonderful meal and I think the jobs of the chefs are safe, as delicious steaks in pepper sauce, fish dishes dressed with lemon and parsley, and beef stifado all roll out of the kitchen. Even Alex is impressed as he washes his steak down with a Mythos beer, nodding and making appreciative noises as he chews his steak.

'It has been so lovely meeting you,' says Alana as she and Linus stand to leave, just after ten thirty.

'Sorry to be the first to leave the party, but we have a young babysitter and I said we would only be a couple of hours,' explains Linus. They kiss us on both cheeks and depart, leaving the four of us chatting over ouzos served at the end of the meal.

'I'm going to miss this place.' I sigh.

'Maybe you can return again soon.' Kyros looks at me hopefully.

'There's nothing I'd like more, but I have my business back home. I don't want to abuse Mum's kindness.' I smile, but my heart sinks at the thought of this being my last evening with Kyros and not knowing when I will see him again.

We take our drinks to an outside table, and an hour later things quieten down in the restaurant as the staff clear up for the end of the night. Kyros disappears for a short while to cash up at the till and I sit and chat with Henry and Alex.

'My son, I think he likes you very much,' says Alex, with a warm smile on his face.

'I like him too.'

I more than like him. I'm pretty sure I've fallen in love with him, but maybe that's not possible in such a short space of time?

'The first time I see my wife shopping in a market I know that one day I marry her.' He lights up a cigarette, before glancing around to make sure Kyros isn't watching. 'My son does not like me to smoke,' he explains. 'Anyway, what I tell you is: love is something you cannot fight.' He looks at me knowingly.

For some reason, talk turns to chess and Henry tells Alex that I'm quite a player. Alex's eyes light up at this news.

'I have a chessboard. And some good brandy. Would you like to come to my house and have a game?'

'I didn't realise you played chess, Alex.' Henry rubs his hands together. 'I'm definitely up for that.'

I look at the two pensioners in front of me, raring to go, and wonder where they get their energy from.

'Thanks, Alex, but I'm a little tired so I don't think I'd be able to fully concentrate.'

Kyros reappears at that moment.

'Able to concentrate on what?' he asks.

Henry explains about the invitation to play chess and Kyros grins and warns Henry that Alex is very competitive.

'You two go and have a game. I'll make sure Becky gets home,' says Kyros, locking eyes with me and I wonder where on earth this is leading.

We head off for a walk towards the new harbour, where yachts threaded with lights are moored up and the sound of laughter rings out as groups sit chatting and socialising on deck.

Heading away from the bustle of the harbour, we walk along the stone pier where the ships come in and sit down on a bench. It's dark here in the shadows of the yachts, the only light coming from the bright moon and stars above and a few solar lights at the far end of the pier. It's surprisingly cooler here too, and I shiver a little, slightly regretting wearing a sleeveless top.

Kyros instinctively places his arm around my shoulders and draws me close to him.

'You are cold?' He gently rubs his hand up and down my arm, before turning my face towards him and kissing me. It's as if fireworks are going off somewhere in the harbour close by, as I am filled with longing and desire. When he suggests we head to his apartment above the restaurant, I know there is no way I can resist this time and we stand up to leave, walking hand in hand, with a growing feeling of anticipation.

The huge apartment is stylishly decorated, and Kyros was right about that spectacular view of the harbour from the large window in the lounge. I don't have time to take too much of it in, though, as Kyros takes me by the hand and guides me slowly to the bedroom. I'm leaving tomorrow, and a part of me wonders why on earth I am going through with this, yet I feel utterly powerless to resist.

Later, I lay wrapped in the arms of Kyros, feeling happier than I have in a long time, yet completely confused. I don't want to leave him and head home tomorrow, yet I know I must. Perhaps this is nothing more than a holiday romance, although I guess I'll find out the answer to that when I'm home and getting on with my life.

'I will miss you when you leave,' says Kyros, pulling me closer to him and planting a kiss on my forehead.

'Will you?' I snuggle into him, enjoying the feeling of our skins touching, his smell, everything.

'But, of course. I felt attracted to you the day we first met, but I never expected to feel this way.'

He looks at me seriously.

'What way? How do you feel, Kyros?' I press, my heart soaring yet sinking at the thought of being away from him.

'I think I have fallen for you. In fact, I do not think, I know. I love you, Becky.'

I'm so surprised that, for a moment, I am barely able to speak.

'Are you alright? Did I say something wrong?' A look of panic crosses his face.

'No, of course not. I feel the same way too. I just wasn't sure if you—'

He silences me with a kiss and suddenly there's no more talking.

I'm sleepily wondering if Henry will be expecting me home when I receive a text message from him saying he is staying the evening with Alex as they are only halfway through a game and enjoying the brandy. He tells me he will be back before noon to take me to the airport, which makes me face the reality. Tomorrow I'm leaving.

Chapter Twenty-Nine

I wake the next morning to the smell of freshly brewed coffee.

'Good morning, beautiful.' Kyros kisses me as he places a drink on the bedside table.

I glance at my watch, which shows the time is just after eight o'clock.

'Morning. I suppose I'd better get going. Henry will be back at the villa soon.' I take a long sip of my coffee.

We say very little as we drive to the villa, my stomach in knots. Kyros offers to drive me to the airport but I decline, as I don't want to be a blubbering mess in the departure lounge, so we say our goodbyes here.

'I will miss you, Becky.' Kyros kisses me one last time.

'I'll miss you too,' I almost whisper, my voice choked with emotion.

I can't believe that despite my reservations, I've fallen for Kyros. It seems Paige was right about not all blokes being like Scott.

'Have a safe flight; call me when you get home.'

'I promise I will.' We have a lingering hug, neither of us wanting to prise ourselves away, before he climbs into his car and it disappears out of sight.

Having showered and changed, I'm outside, leaning on the balcony fence taking in the view and wrestling with my emotions, when Henry arrives home, carrying a paper bag with a bakery logo.

'Morning, Becky, I hope you haven't had breakfast. These are the finest pastries on the island.'

He sets the contents of the paper bag onto a plate and I sink my teeth into a Danish pastry, but it seems to stick in my throat.

I go to pack the final things into my bag and retrieve the pretty ship in a bottle – the gift from me and the girls for Henry – from my wardrobe and hand it to him.

'What did you go and spend your money on me for?' asks Henry, although he's beaming as he turns the bottle that sits on a polished wooden stand over in his hand.

'We clubbed together. And you deserve it.'

'Well, I love it. Thank you so much and be sure to express my gratitude to Abby and Paige.'

'Of course I will.'

A while later, we're heading towards the airport and I'm quietly lost in my thoughts, when Henry asks me if I am alright.

'Yes, I'm fine, thanks, Uncle Henry.' I paint on my brightest smile. 'I'm just thinking about how I'm going to miss this place. And you, of course.'

'I was away for most of your time here, but it's been lovely catching up since I've been back. Next time you visit, I'll make sure I'm here for the duration.' He smiles.

I realise with a heavy heart that I'm not sure when I'll be able to come here again. For the very first time, I almost regret ever coming here in the first place and wonder whether it might have been better if Henry had advertised on an Airbnb site after all. I silently admonish myself for thinking that way, as I did have a wonderful time with my friends, and it was my decision to let someone into my heart after all.

Soon enough, Henry has dropped me at the airport terminal and hugged me tightly before he says goodbye.

'Thanks for everything, Uncle Henry,' I tell him. 'I hope you keep your friendship up with Alex.'

'For sure, we need a return chess match for a start. He beat me last night, so I'm sure I'll never hear the end of it otherwise.' He smiles.

I'm grateful there's no one sitting next to me on the plane, as the tears I've been suppressing fall freely down my face. I gulp down a gin and tonic when the drinks trolley appears, before immersing myself in a book, although I find it hard to concentrate. Thankfully, the flight goes pretty quickly and soon enough, I'm stepping out onto the tarmac at Manchester Airport, welcomed by a grey, cloudy sky. Inside the airport I retrieve my case as it chugs towards me, and smile to myself as I recall Paige's story about falling onto the baggage carousel.

Mum and Dad are outside waiting to give me a lift home and they kiss me on the cheek, before Dad heaves my case into the boot of the car.

'My goodness, you look well – that's a lovely tan you have there,' remarks Mum as I climb into the car. 'You'd never have got that here. We've had two lovely sunny days since you've been away, so we headed into Southport last Sunday and had a lovely day out,' she tells me.

I'm glad one of those sunny days was a Sunday, as the shop is closed then and I often catch up on making new stock.

'Hopefully I've brought a little bit of sunshine back with me.'

It's just after eight in the evening when I arrive home. Mum has thoughtfully placed some milk and a few breakfast items in the fridge for tomorrow morning. I make them a brew and hand over the gifts I bought for them in Skiathos and they thank me warmly.

'I know it isn't much, especially after all you've done looking after the shop,' I say.

'Don't you worry about that. I've loved every single minute of being in the shop. In fact, I don't know what I'm going to do with myself now that you're back.'

'Maybe you could still help out from time to time, if you want to? We can talk about it tomorrow.'

'Oh right, shall I pop into the shop in the morning then?' she asks enthusiastically.

'Of course, Mum, but don't you want a day off?' I ask.

'No, I'll be fine. It's Tuesday tomorrow; it might get busy with it being market day,' she says.

I get the impression being in the shop has given her a new lease of life.

When Mum and Dad leave, I text Kyros to tell him I've arrived home safely, and he asks if he can call me tonight when service at the restaurant has quietened down a little.

Later, I've put some clothes into the washing machine and I'm settled on the sofa with a cuppa watching a quiz show on the TV, when my phone rings.

'Becky, hi, how are you?' Just the sound of his voice makes me melt.

'Kyros, hi. I'm fine thanks, missing you already.' I wonder if saying that sounded a little needy, but then it is something people say.

'Me too. I am so sorry I am so late phoning; the restaurant was crazy busy tonight.'

'It's only just after ten o'clock here but it must be past midnight in Greece.'

'Of course, I forgot about the time difference. I am glad I am not disturbing your sleep.'

It's wonderful to hear his voice and strange to think that less than twelve hours ago I was wrapped in his arms, lying in his bed.

We chat for a while and he tells me he will give me a video call tomorrow evening.

'Won't you be busy at the restaurant?' I ask and he tells me there are enough staff to allow him a break to head upstairs and call me. I can't wait to look at his face tomorrow, but with a sudden stab to my heart I wonder how long this communication will last. A few days? Weeks, maybe? Soon enough I imagine we will all get back to our lives and the urgency to stay in contact with each other may fade with every day that passes. Somehow, though, I don't think I'll ever forget him.

I head to bed a short while later, but despite feeling tired, sleep doesn't come easily. I toss and turn before I must have eventually dozed off, as the next thing I hear is the sound of the alarm the next morning, reminding me it's time to get ready for work.

*

Mum has arranged to meet me outside the shop in the morning, and when I arrive, she's already there waiting, clutching two takeaway coffees. The market is a flurry of activity as the market traders put finishing touches to their stalls.

'Morning, love, I've only just arrived, so don't worry as your coffee will still be hot.' She smiles.

I open up and the familiar floral smell wraps me in a hug as I step inside. I take in the trailing flowers on the shelves, which look prettier in real life, the photos Mum sent me hardly doing them justice. Mum has slightly rearranged the display of candles and goods from other suppliers and displayed the scarves on a stand that she tells me Dad knocked up in the garage. I also spy the chalkboard behind the door that Dad also made. It all looks so pretty and inviting.

'It looks lovely in here, Mum. It's surprising how much these little touches make all the difference,' I tell her gratefully.

I barely used to have time to do anything other than keep the shelves stocked with my produce, so I'm truly grateful for the help Mum and Dad have provided.

We enjoy our coffee and I set the till up for the day with a float, and Mum sits beside me on a stool, sipping her coffee.

'So how would you feel about running the shop for a day or two during the week? I could do with spending more time making my produce, maybe even expand the range a little.' I recall the day Dad was chatting to a bloke about soap to use with old-fashioned razors, for example.

'Really? I'd love to. Of course I would. I can't do Wednesdays, though, that's the day I do my hospital volunteering and I can't let them down.'

'No, I know that, Mum. You can decide what days are best for you, although I'll definitely be here on Tuesday and Saturday as they're market days.'

Mum stays for a couple of hours and one or two returning customers compliment me on some magnolia products that 'smell heavenly'. So I'll add that to my list of products to continue selling.

I ring up quite a few sales before lunchtime and at one o'clock I close the shop for half an hour and head outside into the sunshine. I call at the wool stall and give Sheila a fridge magnet, as she collects them, of Skiathos harbour and she thanks me gratefully.

'So how's business been?' I ask.

'Actually, I was really busy last week, I don't know what happened, but I had to stock up on more wool. New faces too, everyone seems to have taken up knitting. I'm not complaining, though.' She smiles.

'Well, I'm really pleased for you. Let's hope people are starting to realise just how good local markets can be.' I remember Melanie from *Lancashire Life* being impressed with the market the day she came to interview me.

I purchase a sandwich from a local deli and head to the nearby park, where I find an empty seat on a bench and let my mind wander to Greece, thinking of Henry and Alex and wondering what they might be getting up to in the coming days. And, of course, I think of Kyros, who will probably be busy at the restaurant. I'm so looking forward to seeing his face this evening when he calls. I'm pulled out of my thoughts by the sound of my phone ringing and the caller display shows it's Paige.

'You're back then, how's things?' she gushes.

'Hi, Paige I'm okay, thanks, apart from the post-holiday blues.'

'Oh, I know what you mean. I was so excited to see Rob, but it poured down for two days straight when we arrived home and I longed to be back in Greece.' She giggles.

It's Tuesday today so we arrange a night out for a couple of cocktails on Thursday evening in Liverpool, where Abby can join us for an hour or two.

'And they're on me,' says Paige. 'I'll treat us after my little windfall.'

It feels so good to be reminded that I have such good friends and that no matter what happens in my love life, they will always be there for me. I look forward to Thursday evening, returning to the shop with a spring in my step.

When Kyros calls later that evening, I have an urge to book the next flight over to Skiathos, but I know that isn't possible. He chats about life in the restaurant, telling me Henry and Alex dined there for lunch and that he is having a get-together on Thursday evening with some old friends in the village, as one of them is getting married.

'Is it a stag party?' I ask.

'Kind of. Although it will be more of a leisurely meal in a restaurant. There will not be any wild antics.' He smiles.

'It sounds nothing like a British stag do then. At least not the ones I've heard about.'

I tell him I'm also heading out on Thursday evening for cocktails with the girls in town.

'We can raise a distant toast to each other,' I say.

'Have a good time, although don't make yourself look too beautiful; I can't bear the thought of all those men looking at you.' He laughs but for a split second I don't return the smile, as memories of Scott flood into my mind and how he tried to control the way I looked. I shrug the feeling away, and smile into the camera. Kyros is nothing like Scott; it was just a little joke.

'The same applies to you. All those women looking at you. I can't stand it.' I pout.

'At a bachelor party?' He smiles and I want to reach into the camera and kiss his lips.

He asks me about the shop and I tell him about Mum and Dad's help.

'It is nice that you are close to your parents. Family is important.'

'It really is.'

'I will email you in a day or two, or maybe I will do the old-fashioned thing and send you a letter,' Kyros says. 'Something to keep in a drawer. You cannot do that with an email.'

'I don't think it's old-fashioned at all. I would love to receive a letter from you. I will send you my address.'

'I warn you, though, my written English may not be so good,' he tells me, which I think will make it all the more endearing.

When we say good night, I feel cheered, my spirits lifted just by talking and looking at his face.

Chapter Thirty

It's been a busy couple of days at the shop as the sun is shining and people are out and about, some seated at outdoor cafés enjoying the warm sunshine. The front door of the shop is wedged open and people have been lured inside by the enticing smells, so I've had several good sales.

I close up just after five, and head home to get ready for cocktails with the girls this evening. Abby texted me yesterday saying she couldn't wait to see us and that she has some news about her and Joe. For a minute my heart sank, and hoped it wasn't bad news, although I suppose she would have phoned me straight away if it was. The twins are so young; I hope it doesn't have anything to do with Joe's jaunts to the neighbour next door when we were on holiday.

I choose a pair of light blue jeans and a pretty white broderie anglaise top, as the warm weather seems to be continuing into the evening. I arrange to meet Paige at the train station and we arrive at almost the same time and she hugs me tightly in greeting.

'You look fabulous! Look at that tan,' she says.

'So do you,' I tell her honestly. She's wearing a gorgeous dusky pink dress that matches her lipstick and a fashionable floral denim jacket over the top, her lean legs still sporting a light tan.

We find a seat on the train and she tells me that she also received a text from Abby and wonders what it is all about.

'I guess we'll find out soon,' I say as we approach Central Station.

Abby is already waiting outside the restaurant looking stunning in a black jumpsuit and her auburn hair pinned up loosely.

We all embrace each other and sit down, and, of course, the first thing the girls ask me about is Kyros. I fill them in on all the details – well, most of them – and Abby clasps her hands together.

'I'm so happy for you. I knew there was something there after you mentioned him the first day you met,' she says.

'Me, too. There was just something about you after that day, mooning around in a daydream.' Paige winks at Abby.

'I was not!' I protest.

'I'm only teasing.'

'Anyway, come on, ladies, what do you fancy? My treat, remember,' says Paige.

'Oh yes, I forgot about your little reward. Don't go wasting it on us, though, you said you were going to put it towards a holiday,' I remind her.

'And I will. But I can treat my best friends to a drink or two.'

We each lift a cocktail menu from a wooden menu holder in the middle of the table and study it.

'Is it Sex on the Beach you're after?' asks Paige. 'Or maybe you've already had that, Becky.'

Her infectious laugh attracts smiles from a couple sitting at the next table.

'Behave yourself, and no I haven't as it happens.'

We place our orders with a young waiter. I opt for a strawberry daiquiri, whilst Paige and Becky go old school and order a Harvey Wallbanger.

'This is lovely, isn't it? It makes such a change to be able to sit outside in the warm weather,' says Paige as we sip our cocktails when they arrive. 'I've got the day off tomorrow too, so I can soak up some sun in the garden as it's meant to be continuing for a few days.'

Settling in, we remind Abby that she has something to tell us.

'I was just coming to that,' she says excitedly. 'The thing is…' She takes a sip of her drink, leaving us hanging for a second. 'Joe and I are getting married!'

Paige lets out a little squeal, whilst I'm speechless for a moment, as I certainly wasn't expecting that. We hug Abby before clinking our glasses together.

'Abby, that's wonderful! I'm so happy for you. I must confess, I'm relieved,' I tell her honestly. 'Especially after you having niggling doubts about Joe on holiday.'

'I know, I've been such a fool. It seems Joe's trips next door to Priya were to consult her about my wedding dress. She's a dressmaker, and while I was out of the way, she was working on it. Joe actually designed it,' she tells us proudly.

'Really? Wow that's amazing. And how romantic.' Paige sighs.

'It really is,' I add. 'Have you seen it yet?'

'I have. And it's absolutely perfect. He said he had to show it to me, in case I hated it.' She laughs. 'In fact, that was how he proposed. He asked me to close my eyes for a minute, before nipping out of the room. Heather and the twins were there, Heather with a big grin on her face, so she obviously knew what was going on. Then he got down on one knee and presented me with the ring, before saying, "Please say yes to the dress." I burst into tears at that point. The dress is totally stunning. I've got a photo of it.'

The photo shows a cream, stylish dress with a slight fishtail end, the upper body studded with shimmering crystals around a sweetheart neckline.

'Oh my goodness, Joe did well. It's absolutely perfect. You are going to be one beautiful bride,' I tell her, my heart bursting with affection for Abby and her gorgeous family.

We catch a train home afterwards and Rob is waiting at the train station to collect Paige, and insists on dropping me home first, even though my house is around the corner from the station.

'You never know who's hanging around,' he says protectively.

Settled inside, I get ready for bed, thinking of how lucky Paige and Becky are having such lovely men in their lives. Then it dawns on me that maybe I have met someone like that too. It's just that he happens to be thousands of miles away…

Chapter Thirty-One

The next few weeks seem to fly by, and luckily business in the shop is good. Mum works Tuesdays, after she's had a browse around the market looking for bargains, and occasionally on a Thursday. I've been busy making some new products on my days off, including an allergy-free shaving soap that has proved popular. I've also sourced some frankincense and myrrh oils to have a go at some soaps and the scent evokes such strong memories of my time in Greece, it's almost difficult to bear.

It's been a busy Saturday and I'm heading home when I call into the local newsagent for a magazine. My eyes scan the rows of magazines when my eyes fall upon the latest edition of *Lancashire Life*, and for a second my heart thumps in my chest, realising the feature about the shop will be inside. Once again, I wonder if I've done the right thing and hope the article isn't too prominent.

I pay the shop assistant and race home and flick through it, and all my fears are confirmed when I see a full-page spread featured in there, my smiling face out for all to see as I stand outside my shop. I make myself a cup of camomile tea and try to compose my thoughts. The magazine is out there on newsagents' shelves for all to see and I wonder what on earth I was thinking. Admittedly, things have been a little busier this past week, so maybe the advertising has worked, but perhaps that's just a coincidence. I steady my breathing and tell myself to stop worrying. Scott would never purchase *Lancashire Life*; it wouldn't be on his radar, surely? I decide to put the magazine away and forget about it. I have an urge to call Kyros, who I'm still in touch with regularly, but it's Saturday evening and I know he will be busy at the restaurant and besides, he's FaceTiming me on Monday and I don't want to come across as anxious and needy. Instead, I pour myself a glass of wine and find a romantic comedy on Netflix, in an effort to try and forget all about things.

Two days later, I'm in the shop when a man walks hurriedly past the window and a strange feeling creeps over me. I tell myself it's all in my imagination, and to stop being so nervous, even though a fleeting glimpse of the man reminded me of Scott, but then again, it's been more than three years since I've seen him, and he might have changed a lot. Why was the man rushing past? Maybe he was late for an appointment; there could be so many reasons, I tell myself. But all the same, I know that Scott is out there. He's free.

I distract myself with rearranging some of the displays slightly, in between serving customers, and soon enough it's time to lock up for the end of the day. I'm meeting Paige outside the estate agent's today, as she's invited me to have dinner with her and Rob.

'It's coq au vin. It's Rob's speciality and it's absolutely gorgeous,' she tells me as she links arms with me and tells me stories of her day at work and how she felt sorry for a couple who were selling their house after the wife had an affair with their gardener. 'The husband told me that particular nugget of information when the wife was out of the room.'

'A real-life Lady Chatterley, hey?' I say, suddenly feeling sorry for the guy and wondering why some marriages don't last.

'They're selling their house, which is absolutely gorgeous, but do you know something? The wife told me she never did like living there and preferred the very first flat they had when they first got married.'

'Maybe that's where all the happy memories of the marriage are. Perhaps they got married during the lust phase.' I raise an eyebrow. 'And they're still living together until the house sale?' I ask in surprise.

'Yep, the husband has nowhere else to go. You'd be surprised how common that situation is,' she reveals as we arrive at her house. She puts the key in the front door and we're greeted by the smell of something delicious coming from the kitchen.

'Hi, ladies, I hope you're hungry.'

Rob carries the casserole to the dining table and pours us all a glass of wine.

'Mmm, this is absolutely delicious, Rob. Is there anything you can't cook?' I ask in between mouthfuls of tasty garlicky chicken in a thick red wine sauce. Rob often cooks when I'm invited for dinner, although Paige is a pretty decent cook herself.

'Fried rice. I don't know why, but I just can't get it right,' he says.

'Maybe it's the pan you use. Although with so many Chinese takeaways nearby, maybe I'd just cheat and buy it,' I say.

'I do.' He laughs. 'It just niggles me, though. One day I'll get it just perfect,' he says, and I've no doubt that he will.

It's just after eight o'clock when I hug my friends goodbye, thanking them for a lovely dinner and head off home.

Kyros is calling me in an hour and I'm so looking forward to seeing his handsome face as we speak. I can't believe how the time has passed since I've been back home, the nights now getting a little cooler as September is only a few days away. I'm thrilled we've maintained such regular contact, spending hours on the phone where we've learnt so much more about each other. Once a week we FaceTime and it almost feels as though Kyros is here in the room with me. Almost. But it doesn't allow me to touch his face, and inhale his masculine scent that I miss so much, or feel the thrill of his kiss.

I shower and change, and set my laptop waiting for a call from Kyros but the minutes tick by and there's nothing. Half an hour later, I tell myself he must be busy at the restaurant as a feeling of disappointment wraps itself around me. An hour later I glance at my phone to see if there's a text message, but there's nothing. I decide to head to bed and give Kyros a call in the morning, settling down into bed with a sinking feeling in my stomach, hoping this isn't the beginning of the end.

I'm dreaming of Greek beaches and cocktails, when I'm awakened by the sound of my phone ringing on the bedside table beside me. Rubbing my bleary eyes, I sit up and press the phone to my ear. It's Kyros.

'Becky, were you asleep? I am so sorry it's so late.'

At the sound of his voice, I'm suddenly wide awake.

'No, it's fine, is everything alright?' I glance at the clock that shows it's just after eleven o'clock.

'It is now, yes. We had a power cut earlier. I had no laptop and would you believe the battery on my phone had died.'

Would I believe it? Of course I would. The realisation that I fully trust Kyros surprises and delights me.

'A power cut, oh no. Was it during restaurant service?'

'We'd almost finished up for the evening thankfully, which was when I'd planned to call you. Then we were plunged into darkness. It happens here sometimes,' he tells me. 'It's not normally off for more than an hour or two; you get used to it.'

A feeling of relief floods through me as I realise Kyros had no way of contacting me earlier. We talk for a while and this time at the end of the call, he tells me that he misses me.

'I miss you too,' I tell him, before I ring off. *More than you'll ever know.*

It's early October and there's a nip in the air as the leaves on the trees slowly turn from green to shades of red and gold. The market traders' stalls are groaning with Halloween merchandise and dressing-up outfits and the vegetable stall is laden with bright orange pumpkins. It's particularly cool today, and the stallholders rub their hands together in an effort to keep warm.

I've nipped out for spiced pumpkin latte, when I pass Sheila shivering and stamping her feet behind her stall. She's dressed in a thick woollen coat and bobble hat and I can't help wondering how she'll survive once winter really sets in.

'Morning, Sheila, would you like a hot coffee to warm you up?' I offer.

'Oh yes, please, love, that would be lovely. It's a cold one today, isn't it? I might close up early. I'm not sure how I'll survive in the winter,' she says, echoing my thoughts. 'Maybe I'll just trade online if the weather gets really bad,' she muses.

A short while later, when I drop Sheila's coffee to her on the stall, a woman seems to be buying a large quantity of wool, so maybe it was worth Sheila being out in the cold today after all.

Back in the shop, I've nipped into the back for a second, to retrieve a couple of cinnamon and orange gift sets to replenish a shelf, when there's the tinkle of the doorbell at the front of the shop.

'I'll be with you in a second,' I call out.

'Sorry about that,' I say, heading back behind the counter.

'Not a problem,' says a male voice I recognise, and my heart jumps into my mouth because smiling at me from the other side of the counter is my ex-boyfriend Scott.

Chapter Thirty-Two

My mouth goes dry as I try to say something, but I can't seem to put any words together.

'What are you doing here?' I eventually manage to ask him.

'I came to see you, of course. You look good, Becky.' He looks me up and down and it makes my skin crawl.

'How did you find me?' I ask, although I already know the answer to that.

'An article in a magazine. Nice photo of you. It was on a table in a dentist's surgery; I'd gone for a check-up,' he tells me as he glances around the shop.

I should have known he could have come across that magazine anywhere, even if it isn't the type of thing he would normally read, and I curse myself for ever allowing the interview to take place. I try to compose myself, even though my palms are clammy and my heart is racing wildly.

'Nice place you've got here. How's business?' he asks casually, as though nothing bad has ever passed between us.

'Not too bad thanks, ticking over.' I manage to keep the nerves from my voice but I can feel myself shaking inside.

'It really is good to see you, Becky, I've missed you.'

I steel myself, determined not to let his presence intimidate me. 'What exactly do you want, Scott?' I stare at him.

'I've told you, I wanted to see you. I thought maybe we could have a catch-up,' he says.

'No, thank you. What would you like to catch up on exactly? Do you want to go through the details of the night you left me bleeding on the doorstep?'

'I am sorry about that, Becky. I've had years of living with that guilt. I've thought about us a lot.'

'I'd rather you didn't. There is no us.' I try to keep my voice even.

'That's not very nice, is it? You must remember the good times we had. I'd never hurt you again.'

He picks up a soap from a basket nearby and sniffs it, before placing it back and smiling at me. I'm feeling increasingly unnerved by his presence, and wondering what's going to happen next, when there's a tinkle of the doorbell and two people enter the shop. I've never been so happy to see anyone in my whole life. I'm inwardly shaking as I greet the customers, a couple who look in their forties, and thankfully Scott takes it as his cue to leave.

'I'll see you again, Becky.' He winks as he heads for the door.

'I don't think so, Scott.' I muster every bit of strength I have. I'm not the person I was when I was with him and there's no way he's going to drag me down again.

'You don't mean that. We were good together, don't you remember?' His eyes meet mine.

'You're deluded. It's only with hindsight that I realise our relationship was completely unhealthy. I don't want to see you around here again.' I stand close to him, almost spitting the words in his ear, as I don't want my customers overhearing the conversation.

'It's a free country.' He smirks, completely unfazed.

'I mean it. I'll get a restraining order if you turn up again. I don't want you anywhere near me.'

He opens the door, before turning to me with a smile on his face. 'See you around,' he says. 'You can be sure of that.'

When he leaves, I realise I'm shaking and the woman in the shop asks me if I'm okay.

'I'm fine,' I tell her, forcing a smile. I pull myself together and assist her in what she is looking for and she purchases a lavender bath set.

When the couple leave, I turn the shop sign to closed and head into the toilet at the back of the shop, where I promptly throw up. But I did it. I stood up to Scott and it felt good.

After I've composed myself, I call Mum and ask her if she can look after the shop for an hour. I don't tell her Scott has been here, but mumble something about leaving my mobile phone at home.

I head off after she's arrived, and once home, I check every lock and window in the house, but thankfully everything seems secure. I suddenly shake myself; just because Scott knows where the shop is, it doesn't mean he knows where I live, does it? Then again, if he's been hanging around, he could have followed me home from work in the evening. Perhaps he does know where I live.

Walking back to the shop later, it crosses my mind that Scott might leave me alone after not getting the welcome he had clearly hoped for, which in itself is strange given how things ended between us. I do consider reporting him to the police, but what would they be able to do? He's served his time and hasn't actually broken any laws calling into my shop. He hasn't threatened me in any way, so I imagine there would be little the police could do. I can only hope that he doesn't pay me a return visit at the shop. But if he does, I won't hesitate in finding out more about a restraining order.

I'm looking over my shoulder for the next week, but Scott doesn't appear at the shop again, so I cautiously allow myself to relax a little, hoping he's got the message.

I'm grateful that apart from being busy in the shop, I've also been helping Abby with preparations for her wedding, which is next spring at St George's Hall in Liverpool. I'm thrilled that she's asked me and Paige to be bridesmaids, along with her daughter Heather; the twins will be little pageboys. A party will follow at a local football club in Crosby and I can hardly wait. It's been so much fun helping her decide on flower choices and the colour of the bridesmaids' dresses, eventually settling on dusky pink satin which will contrast beautifully with the cream and rose-coloured bouquets.

It's a fairly quiet Saturday afternoon in the shop, and I'm just sorting through some stock, when the doorbell rings and the familiar tones of Paige's voice ring out.

'Becky, are you about? I've found some strange bloke lurking outside the shop asking for you.'

My hands tightly grip the box I'm carrying and my heart sinks as a feeling of dread and déjà vu hits me.

I head out to the front of the shop slowly, with a sense of foreboding.

'Surprise!' says Paige, and I drop the box of soaps to the floor in shock.

'Hello, Becky, how are you?' asks Kyros, standing beside her, smiling.

Chapter Thirty-Three

'Kyros, am I dreaming, is it really you?' I ask, when I finally prise myself apart from his hug. 'What are you doing here?'

I'm so shocked I can barely speak, but I can feel my eyes welling up with emotion.

'I'll leave you to it,' says Paige, who discreetly disappears and was clearly in on his surprise visit.

'I can't believe it, how long are you staying?' I ask, bursting with excitement.

'Maybe two weeks, if you can put up with me that long.' He smiles. 'The season is over back home now, so things are very quiet. It seemed like a perfect chance to come and visit.' He circles his arms around my waist and pulls me in for a kiss, when I fleetingly notice a man looking through the window, but when I glance again, he's gone. I tell myself I'm being paranoid as I haven't heard anything from Scott in the last week. Besides, I have Kyros here with me now so I'm sure I'll sleep easier at night.

I close a little early and we go for a drink in a local pub and I proudly introduce him to Sheila and some of the other stallholders as we pass through the market square en route. His good looks and accent attract admiring glances from some women in the pub, and

I feel really proud to be seen with him. Mum and Dad join us a while later and introductions are made, before Mum invites him for Sunday lunch tomorrow.

'You never told me he was so good looking,' says Mum, and I laugh. She's followed me into the pub toilet where she's touching up her lipstick.

'So what would you like to do this evening?' I ask as we stroll home in the moonlight. The nights are drawing in, and Kyros pulls the collar up on his jacket, which seems a little thin for this weather.

'Sit by a fire with a brandy. It's freezing here.' He shivers.

'This is nothing,' I tell him, although when we get home, we do exactly that. We have an Indian takeaway, which Kyros enjoys, and sip brandy snuggled up on the sofa. Before we head upstairs, to bed, if not to sleep.

Chapter Thirty-Four

Henry rings the next morning to say hi and ask if Kyros arrived okay.

'Yes he has. Did you know he was making a surprise visit?' I ask.

'Whatever gave you that idea?' Henry laughs and we chat and catch up, before Kyros takes the phone and speaks to him for a minute.

Henry tells me that he's going on holiday to Italy next May with Alex, 'To sample some good wine and pasta,' and wonders if I fancy staying at the villa again. I expect my next visit to Skiathos may be spent with Kyros in his apartment, but I make a suggestion.

'Actually, Uncle Henry. Abby is getting married next April. If it's not too cheeky, maybe she could look after your villa and have a honeymoon at the same time.'

I know Joe and Abby are saving hard for the wedding and she's told me a honeymoon will have to wait.

'By all means, in fact, that's a wonderful idea. What age are the children?' he asks.

'The twins will be almost three years old by then, and Heather will be sixteen.'

'Right, well I'll have the pool fenced off before they arrive,' he says decisively.

'You don't have to do that, surely? I'm certain Abby and Joe will keep their eye on the little ones.'

'I've been meaning to do it for a while actually. At least I won't have to worry about me falling into the pool after a few too many ouzos.' He guffaws.

'Uncle Henry, I wish you hadn't told me that, I'll be worrying about you now.'

Later, we head into town to buy Kyros a warmer jacket, before heading to Mum and Dad's for Sunday lunch.

The table is groaning with the usual Sunday fare and we tuck into roast beef and Mum is thrilled when Kyros says her home-made Yorkshire pudding is delicious and maybe she could give him the recipe.

We spend a lovely few hours with Mum and Dad, with Kyros telling Mum all about the restaurant in Skiathos and how Uncle Henry and Alex have become close friends again.

When we are about to depart, Dad hands Kyros a pair of spare gloves.

'I noticed you rubbing your hands together when you first walked in. I don't expect you're used to this weather.'

Kyros gratefully accepts the black gloves and puts them on his hands as we head outside into the night air.

'Fancy a drink?' I ask. 'It won't be quite the same as sitting in the sun with the sand between your toes, but I know a place that serves real ale if you want to try a pint of English beer.'

'Lead the way.'

We're snuggled in the corner of a cosy pub that has bookcases and brass fixtures and fittings, sipping a speciality beer, brewed locally. Kyros enjoys it, but admits his preference is a glass of wine.

'I still can't believe you're here,' I tell him, peering across a table that has a lit chunky candle between us.

'Well, it's true. And I am so happy to be here. Even if it is a little chilly, my heart is warm when I am close to you.' He touches his chest.

'That is so cheesy,' I tease.

Strolling home later, I have the feeling someone is watching us, but every time I turn around there's no one there. I give a final look around before I let us into my house, but there is not a soul in sight, so I put it down to my imagination. I don't mention anything to Kyros as I want him to relax and have a good time while he is here. I want to show him the sights, just as he did when I was in Skiathos.

Mum was more than happy to look after the shop for a few days, so I could show Kyros the best the local area has to offer. We've toured museums and art galleries, met up with Abby and Paige and their other halves, and had dinner together at an award-winning restaurant in Liverpool – the men bonding over football, which I hadn't realise Kyros enjoyed. It's such a joy finding out more about him. There have been afternoon walks through leafy parks, with scrunchy leaves underfoot, and I booked an afternoon in an escape room, which Kyros thought was a lot of fun.

Today has been a sunny autumnal day and a lot warmer than the day he first arrived here. We've just got off the train from Liverpool, having had a day out shopping at the Albert Dock.

'You live in a great place,' Kyros says as we stroll along together. 'Living in a small town, yet so close to a big city.'

'I know. It's great to have the best of both worlds.'

I decide I'm going to cook for Kyros this evening, so we head to a local butchers to pick up a couple of steaks.

'Maybe I should give you a job in my restaurant,' says Kyros when we're cuddled up on the sofa sipping a glass of wine after a delicious dinner of steak in peppercorn sauce. 'That meal was delicious.'

A part of me wishes he wasn't joking.

'I'll have to work on Saturday, so what do you fancy doing tomorrow?' I ask.

'Don't worry about keeping me entertained every day.' Kyros smiles. 'I'm perfectly happy just being here.'

'Okay, we can have a really lazy day then,' I tell him, snuggling into him.

Kyros pours the remains of the red wine into our glasses, from a half bottle that was in the cupboard, and I realise I don't have any more in the house.

'I'm just going to nip to an off-licence for some more wine, I won't be long.'

'I will come with you.' Kyros jumps up. 'Walk off a little off this food.' He pats his stomach.

'It's only a few minutes' walk away.' I smile.

Walking along, my arm linked through his, I feel as though I could burst with happiness. I never imagined when I went to Greece that things would develop between us, despite the miles separating us. I never thought that he would be here with me, staying in my house. It all feels like a wonderful dream.

Heading back towards the house, a car seems to be crawling along behind us and it unnerves me slightly, although Kyros doesn't seem to notice. A minute later, a black car pulls up alongside us, and for a minute I think it might be someone about to ask for directions, but when the driver winds his window down, my heart sinks. It's Scott.

'Alright, Becky, who's your friend?' he asks, eyeing Kyros up and down.

'None of your business,' I reply.

Kyros is about to say something to him, but I steer him away.

'I take it that was your ex,' says Kyros as Scott speeds off, tooting his horn. 'Are you okay?'

'I'm fine. He doesn't frighten me anymore.

I tell Kyros all about him paying a visit to the shop. 'But I haven't seen him since then, so I assumed he'd got the message.' I sigh.

As we reach a busier road, we're just about to cross when the glare of a car's headlights comes speeding towards us. I stare at the beams of light, almost rooted to the spot when I feel myself being pulled backwards.

'Watch out.' Kyros grabs me, and I stumble onto the pavement, but Kyros doesn't get away in time, taking the full force of the car. I can hear the scream in my head, although nothing seems to come out of my mouth as Kyros lies motionless in the road.

Chapter Thirty-Five

'I have to admit, this is not the type of relaxation I had in mind.'

Kyros is sitting in a side ward of the local hospital, after he miraculously escaped serious injury, although he is being monitored for concussion.

We're expecting an overnight stay and a doctor appears several hours later after preliminary checks have proved good.

'You're a very lucky man,' says the doctor. 'There was nothing concerning on the head scan, so it seems that apart from a few scratches and no doubt a headache, you should be fine. It's late, so you can stay in overnight, but all being well you will be free to go tomorrow morning.'

'Thank you, Doctor,' says Kyros and relief floods through me that he's going to be okay.

'Oh my goodness, is Kyros alright? Are you alright?'

I'm talking to Mum the next morning, telling her what happened.

'Can we do anything? Shall we pop over?' she offers.

'Mum, he's fine, he was lucky, just a bit shaken up. He's not really up to visitors; he needs his rest,' I say firmly. 'Can you just take care of the shop for me?'

'Of course we will. Okay, well if you're sure.'

'I am. Thanks again, Mum, I'll speak to you tomorrow.'

I feel sick every time I think about what happened. Was it an accident? Surely Scott hadn't intended to kill me? Although maybe he became jealous with rage when he saw me with another man. I'm mulling these things over when I receive a phone call. It's the police. We made a brief statement at the hospital, but I'm surprised they've contacted me so quickly.

'Luckily, there was a speed camera at the location, so we've been able to identify the vehicle. And a man has been arrested,' the female police officer informs me.

I allow myself to relax a little, knowing Scott is in custody but still feel shaken by the turn of events, not to mention feeling sorry for Kyros.

Later that evening, tucked up in bed beside him, I thank goodness Kyros wasn't seriously injured and shudder at the thought of how things might have turned out.

A few days later, we receive the news that Scott will remain in custody until he appears in court and is likely to be returning to prison for a long time, with no chance of an early release this time.

I weep tears of relief and Kyros wraps me in his arms. Thankfully his headache has disappeared and he's feeling fine now. I can't describe how I feel knowing Scott is behind bars again and my anxiety has lifted, knowing I won't need to be glancing over my shoulder all the time. Maybe my gut feeling of someone watching me had been right all along.

I have to head into work the next day and Kyros insists on coming with me.

'Aren't you supposed to be taking it easy?' I remind him as he helps me unload some stock from my car, carrying it into the shop.

'I am fine. The doctor has given me a clean bill of health, remember.' He shrugs off my concerns.

Once inside the shop, he chats to the customers, who are all charmed by his looks and easy manner, just as I was when we met in Greece. Evelyn from the hairdresser's next door has been in 'browsing' and Sheila called in and asked him for a recipe for moussaka, which he was only too happy to divulge.

At lunchtime, Kyros turns the shop sign to closed, and pulls me into the back of the shop, where he kisses me passionately.

'I've been dying to do that all morning,' he says. 'I'm so glad we are finally alone.'

'Me too. And I suppose we have to make the most of our time together. I don't know what I'll do when you go home,' I tell him honestly.

'We'll figure it out.' He's kissing my neck and my stomach is doing little flips. 'I will be back soon, I promise, and you must visit me in Skiathos again.'

'Of course I will, as long as you promise to come here for Christmas,' I say. 'If you think Mum's Sunday lunches are big, you should see her Christmas lunch.'

'Will there be Yorkshire pudding?' he asks, kissing my hand and working his way up my arm, which makes me giggle.

'Not usually, but I can make a special request to Mum,' I tell him.

'In that case make sure there is a place at the table for me.'

'There will be a place at the table for as long as you want one,' I tell him, in between kisses.

He pulls away from me for a second and looks into my eyes.

'One day, I hope to share the same table with you forever. And I can't lie, I would love it to be in Greece. But, of course, I would stay here rather than lose you. I would live on Mars if it was your desire.'

'We'll figure something out,' I say, echoing his words earlier as I sink into his arms, knowing that wherever we end up, I feel certain our love will last a lifetime.

THE FOLLOWING SPRING

Abby is the epitome of a beautiful bride and when she makes her vows, I have to bite my lip to stop myself from blubbering and ruining my carefully applied make-up. Heather looks beautiful too in dusky pink satin in and the little pageboys are a picture of cuteness in navy sailor suits.

It's a joyous occasion and as we take our seats at the reception, Kyros takes my hand in his. He spent Christmas here, his father spending time with Linus and his family and, of course, Henry, and we enjoyed the lights in the City of Liverpool and Christmas carols in the cathedral.

The season is opening up in Greece in a couple of weeks, so I know Kyros will not be such a frequent visitor here, but I hope to go and stay with him from time to time. Mum has made it clear she is more than happy to look after the shop in my absence and has been happily spending a little more time behind the counter. She's made friends with everyone in the market and enjoys her lunchtime chats with Evelyn at the hairdresser's next door.

'Listen to your heart,' she told me one afternoon as we had coffee and cake in a local café. 'If you want to live in Greece, go to Kyros.

He's a good man and anyone can see how much he loves you. Me and your father have a good life here; it's time to follow your dreams.'

'Oh, Mum, thanks.' I gripped her hand and squeezed it, swallowing down a lump in my throat. In truth, I had been worrying about leaving my parents with being their only daughter, and also because they had already uprooted their life for me once, so it feels so good to have Mum's blessing. My friends are settled here in happy marriages, and much as I'll miss them, maybe it is time to go after my own happy ending.

'If I did move to Greece, I promise I'd come and visit,' I told mum that afternoon in the café. The thought of it even being a possibility and not a daydream filled me with excitement.

'You promise?'

'Of course. There's only so long I could stay away from one of your fabulous roasts.' I smiled as I covered her hand with mine.

'That's good enough for me, love,' Mum said, her face breaking into a huge smile. 'You're a wonderful daughter but you have your own life to live and it would be selfish of me to expect you to stay here. Me and your father only want what's best for you.'

It was a huge relief to hear that and I mulled over Mum's words, thinking of how I might regret it if I don't at least give living in Greece a try. After all, everyone should have the chance to find their happy ever after right? I think it might finally be time to go in search of mine...

A Letter from Sue Roberts

Dear reader,

I want to say a huge thank you for choosing to read *Greece Actually*. I've had so many messages from readers, telling me how my sunshine reads have lifted their spirits recently, which is just lovely! Thank you so much for buying this book; I do hope you enjoyed reading it. If you did enjoy it, and want to keep up to date with all my latest releases, just sign up at the following link. Your email address will never be shared and you can unsubscribe at any time.

www.bookouture.com/sue-roberts

I hope you loved *Greece Actually* and if you did, I would be very grateful if you could write a review. I'd love to hear what you think, and it makes such a difference helping new readers to discover one of my books for the first time.

I love hearing from my readers – you can get in touch on my Facebook page, through Twitter, Goodreads or my website.

Thanks,
Sue Roberts

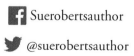

Suerobertsauthor

@suerobertsauthor

Acknowledgements

As ever, I would like to say a huge thank you to everyone at Bookouture for their tireless work and expertise in helping to achieve the very best for all of my books. A special thanks to my wonderful editor, Emily Gowers, for her advice and guidance, which is always so appreciated.

I would also like to thank all of the readers of my books, many of whom have messaged me during this difficult year, to say how reading my sunshine stories has helped them. It means so much.

Finally, thanks to all of you bloggers and reviewers. Your continued support means everything.